WRASSLE CASTLE

RIDERS ON THE STORM

WRITTEN BY
COLLEEN COOVER & PAUL TOBIN

ILLUSTRATED BY
GALAAD

COLORED BY
REBECCA HORNER

LETTERED BY
ANDWORLD DESIGN

DESIGNED BY
BONES LEOPARD & SONJA SYNAK

EDITED BY
REBECCA TAYLOR

WONDERBOUND

Missoula, Montana
www.readwonderbound.com
@readwonderbound

PUBLISHER, DAMIAN A. WASSEL
EDITOR-IN-CHIEF, ADRIAN F. WASSEL
ART DIRECTOR, NATHAN C. GOODEN
MANAGING EDITOR, REBECCA TAYLOR
DIRECTOR OF SALES & MARKETING, DIRECT MARKET, DAVID DISSANAYAKE
DIRECTOR OF SALES & MARKETING, BOOK MARKET, SYNDEE BARWICK
PRODUCTION MANAGER, IAN BALDESSARI
ART DIRECTOR, WONDERBOUND.W SONJA SYNAK
ART DIRECTOR, VAULT, TIM DANIEL
PRINCIPAL, DAMIAN A. WASSEL SR.

LIBRARY OF CONGRESS CONTROL NUMBER: 2021922724
PRINT ISBN: 978-1-63849-070-8

PRINTED IN THE USA BY VERSA
FIRST EDITION FEBRUARY 2022

10 9 8 7 6 5 4 3 2 1

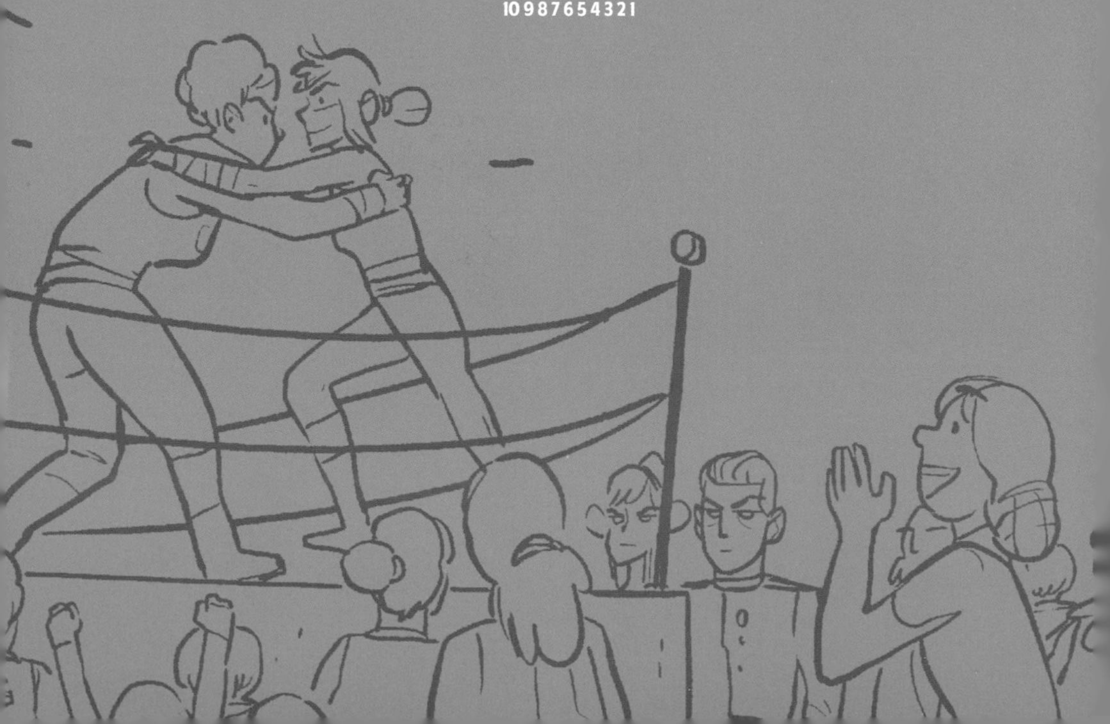

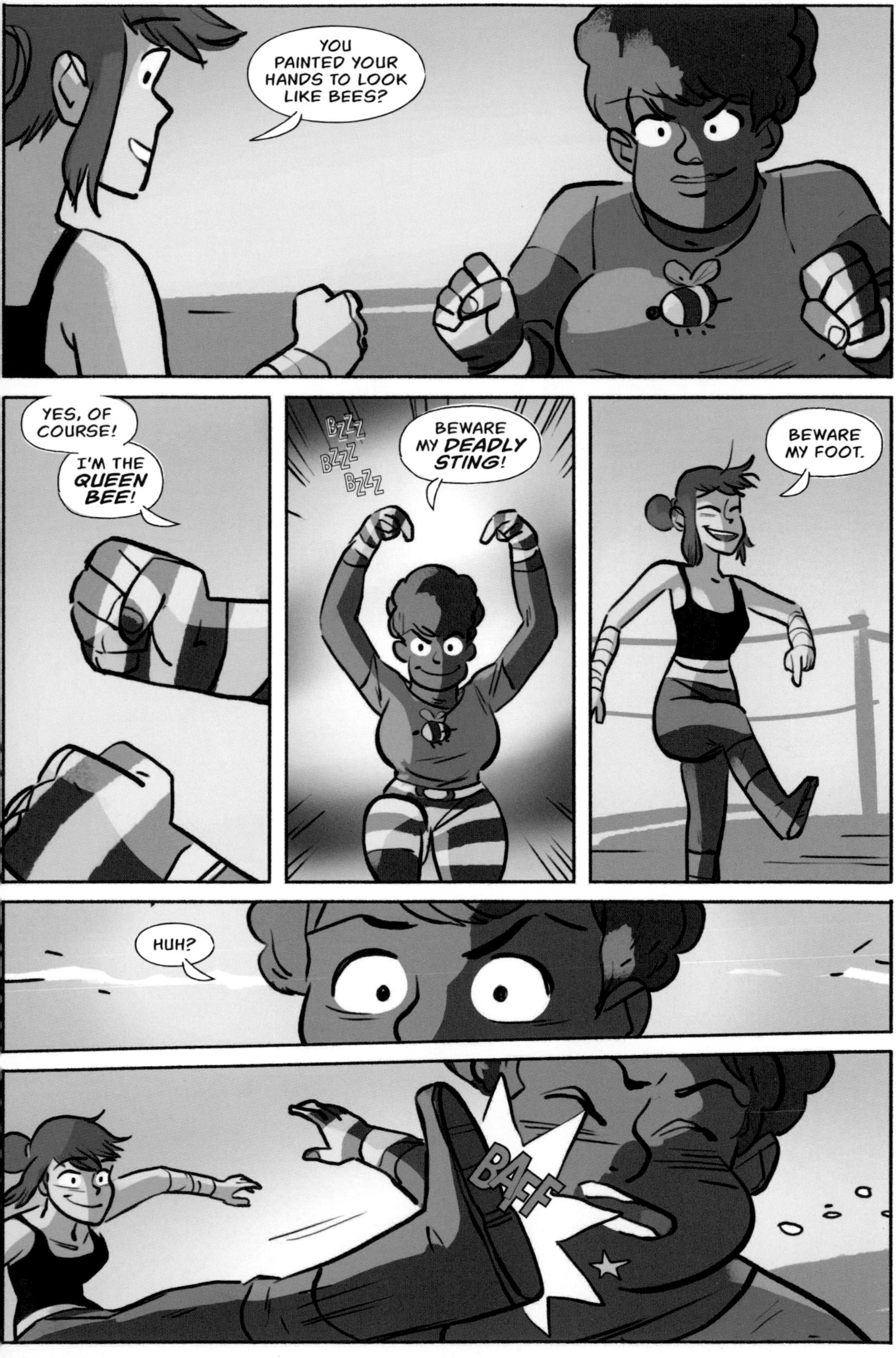
YOU PAINTED YOUR HANDS TO LOOK LIKE BEES?
YES, OF COURSE!
I'M THE QUEEN BEE!
BZZZ BZZZ BZZZ
BEWARE MY DEADLY STING!
BEWARE MY FOOT.
HUH?
BAFF

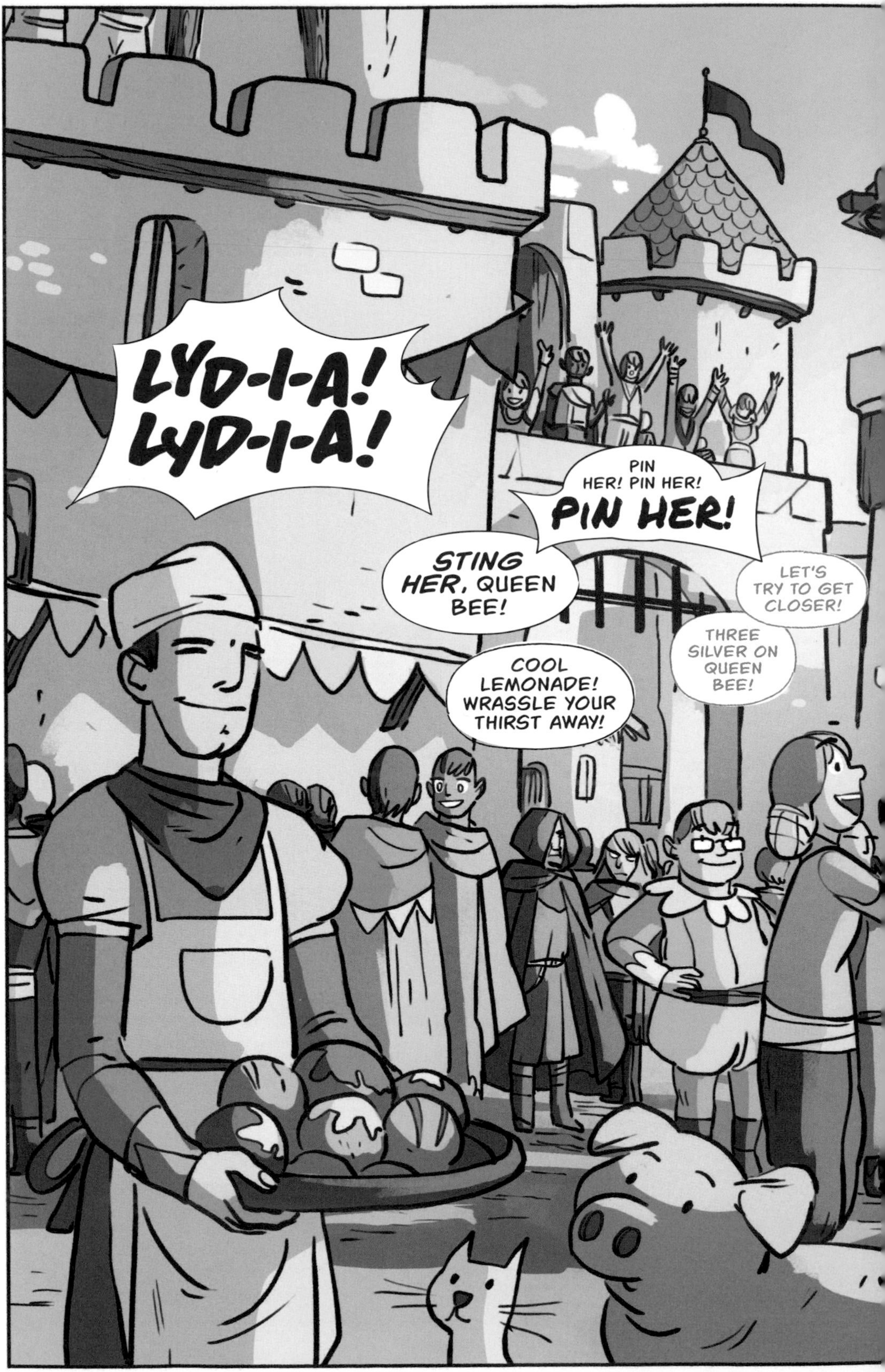
LYD-I-A! LYD-I-A!
PIN HER! PIN HER! PIN HER!
STING HER, QUEEN BEE!
LET'S TRY TO GET CLOSER!
THREE SILVER ON QUEEN BEE!
COOL LEMONADE! WRASSLE YOUR THIRST AWAY!

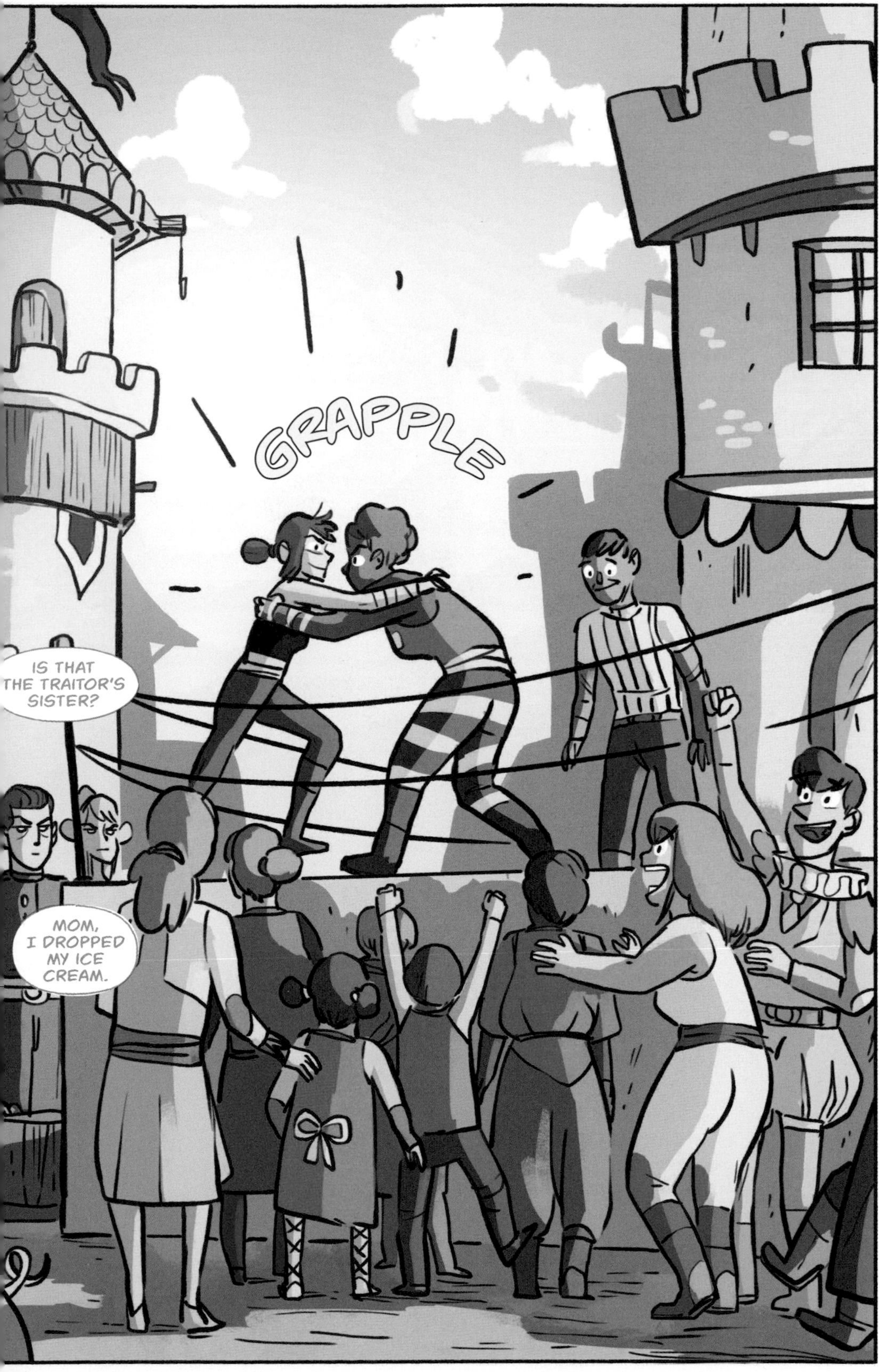
GRAPPLE
IS THAT THE TRAITOR'S SISTER?
MOM, I DROPPED MY ICE CREAM.

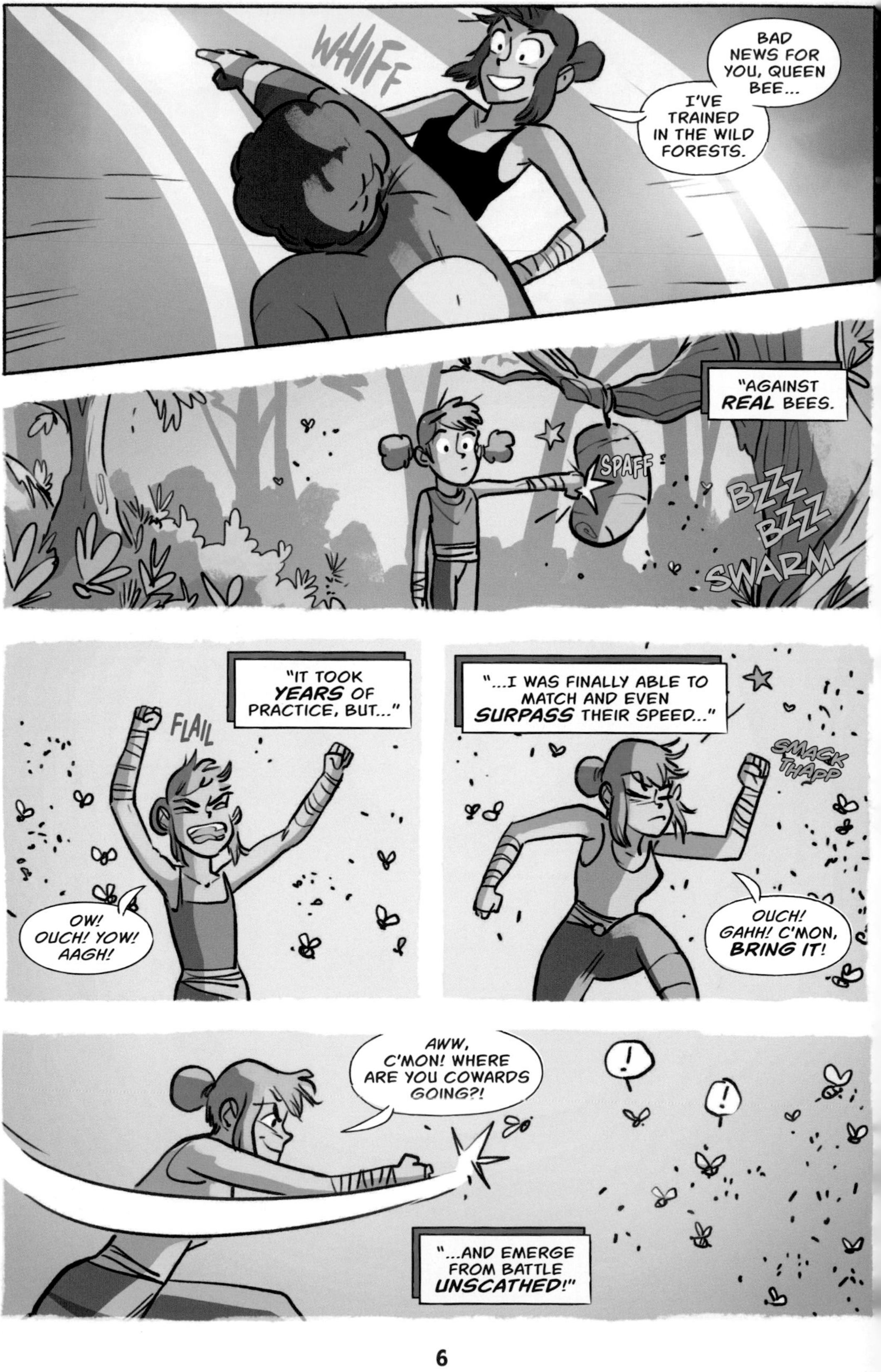
WHIFF
BAD NEWS FOR YOU, QUEEN BEE...
I'VE TRAINED IN THE WILD FORESTS.
"AGAINST REAL BEES.
SPAFF
BZZZ BZZZ SWARM
"IT TOOK YEARS OF PRACTICE, BUT..."
FLAIL
OW! OUCH! YOW! AAGH!
"...I WAS FINALLY ABLE TO MATCH AND EVEN SURPASS THEIR SPEED..."
SMACK THAPP
OUCH! GAHH! C'MON, BRING IT!
AWW, C'MON! WHERE ARE YOU COWARDS GOING?!
!
!
"...AND EMERGE FROM BATTLE UNSCATHED!"

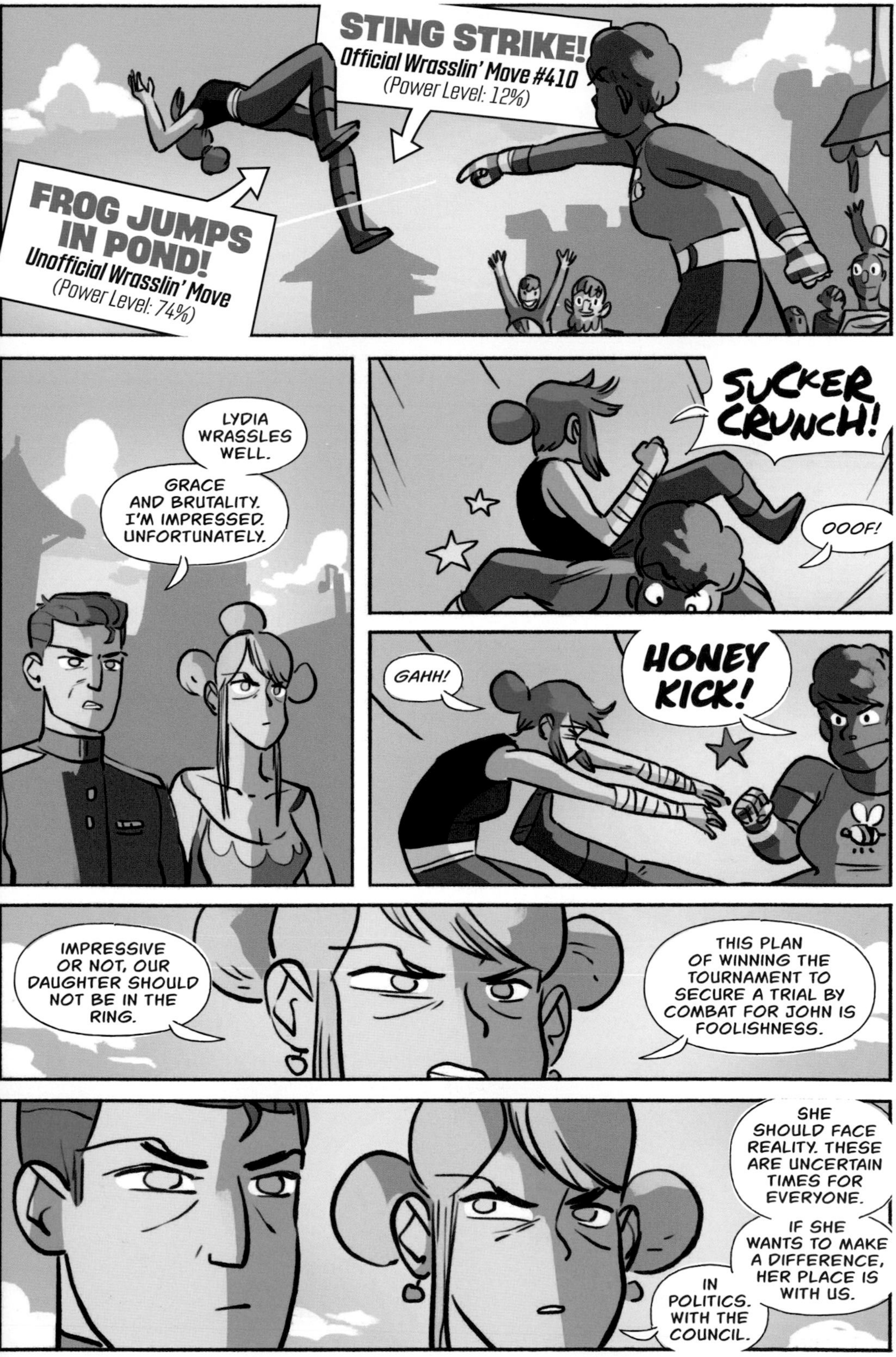
STING STRIKE!
Official Wrasslin' Move #410
(Power Level: 12%)
FROG JUMPS IN POND!
Unofficial Wrasslin' Move
(Power Level: 74%)
LYDIA WRASSLES WELL.
GRACE AND BRUTALITY. I'M IMPRESSED. UNFORTUNATELY.
SUCKER CRUNCH!
OOOF!
GAHH!
HONEY KICK!
IMPRESSIVE OR NOT, OUR DAUGHTER SHOULD NOT BE IN THE RING.
THIS PLAN OF WINNING THE TOURNAMENT TO SECURE A TRIAL BY COMBAT FOR JOHN IS FOOLISHNESS.
SHE SHOULD FACE REALITY. THESE ARE UNCERTAIN TIMES FOR EVERYONE.
IF SHE WANTS TO MAKE A DIFFERENCE, HER PLACE IS WITH US.
IN POLITICS. WITH THE COUNCIL.

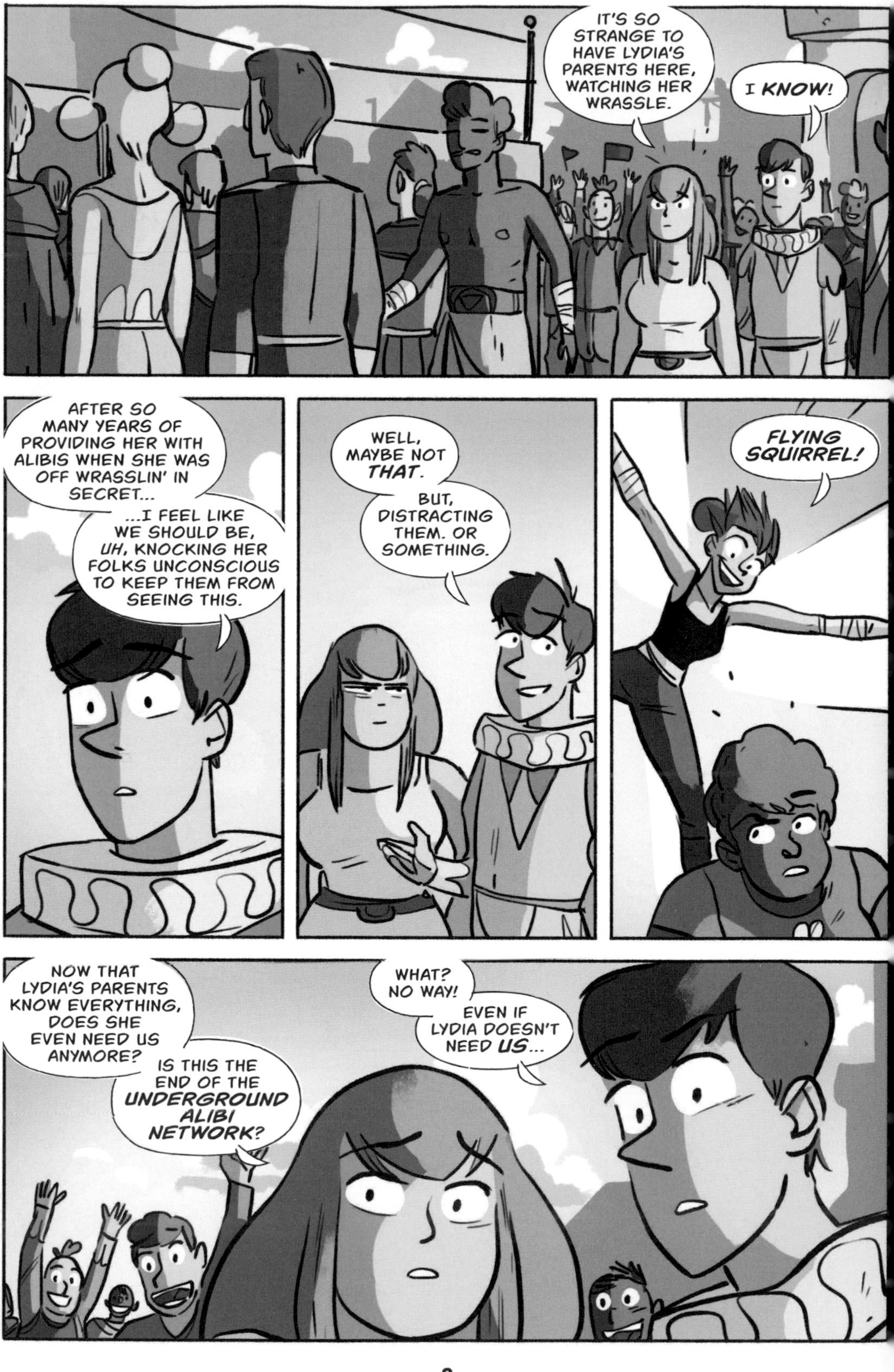
IT'S SO STRANGE TO HAVE LYDIA'S PARENTS HERE, WATCHING HER WRASSLE.
I *KNOW*!
AFTER SO MANY YEARS OF PROVIDING HER WITH ALIBIS WHEN SHE WAS OFF WRASSLIN' IN SECRET...
...I FEEL LIKE WE SHOULD BE, *UH*, KNOCKING HER FOLKS UNCONSCIOUS TO KEEP THEM FROM SEEING THIS.
WELL, MAYBE NOT *THAT*.
BUT, DISTRACTING THEM. OR SOMETHING.
FLYING SQUIRREL!
NOW THAT LYDIA'S PARENTS KNOW EVERYTHING, DOES SHE EVEN NEED US ANYMORE?
IS THIS THE END OF THE *UNDERGROUND ALIBI NETWORK*?
WHAT? NO WAY!
EVEN IF LYDIA DOESN'T NEED *US*...

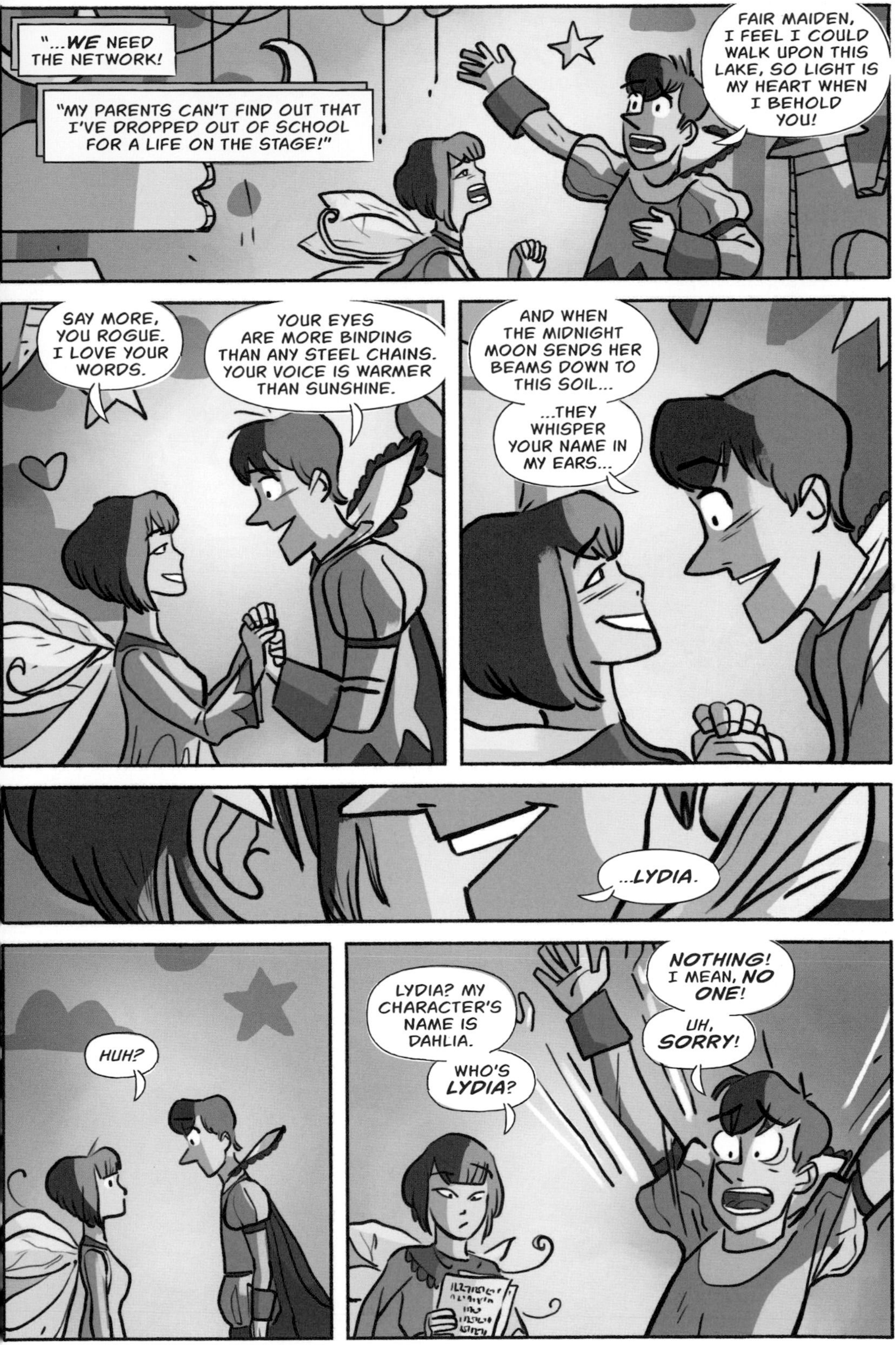
"...WE NEED THE NETWORK!
"MY PARENTS CAN'T FIND OUT THAT I'VE DROPPED OUT OF SCHOOL FOR A LIFE ON THE STAGE!"
FAIR MAIDEN, I FEEL I COULD WALK UPON THIS LAKE, SO LIGHT IS MY HEART WHEN I BEHOLD YOU!
SAY MORE, YOU ROGUE. I LOVE YOUR WORDS.
YOUR EYES ARE MORE BINDING THAN ANY STEEL CHAINS. YOUR VOICE IS WARMER THAN SUNSHINE.
AND WHEN THE MIDNIGHT MOON SENDS HER BEAMS DOWN TO THIS SOIL...
...THEY WHISPER YOUR NAME IN MY EARS...
...LYDIA.
HUH?
LYDIA? MY CHARACTER'S NAME IS DAHLIA.
WHO'S LYDIA?
NOTHING! I MEAN, NO ONE!
UH, SORRY!

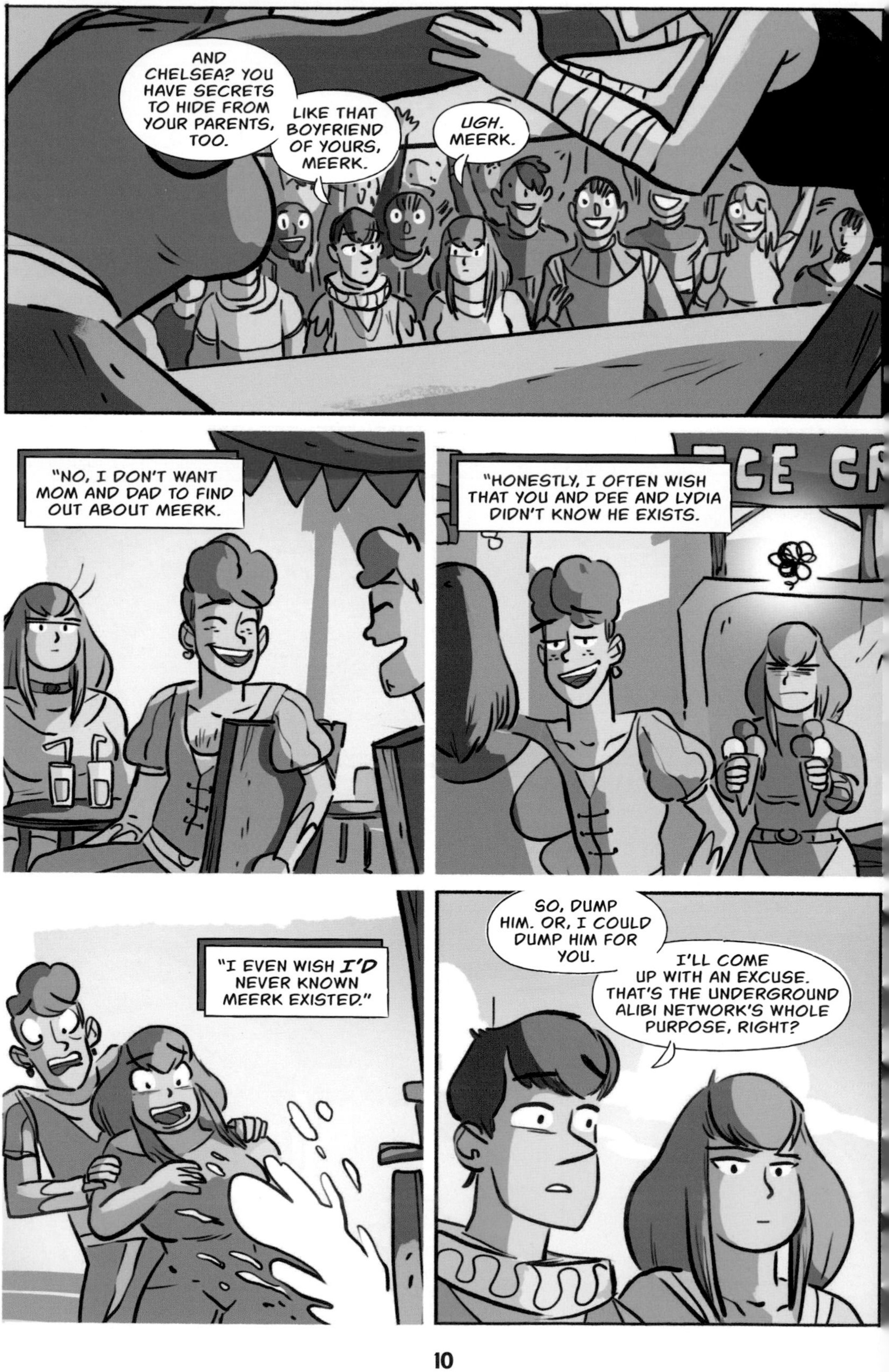
AND CHELSEA? YOU HAVE SECRETS TO HIDE FROM YOUR PARENTS, TOO.
LIKE THAT BOYFRIEND OF YOURS, MEERK.
UGH. MEERK.
"NO, I DON'T WANT MOM AND DAD TO FIND OUT ABOUT MEERK.
"HONESTLY, I OFTEN WISH THAT YOU AND DEE AND LYDIA DIDN'T KNOW HE EXISTS.
"I EVEN WISH *I'D* NEVER KNOWN MEERK EXISTED."
SO, DUMP HIM. OR, I COULD DUMP HIM FOR YOU.
I'LL COME UP WITH AN EXCUSE. THAT'S THE UNDERGROUND ALIBI NETWORK'S WHOLE PURPOSE, RIGHT?

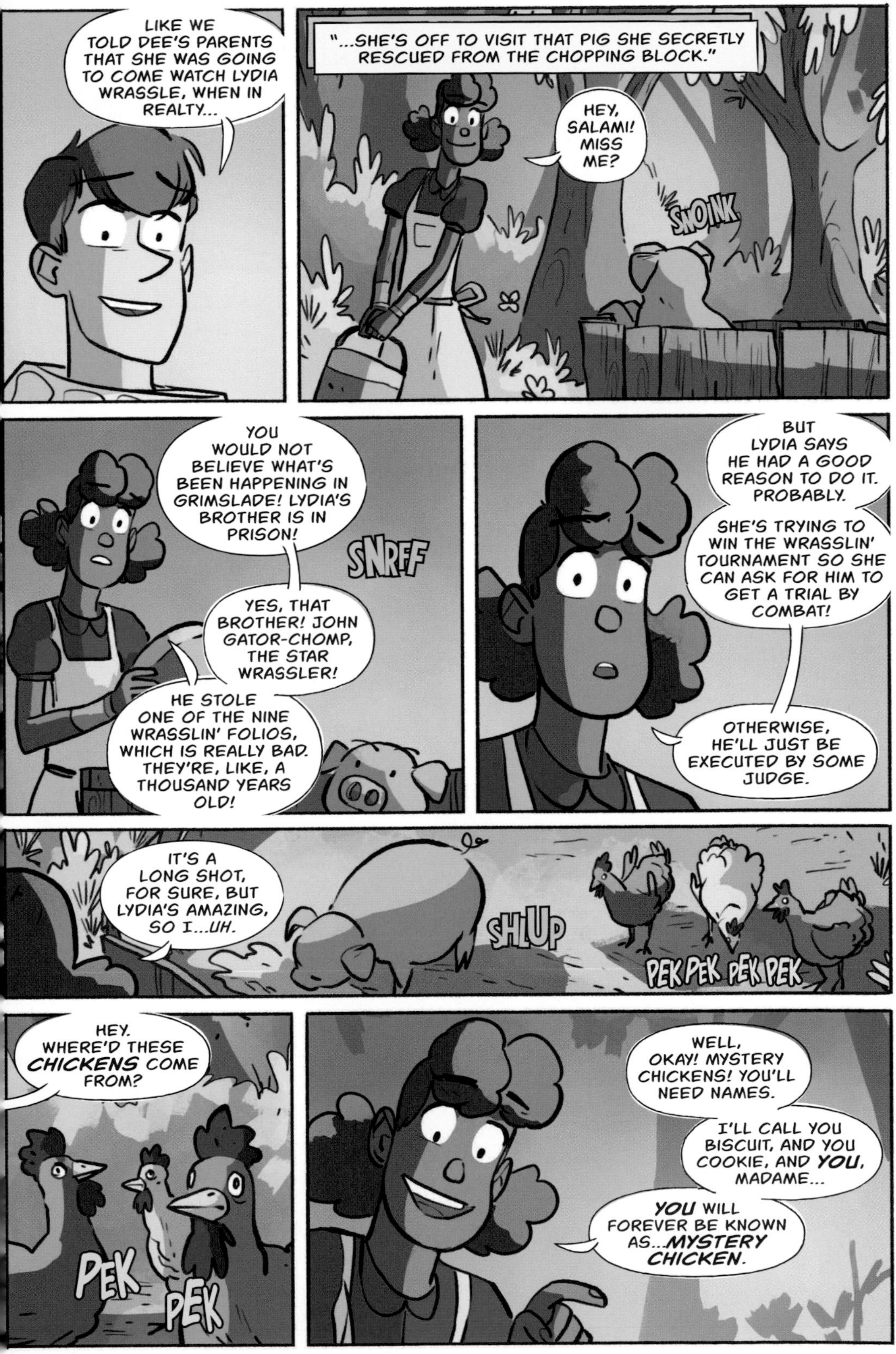

LIKE WE TOLD DEE'S PARENTS THAT SHE WAS GOING TO COME WATCH LYDIA WRASSLE, WHEN IN REALTY...
"...SHE'S OFF TO VISIT THAT PIG SHE SECRETLY RESCUED FROM THE CHOPPING BLOCK."
HEY, SALAMI! MISS ME?
SNOINK
YOU WOULD NOT BELIEVE WHAT'S BEEN HAPPENING IN GRIMSLADE! LYDIA'S BROTHER IS IN PRISON!
SNRFF
YES, THAT BROTHER! JOHN GATOR-CHOMP, THE STAR WRASSLER!
HE STOLE ONE OF THE NINE WRASSLIN' FOLIOS, WHICH IS REALLY BAD. THEY'RE, LIKE, A THOUSAND YEARS OLD!
BUT LYDIA SAYS HE HAD A GOOD REASON TO DO IT. PROBABLY.
SHE'S TRYING TO WIN THE WRASSLIN' TOURNAMENT SO SHE CAN ASK FOR HIM TO GET A TRIAL BY COMBAT!
OTHERWISE, HE'LL JUST BE EXECUTED BY SOME JUDGE.
IT'S A LONG SHOT, FOR SURE, BUT LYDIA'S AMAZING, SO I...*UH*.
SHLUP
PEK PEK PEK PEK
HEY. WHERE'D THESE ***CHICKENS*** COME FROM?
PEK
PEK
WELL, OKAY! MYSTERY CHICKENS! YOU'LL NEED NAMES.
I'LL CALL YOU BISCUIT, AND YOU COOKIE, AND ***YOU***, MADAME...
YOU WILL FOREVER BE KNOWN AS...***MYSTERY CHICKEN***.

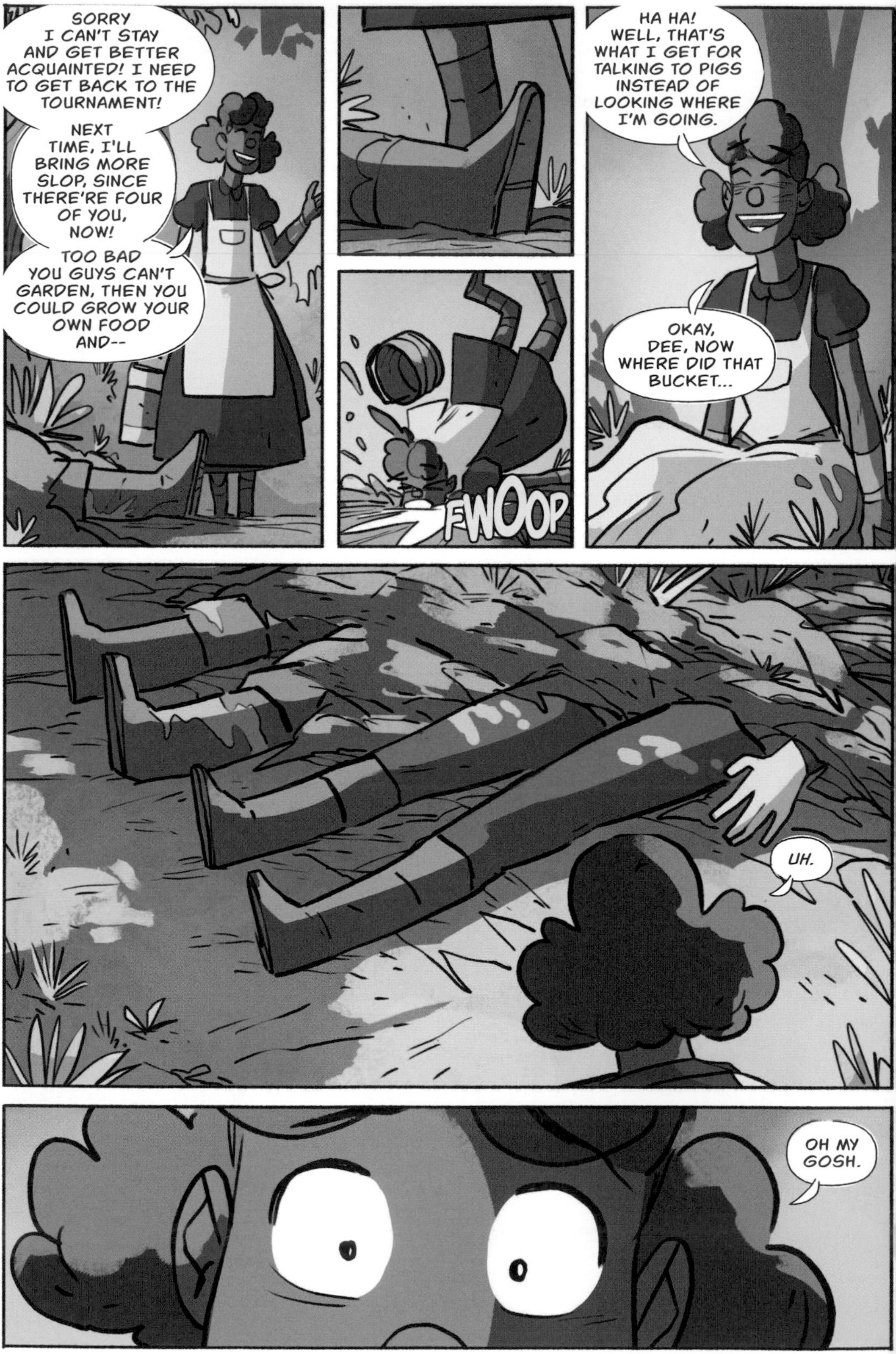
SORRY I CAN'T STAY AND GET BETTER ACQUAINTED! I NEED TO GET BACK TO THE TOURNAMENT!
NEXT TIME, I'LL BRING MORE SLOP, SINCE THERE'RE FOUR OF YOU, NOW!
TOO BAD YOU GUYS CAN'T GARDEN, THEN YOU COULD GROW YOUR OWN FOOD AND--
FWOOP
HA HA! WELL, THAT'S WHAT I GET FOR TALKING TO PIGS INSTEAD OF LOOKING WHERE I'M GOING.
OKAY, DEE, NOW WHERE DID THAT BUCKET...
UH.
OH MY GOSH.

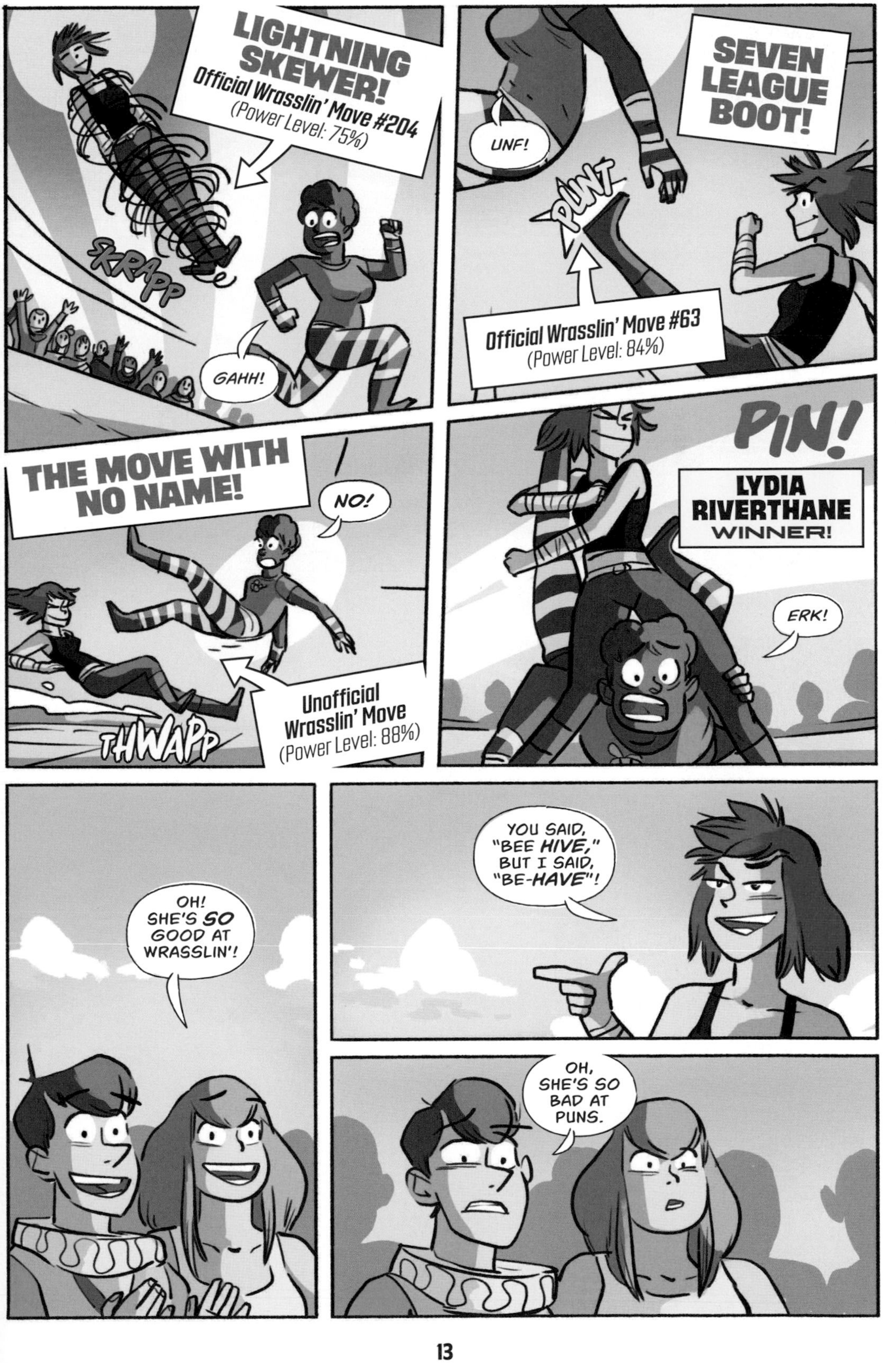
LIGHTNING SKEWER!
Official Wrasslin' Move #204
(Power Level: 75%)
SKRAPP
GAHH!
SEVEN LEAGUE BOOT!
UNF!
PUNT
Official Wrasslin' Move #63
(Power Level: 84%)
THE MOVE WITH NO NAME!
NO!
Unofficial Wrasslin' Move
(Power Level: 88%)
THWAPP
PIN!
LYDIA RIVERTHANE
WINNER!
ERK!
OH! SHE'S SO GOOD AT WRASSLIN'!
YOU SAID, "BEE HIVE," BUT I SAID, "BE-HAVE"!
OH, SHE'S SO BAD AT PUNS.

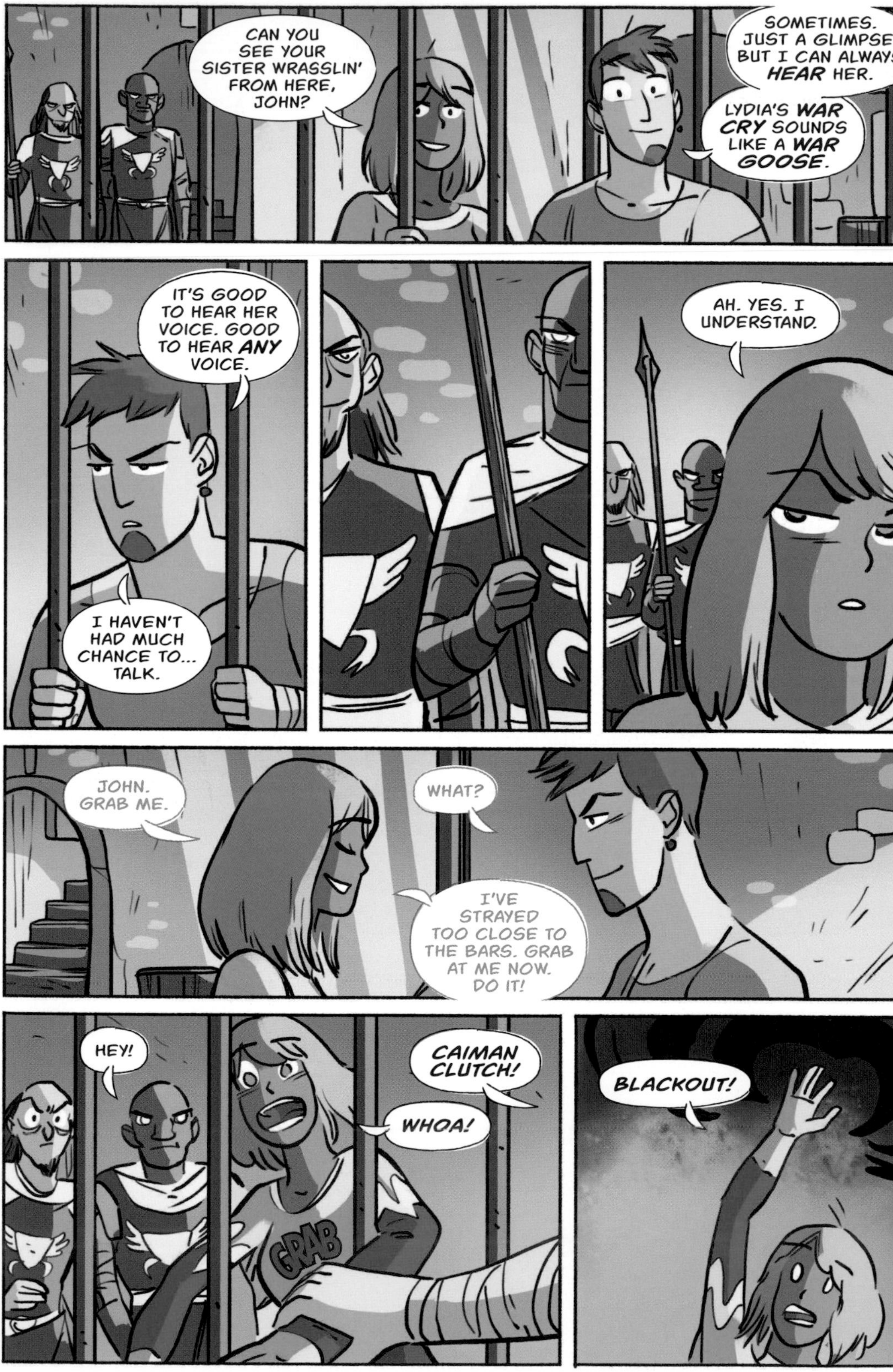
CAN YOU SEE YOUR SISTER WRASSLIN' FROM HERE, JOHN?
SOMETIMES. JUST A GLIMPSE. BUT I CAN ALWAYS HEAR HER.
LYDIA'S WAR CRY SOUNDS LIKE A WAR GOOSE.
IT'S GOOD TO HEAR HER VOICE. GOOD TO HEAR ANY VOICE.
I HAVEN'T HAD MUCH CHANCE TO... TALK.
AH. YES. I UNDERSTAND.
JOHN. GRAB ME.
WHAT?
I'VE STRAYED TOO CLOSE TO THE BARS. GRAB AT ME NOW. DO IT!
HEY!
CAIMAN CLUTCH!
WHOA!
GRAB
BLACKOUT!

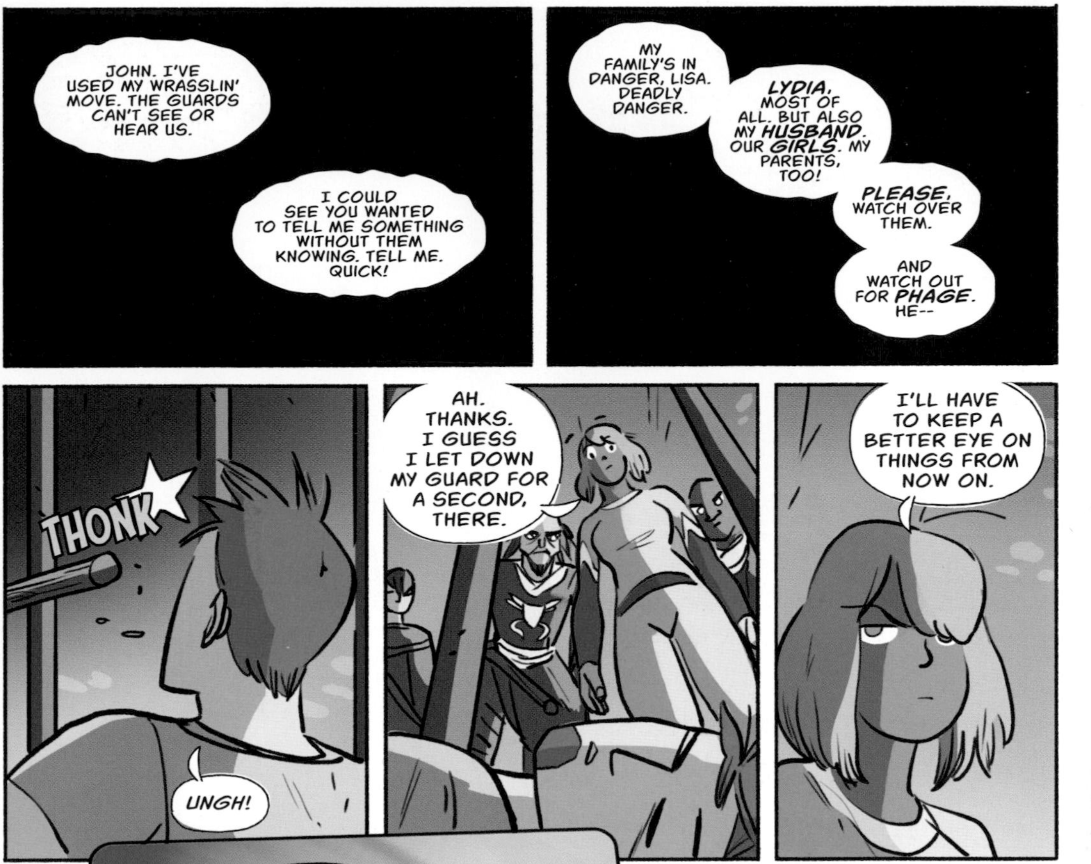
JOHN. I'VE USED MY WRASSLIN' MOVE. THE GUARDS CAN'T SEE OR HEAR US.
I COULD SEE YOU WANTED TO TELL ME SOMETHING WITHOUT THEM KNOWING. TELL ME. QUICK!
MY FAMILY'S IN DANGER, LISA. DEADLY DANGER.
LYDIA, MOST OF ALL. BUT ALSO MY HUSBAND. OUR GIRLS. MY PARENTS, TOO!
PLEASE, WATCH OVER THEM.
AND WATCH OUT FOR PHAGE. HE--
THONK
UNGH!
AH. THANKS. I GUESS I LET DOWN MY GUARD FOR A SECOND, THERE.
I'LL HAVE TO KEEP A BETTER EYE ON THINGS FROM NOW ON.

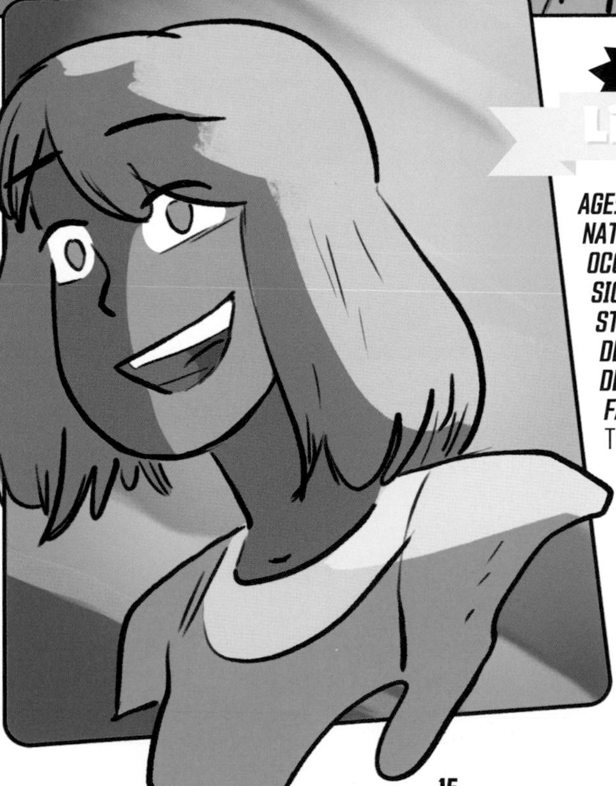

BONUS STAT CARD!

Lisa "Lights Out" Landon

AGE: 26
NATIONAL RANKING: 14
OCCUPATION: Instructor at Wrassle Castle
SIGNATURE MOVE: Blackout
STRENGTH: 13
DEXTERITY: 16
DETERMINATION: 16
FAVORITE FOOD: Cucumber & Tomato sandwich
HOBBIES: Walking in the dark (city or forest)
NOTES: Lisa's signature "Blackout" move summons complete darkness. For the last three years, she's been honing her ability to preclude sound and scent, as well.

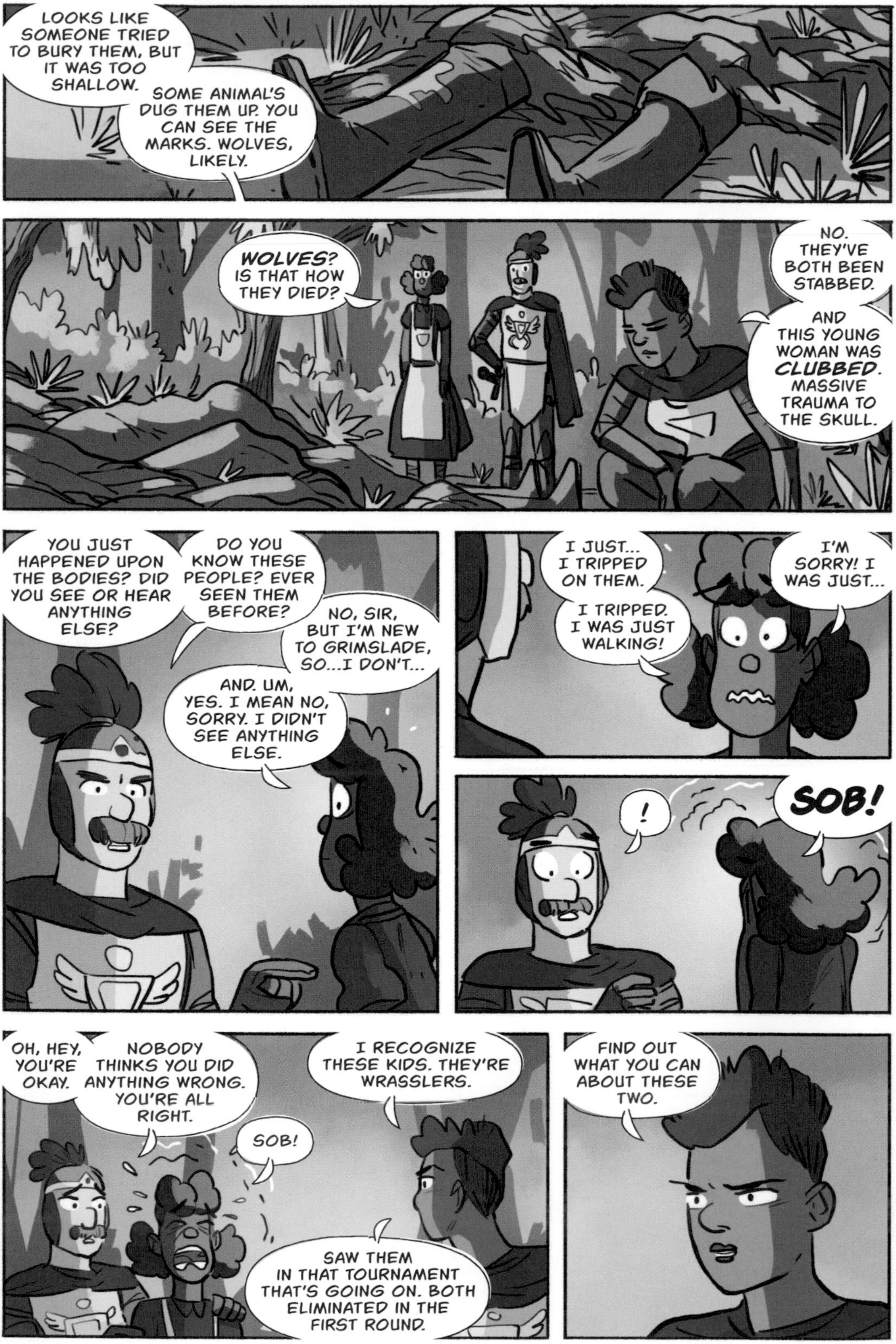
LOOKS LIKE SOMEONE TRIED TO BURY THEM, BUT IT WAS TOO SHALLOW.
SOME ANIMAL'S DUG THEM UP. YOU CAN SEE THE MARKS. WOLVES, LIKELY.
WOLVES? IS THAT HOW THEY DIED?
NO. THEY'VE BOTH BEEN STABBED.
AND THIS YOUNG WOMAN WAS CLUBBED. MASSIVE TRAUMA TO THE SKULL.
YOU JUST HAPPENED UPON THE BODIES? DID YOU SEE OR HEAR ANYTHING ELSE?
DO YOU KNOW THESE PEOPLE? EVER SEEN THEM BEFORE?
NO, SIR, BUT I'M NEW TO GRIMSLADE, SO...I DON'T...
AND. UM, YES. I MEAN NO, SORRY. I DIDN'T SEE ANYTHING ELSE.
I JUST... I TRIPPED ON THEM.
I TRIPPED. I WAS JUST WALKING!
I'M SORRY! I WAS JUST...
!
SOB!
OH, HEY, YOU'RE OKAY.
NOBODY THINKS YOU DID ANYTHING WRONG. YOU'RE ALL RIGHT.
SOB!
I RECOGNIZE THESE KIDS. THEY'RE WRASSLERS.
SAW THEM IN THAT TOURNAMENT THAT'S GOING ON. BOTH ELIMINATED IN THE FIRST ROUND.
FIND OUT WHAT YOU CAN ABOUT THESE TWO.

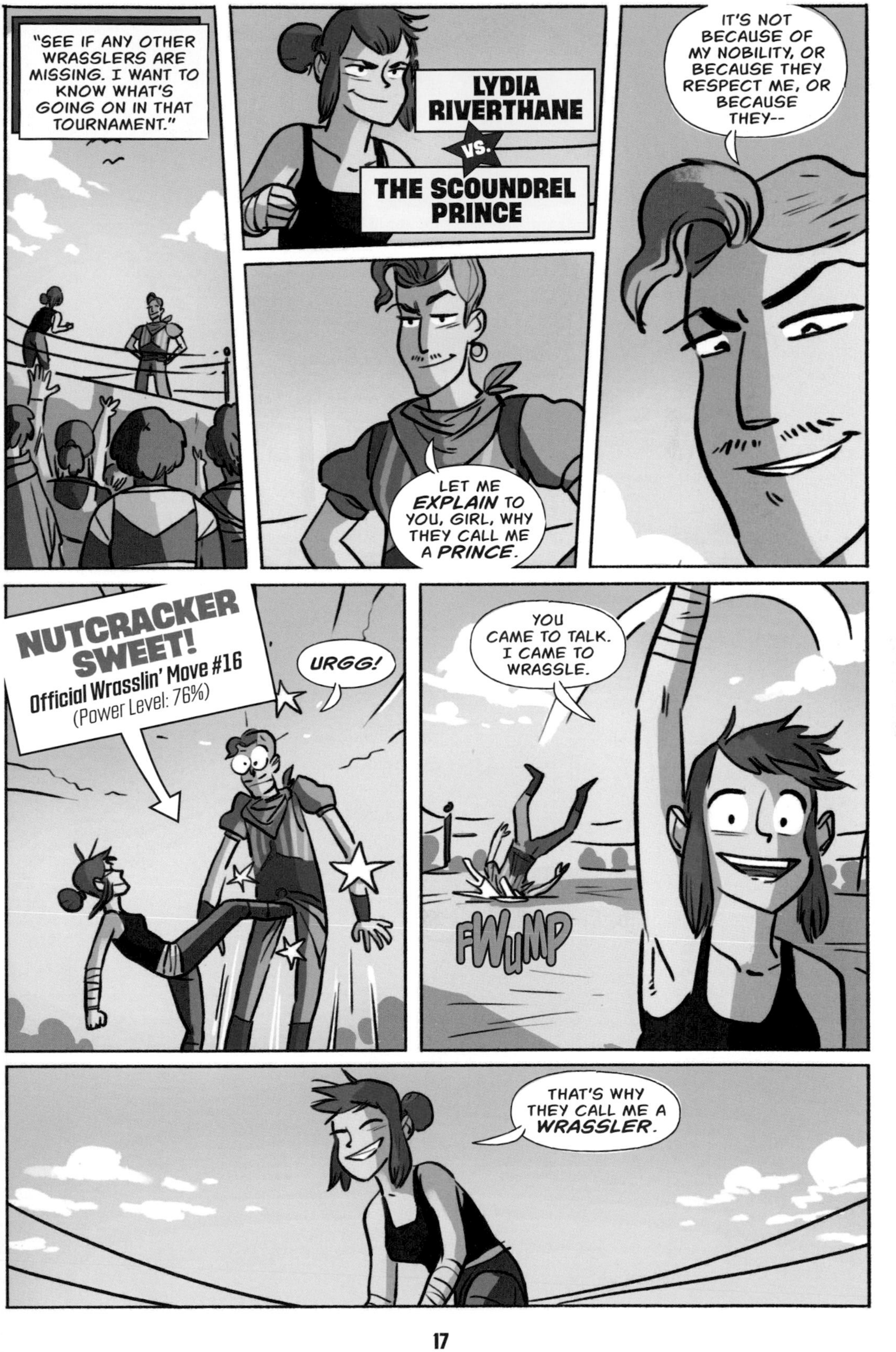
"SEE IF ANY OTHER WRASSLERS ARE MISSING. I WANT TO KNOW WHAT'S GOING ON IN THAT TOURNAMENT."
LYDIA RIVERTHANE
VS.
THE SCOUNDREL PRINCE
LET ME EXPLAIN TO YOU, GIRL, WHY THEY CALL ME A PRINCE.
IT'S NOT BECAUSE OF MY NOBILITY, OR BECAUSE THEY RESPECT ME, OR BECAUSE THEY--
NUTCRACKER SWEET!
Official Wrasslin' Move #16
(Power Level: 76%)
URGG!
YOU CAME TO TALK. I CAME TO WRASSLE.
FWUMP
THAT'S WHY THEY CALL ME A WRASSLER.

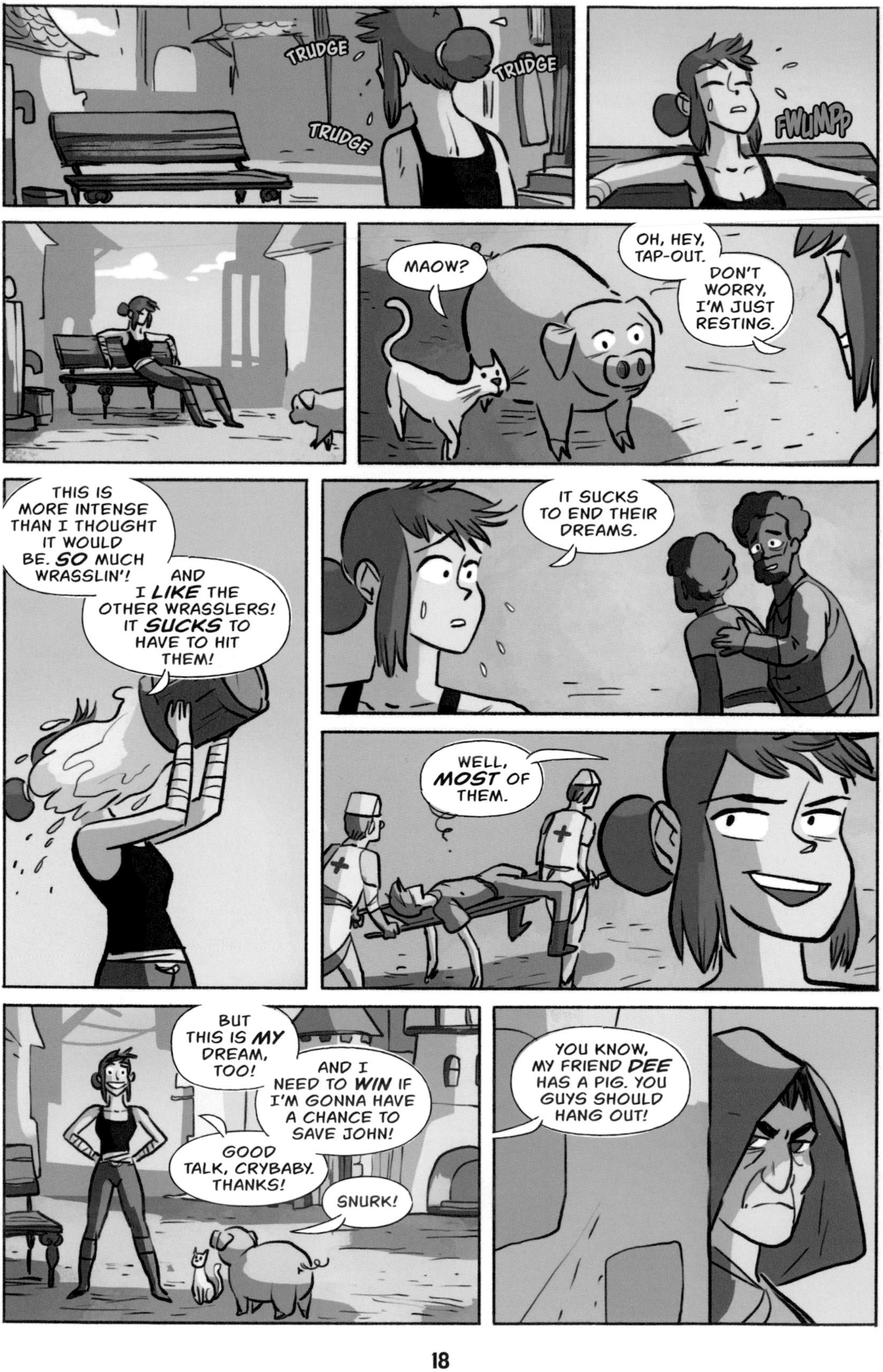
TRUDGE
TRUDGE
TRUDGE
FWUMPP
MAOW?
OH, HEY, TAP-OUT.
DON'T WORRY, I'M JUST RESTING.
THIS IS MORE INTENSE THAN I THOUGHT IT WOULD BE. SO MUCH WRASSLIN'!
AND I LIKE THE OTHER WRASSLERS! IT SUCKS TO HAVE TO HIT THEM!
IT SUCKS TO END THEIR DREAMS.
WELL, MOST OF THEM.
BUT THIS IS MY DREAM, TOO!
AND I NEED TO WIN IF I'M GONNA HAVE A CHANCE TO SAVE JOHN!
GOOD TALK, CRYBABY. THANKS!
SNURK!
YOU KNOW, MY FRIEND DEE HAS A PIG. YOU GUYS SHOULD HANG OUT!

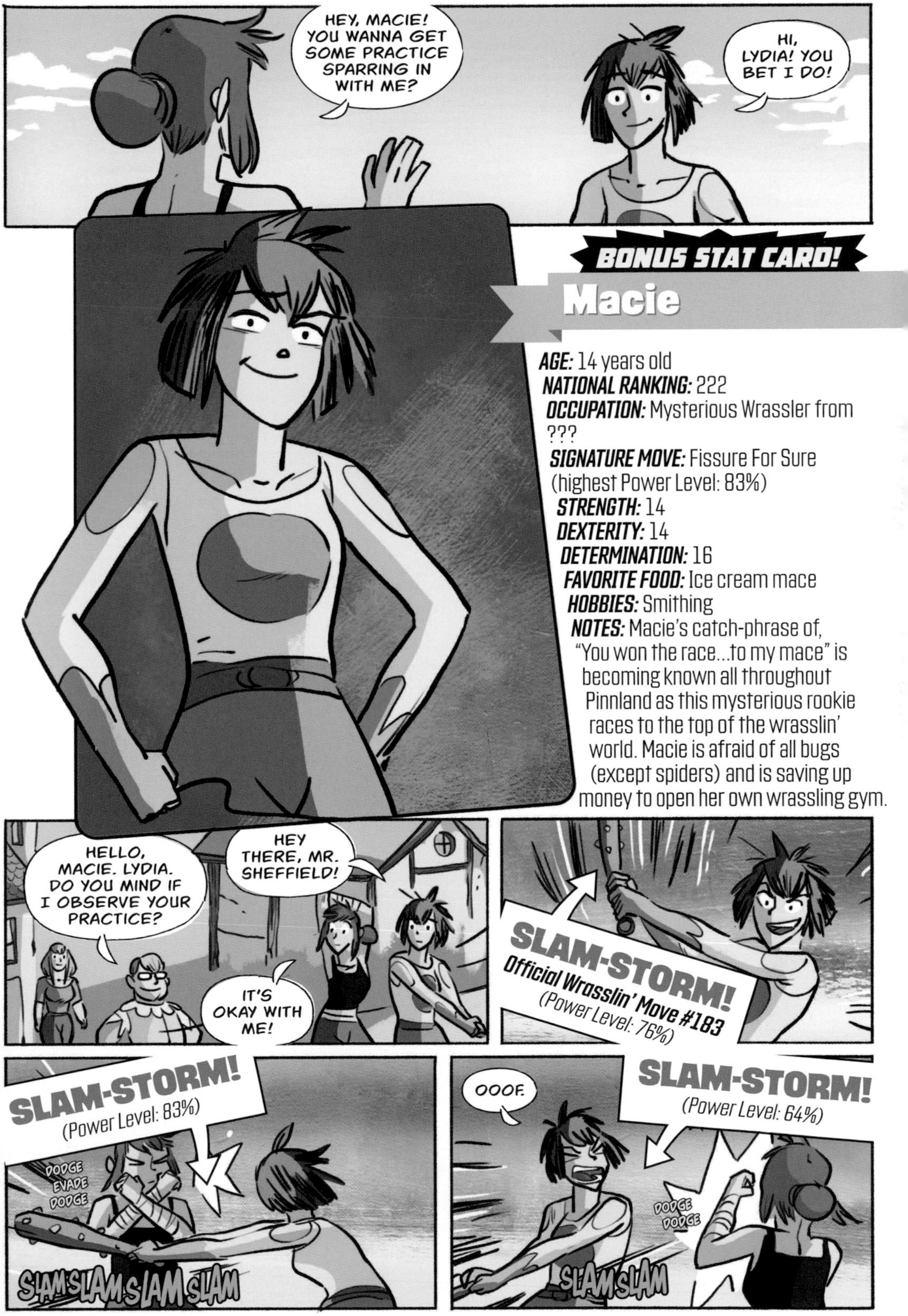
HEY, MACIE! YOU WANNA GET SOME PRACTICE SPARRING IN WITH ME?
HI, LYDIA! YOU BET I DO!
BONUS STAT CARD!
Macie
AGE: 14 years old
NATIONAL RANKING: 222
OCCUPATION: Mysterious Wrassler from ???
SIGNATURE MOVE: Fissure For Sure (highest Power Level: 83%)
STRENGTH: 14
DEXTERITY: 14
DETERMINATION: 16
FAVORITE FOOD: Ice cream mace
HOBBIES: Smithing
NOTES: Macie's catch-phrase of, "You won the race...to my mace" is becoming known all throughout Pinnland as this mysterious rookie races to the top of the wrasslin' world. Macie is afraid of all bugs (except spiders) and is saving up money to open her own wrassling gym.
HELLO, MACIE. LYDIA. DO YOU MIND IF I OBSERVE YOUR PRACTICE?
HEY THERE, MR. SHEFFIELD!
IT'S OKAY WITH ME!
SLAM-STORM!
Official Wrasslin' Move #183
(Power Level: 76%)
SLAM-STORM!
(Power Level: 83%)
DODGE
EVADE
DODGE
SLAM SLAM SLAM SLAM
OOOF.
SLAM-STORM!
(Power Level: 64%)
DODGE
DODGE
SLAM SLAM

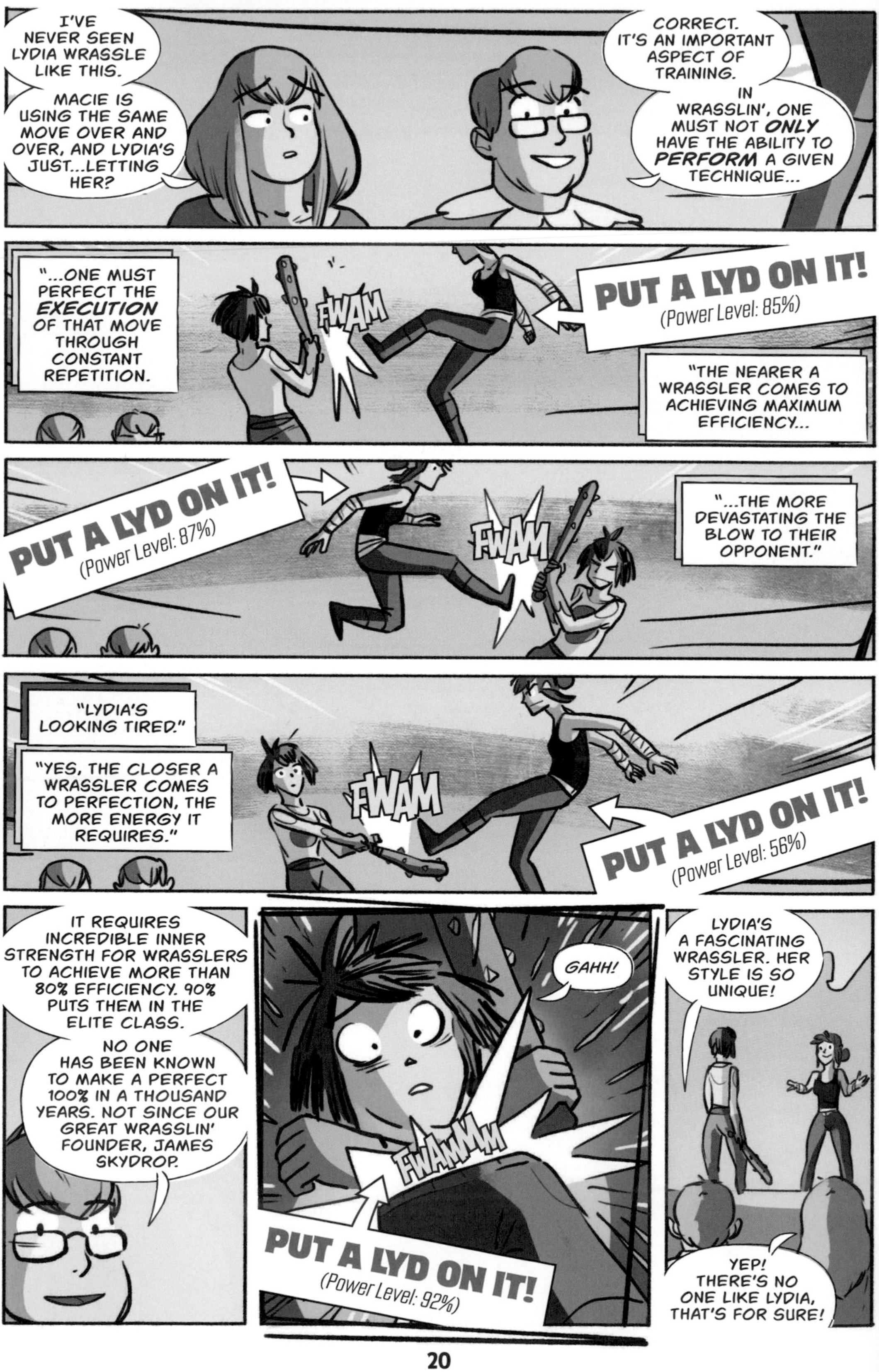
I'VE NEVER SEEN LYDIA WRASSLE LIKE THIS.
MACIE IS USING THE SAME MOVE OVER AND OVER, AND LYDIA'S JUST...LETTING HER?
CORRECT. IT'S AN IMPORTANT ASPECT OF TRAINING.
IN WRASSLIN', ONE MUST NOT ONLY HAVE THE ABILITY TO PERFORM A GIVEN TECHNIQUE...
"...ONE MUST PERFECT THE EXECUTION OF THAT MOVE THROUGH CONSTANT REPETITION.
FWAM
PUT A LYD ON IT!
(Power Level: 85%)
"THE NEARER A WRASSLER COMES TO ACHIEVING MAXIMUM EFFICIENCY...
PUT A LYD ON IT!
(Power Level: 87%)
FWAM
"...THE MORE DEVASTATING THE BLOW TO THEIR OPPONENT."
"LYDIA'S LOOKING TIRED."
"YES, THE CLOSER A WRASSLER COMES TO PERFECTION, THE MORE ENERGY IT REQUIRES."
FWAM
PUT A LYD ON IT!
(Power Level: 56%)
IT REQUIRES INCREDIBLE INNER STRENGTH FOR WRASSLERS TO ACHIEVE MORE THAN 80% EFFICIENCY. 90% PUTS THEM IN THE ELITE CLASS.
NO ONE HAS BEEN KNOWN TO MAKE A PERFECT 100% IN A THOUSAND YEARS. NOT SINCE OUR GREAT WRASSLIN' FOUNDER, JAMES SKYDROP.
GAHH!
FWAMMM
PUT A LYD ON IT!
(Power Level: 92%)
LYDIA'S A FASCINATING WRASSLER. HER STYLE IS SO UNIQUE!
YEP! THERE'S NO ONE LIKE LYDIA, THAT'S FOR SURE!

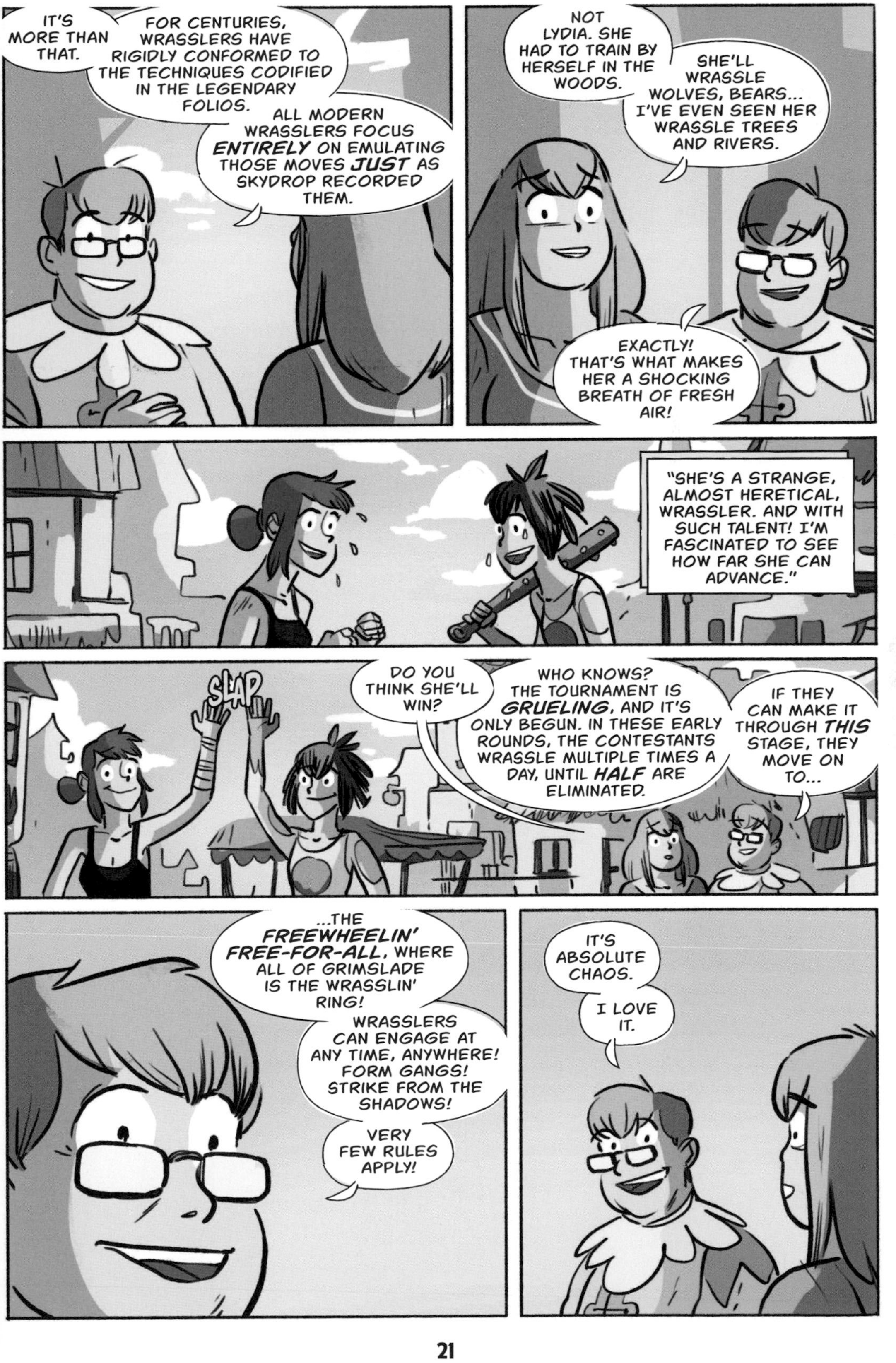
IT'S MORE THAN THAT.
FOR CENTURIES, WRASSLERS HAVE RIGIDLY CONFORMED TO THE TECHNIQUES CODIFIED IN THE LEGENDARY FOLIOS.
ALL MODERN WRASSLERS FOCUS *ENTIRELY* ON EMULATING THOSE MOVES *JUST* AS SKYDROP RECORDED THEM.
NOT LYDIA. SHE HAD TO TRAIN BY HERSELF IN THE WOODS.
SHE'LL WRASSLE WOLVES, BEARS... I'VE EVEN SEEN HER WRASSLE TREES AND RIVERS.
EXACTLY! THAT'S WHAT MAKES HER A SHOCKING BREATH OF FRESH AIR!
"SHE'S A STRANGE, ALMOST HERETICAL, WRASSLER. AND WITH SUCH TALENT! I'M FASCINATED TO SEE HOW FAR SHE CAN ADVANCE."
SLAP
DO YOU THINK SHE'LL WIN?
WHO KNOWS? THE TOURNAMENT IS *GRUELING*, AND IT'S ONLY BEGUN. IN THESE EARLY ROUNDS, THE CONTESTANTS WRASSLE MULTIPLE TIMES A DAY, UNTIL *HALF* ARE ELIMINATED.
IF THEY CAN MAKE IT THROUGH *THIS* STAGE, THEY MOVE ON TO...
...THE *FREEWHEELIN' FREE-FOR-ALL*, WHERE ALL OF GRIMSLADE IS THE WRASSLIN' RING!
WRASSLERS CAN ENGAGE AT ANY TIME, ANYWHERE! FORM GANGS! STRIKE FROM THE SHADOWS!
VERY FEW RULES APPLY!
IT'S ABSOLUTE CHAOS.
I LOVE IT.

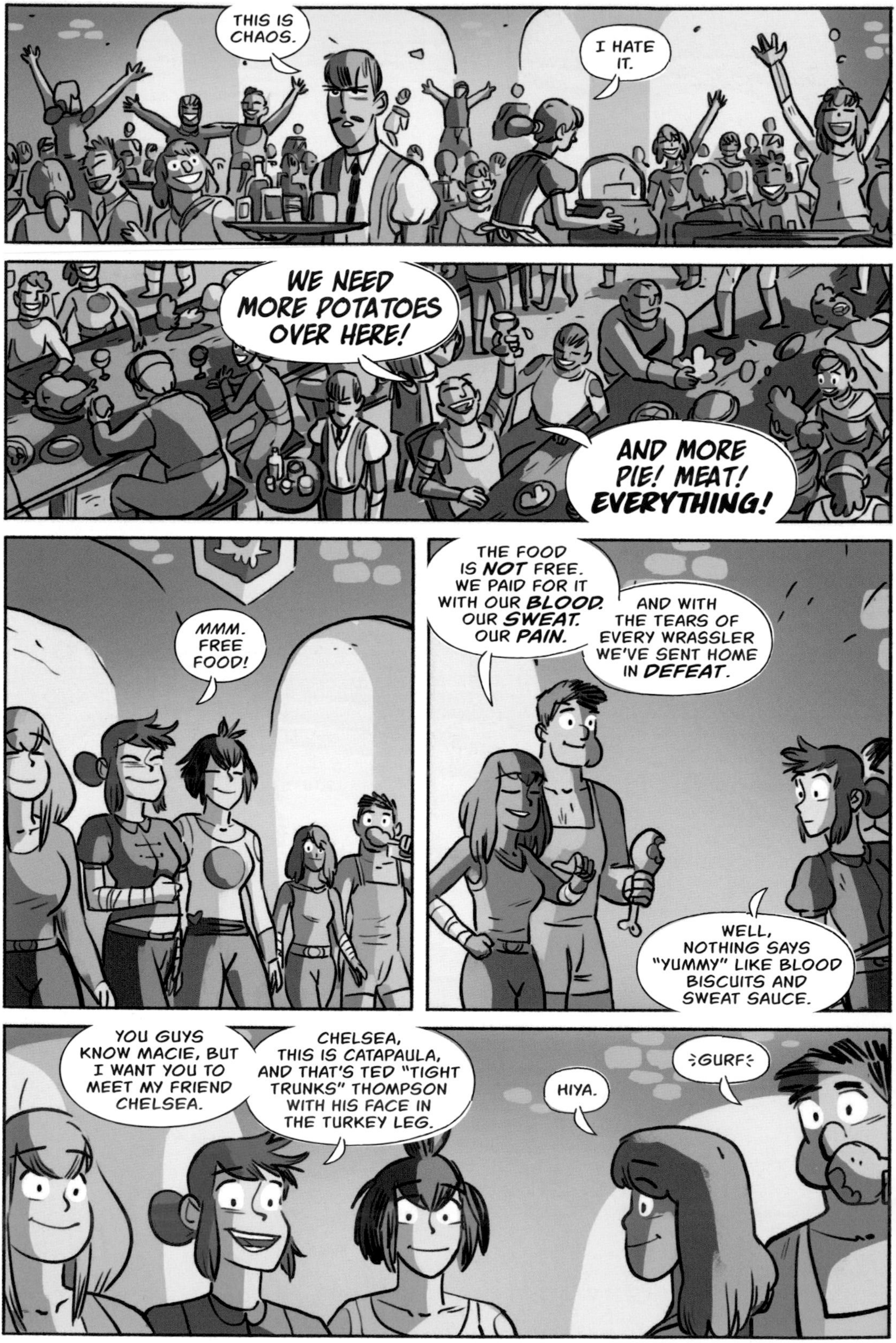
THIS IS CHAOS.
I HATE IT.
WE NEED MORE POTATOES OVER HERE!
AND MORE PIE! MEAT! EVERYTHING!
MMM. FREE FOOD!
THE FOOD IS NOT FREE. WE PAID FOR IT WITH OUR BLOOD. OUR SWEAT. OUR PAIN.
AND WITH THE TEARS OF EVERY WRASSLER WE'VE SENT HOME IN DEFEAT.
WELL, NOTHING SAYS "YUMMY" LIKE BLOOD BISCUITS AND SWEAT SAUCE.
YOU GUYS KNOW MACIE, BUT I WANT YOU TO MEET MY FRIEND CHELSEA.
CHELSEA, THIS IS CATAPAULA, AND THAT'S TED "TIGHT TRUNKS" THOMPSON WITH HIS FACE IN THE TURKEY LEG.
HIYA.
GURF

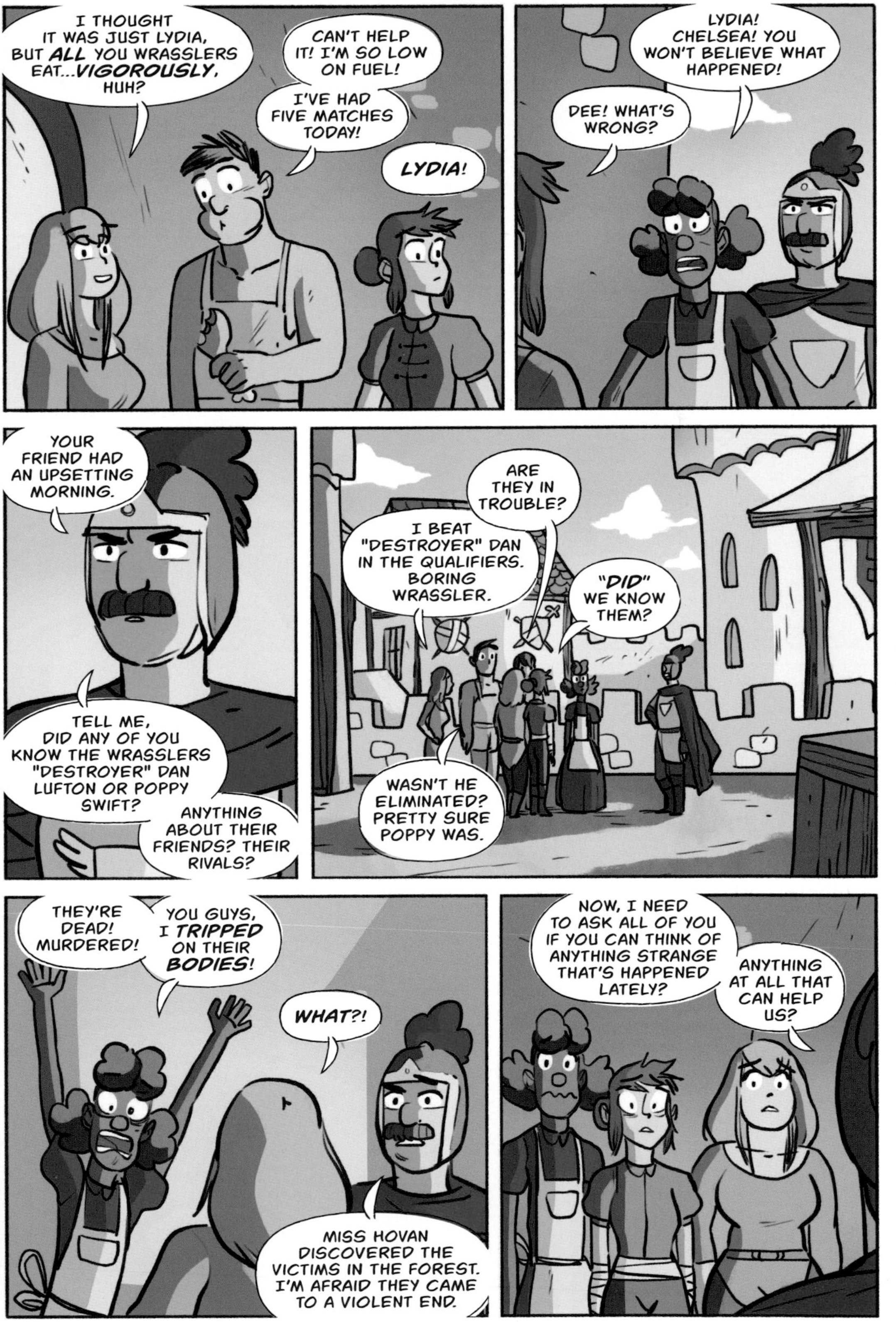
I THOUGHT IT WAS JUST LYDIA, BUT ALL YOU WRASSLERS EAT...VIGOROUSLY, HUH?
CAN'T HELP IT! I'M SO LOW ON FUEL!
I'VE HAD FIVE MATCHES TODAY!
LYDIA!
LYDIA! CHELSEA! YOU WON'T BELIEVE WHAT HAPPENED!
DEE! WHAT'S WRONG?
YOUR FRIEND HAD AN UPSETTING MORNING.
TELL ME, DID ANY OF YOU KNOW THE WRASSLERS "DESTROYER" DAN LUFTON OR POPPY SWIFT?
ANYTHING ABOUT THEIR FRIENDS? THEIR RIVALS?
ARE THEY IN TROUBLE?
I BEAT "DESTROYER" DAN IN THE QUALIFIERS. BORING WRASSLER.
"DID" WE KNOW THEM?
WASN'T HE ELIMINATED? PRETTY SURE POPPY WAS.
THEY'RE DEAD! MURDERED!
YOU GUYS, I TRIPPED ON THEIR BODIES!
WHAT?!
MISS HOVAN DISCOVERED THE VICTIMS IN THE FOREST. I'M AFRAID THEY CAME TO A VIOLENT END.
NOW, I NEED TO ASK ALL OF YOU IF YOU CAN THINK OF ANYTHING STRANGE THAT'S HAPPENED LATELY?
ANYTHING AT ALL THAT CAN HELP US?

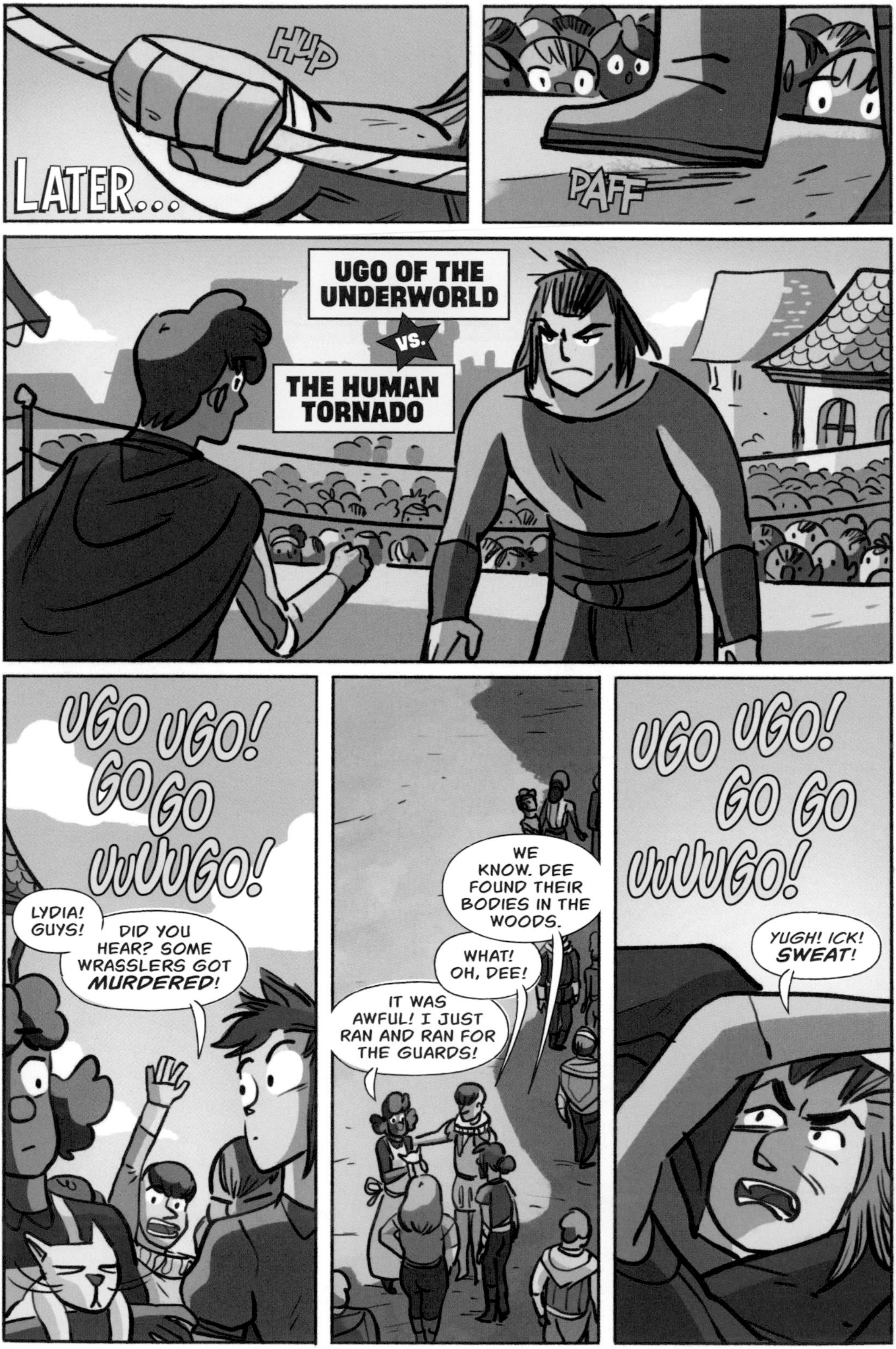
HUP
LATER...
PAFF
UGO OF THE UNDERWORLD
VS.
THE HUMAN TORNADO
UGO UGO! GO GO UUUUGO!
LYDIA! GUYS!
DID YOU HEAR? SOME WRASSLERS GOT MURDERED!
WE KNOW. DEE FOUND THEIR BODIES IN THE WOODS.
WHAT! OH, DEE!
IT WAS AWFUL! I JUST RAN AND RAN FOR THE GUARDS!
UGO UGO! GO GO UUUUGO!
YUGH! ICK! SWEAT!

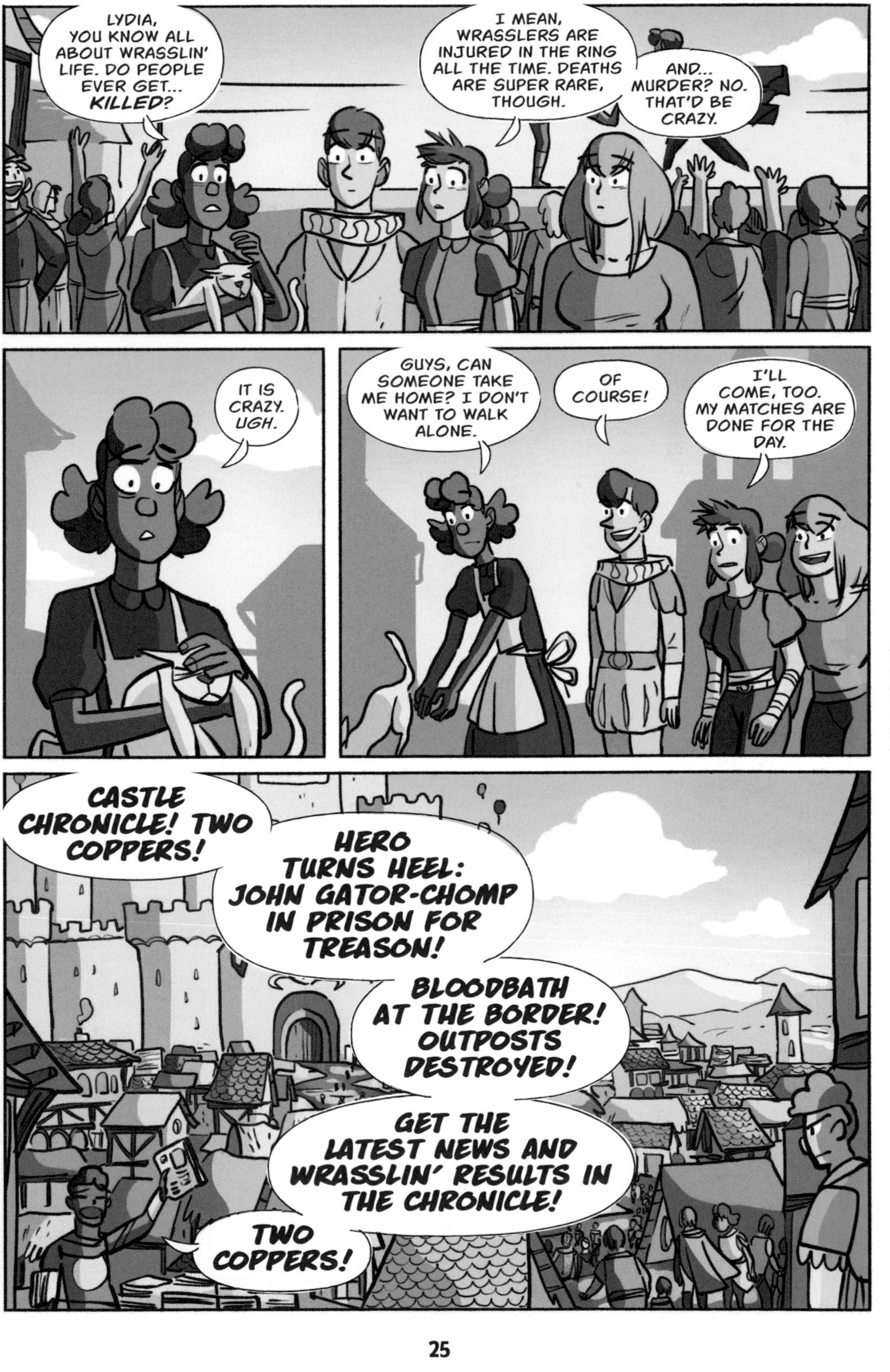
LYDIA, YOU KNOW ALL ABOUT WRASSLIN' LIFE. DO PEOPLE EVER GET... KILLED?
I MEAN, WRASSLERS ARE INJURED IN THE RING ALL THE TIME. DEATHS ARE SUPER RARE, THOUGH.
AND... MURDER? NO. THAT'D BE CRAZY.
IT IS CRAZY. UGH.
GUYS, CAN SOMEONE TAKE ME HOME? I DON'T WANT TO WALK ALONE.
OF COURSE!
I'LL COME, TOO. MY MATCHES ARE DONE FOR THE DAY.
CASTLE CHRONICLE! TWO COPPERS!
HERO TURNS HEEL: JOHN GATOR-CHOMP IN PRISON FOR TREASON!
BLOODBATH AT THE BORDER! OUTPOSTS DESTROYED!
GET THE LATEST NEWS AND WRASSLIN' RESULTS IN THE CHRONICLE!
TWO COPPERS!

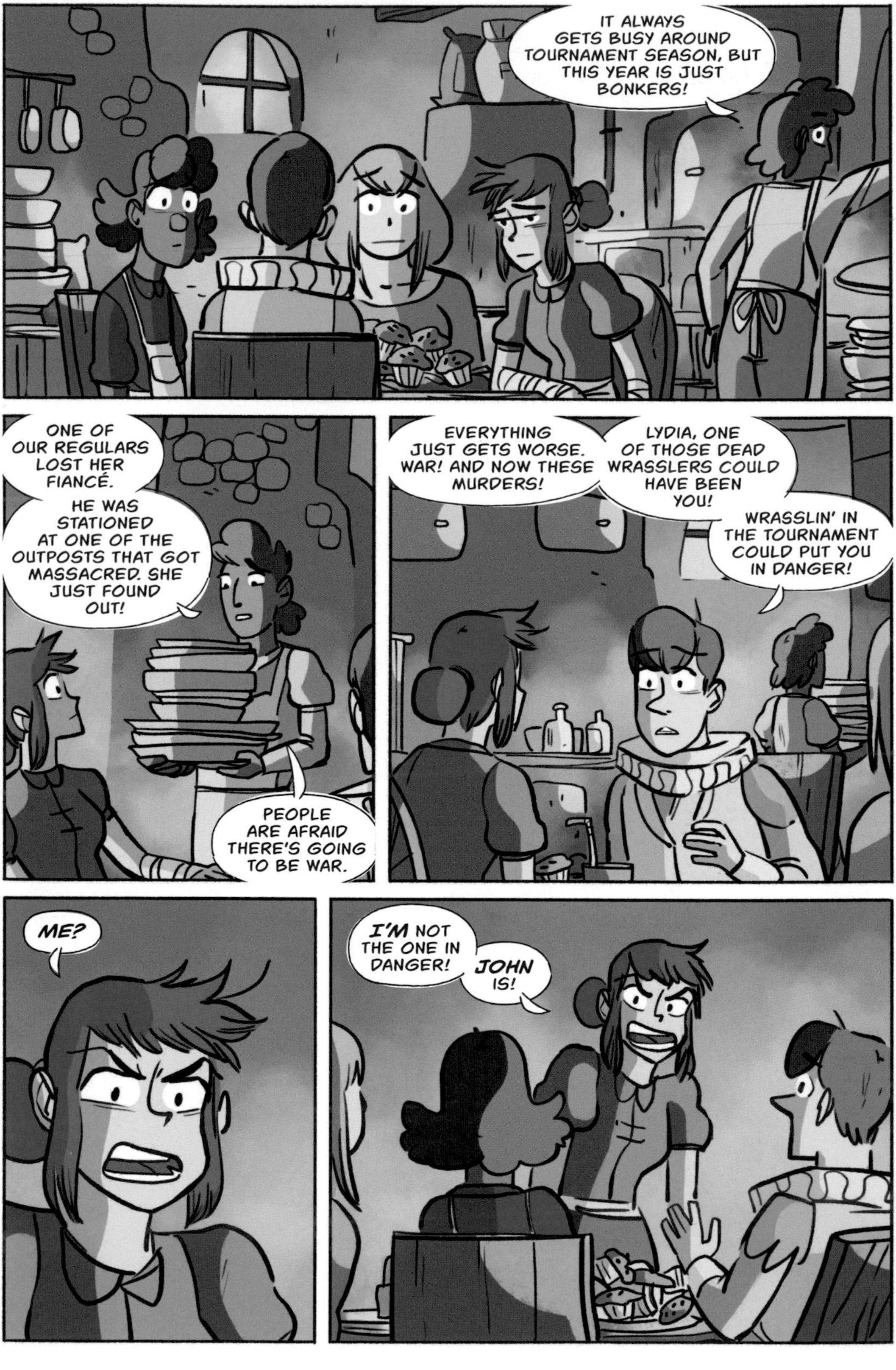
IT ALWAYS GETS BUSY AROUND TOURNAMENT SEASON, BUT THIS YEAR IS JUST BONKERS!
ONE OF OUR REGULARS LOST HER FIANCÉ.
HE WAS STATIONED AT ONE OF THE OUTPOSTS THAT GOT MASSACRED. SHE JUST FOUND OUT!
PEOPLE ARE AFRAID THERE'S GOING TO BE WAR.
EVERYTHING JUST GETS WORSE. WAR! AND NOW THESE MURDERS!
LYDIA, ONE OF THOSE DEAD WRASSLERS COULD HAVE BEEN YOU!
WRASSLIN' IN THE TOURNAMENT COULD PUT YOU IN DANGER!
ME?
I'M NOT THE ONE IN DANGER!
JOHN IS!

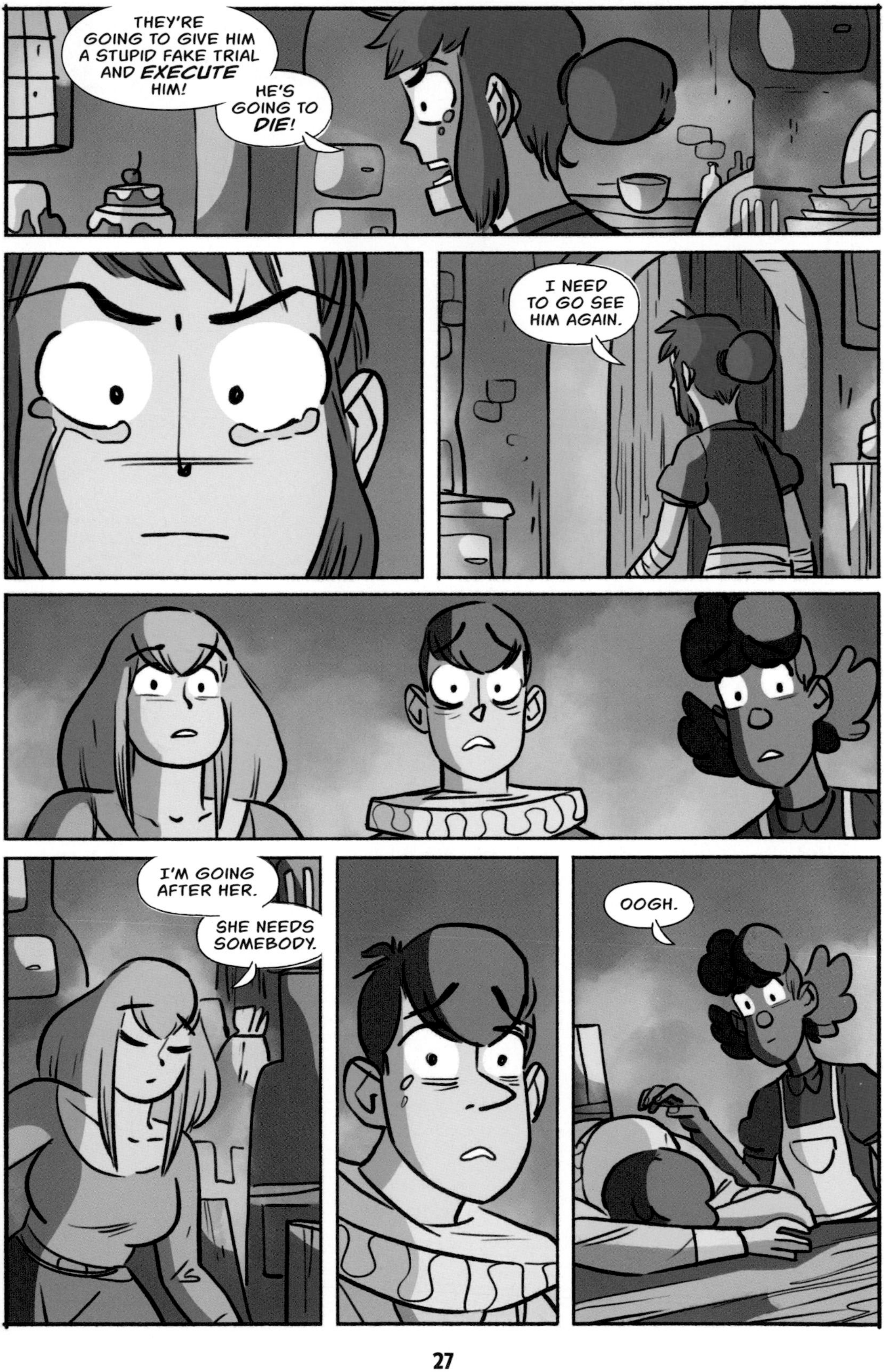
THEY'RE GOING TO GIVE HIM A STUPID FAKE TRIAL AND **EXECUTE** HIM!
HE'S GOING TO **DIE**!
I NEED TO GO SEE HIM AGAIN.
I'M GOING AFTER HER.
SHE NEEDS SOMEBODY.
OOGH.

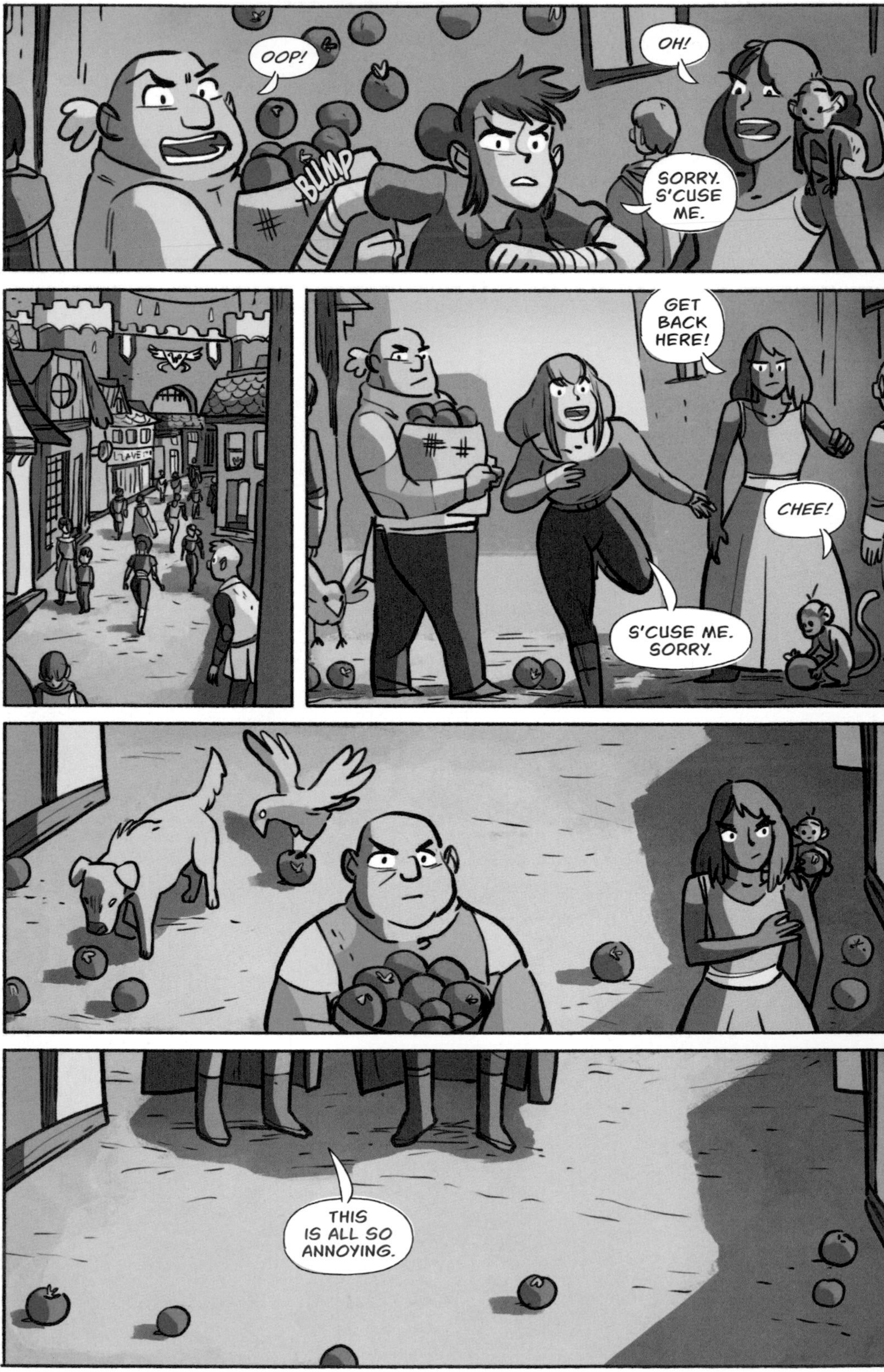
OOP!
BUMP
OH!
SORRY. S'CUSE ME.
GET BACK HERE!
CHEE!
S'CUSE ME. SORRY.
THIS IS ALL SO ANNOYING.

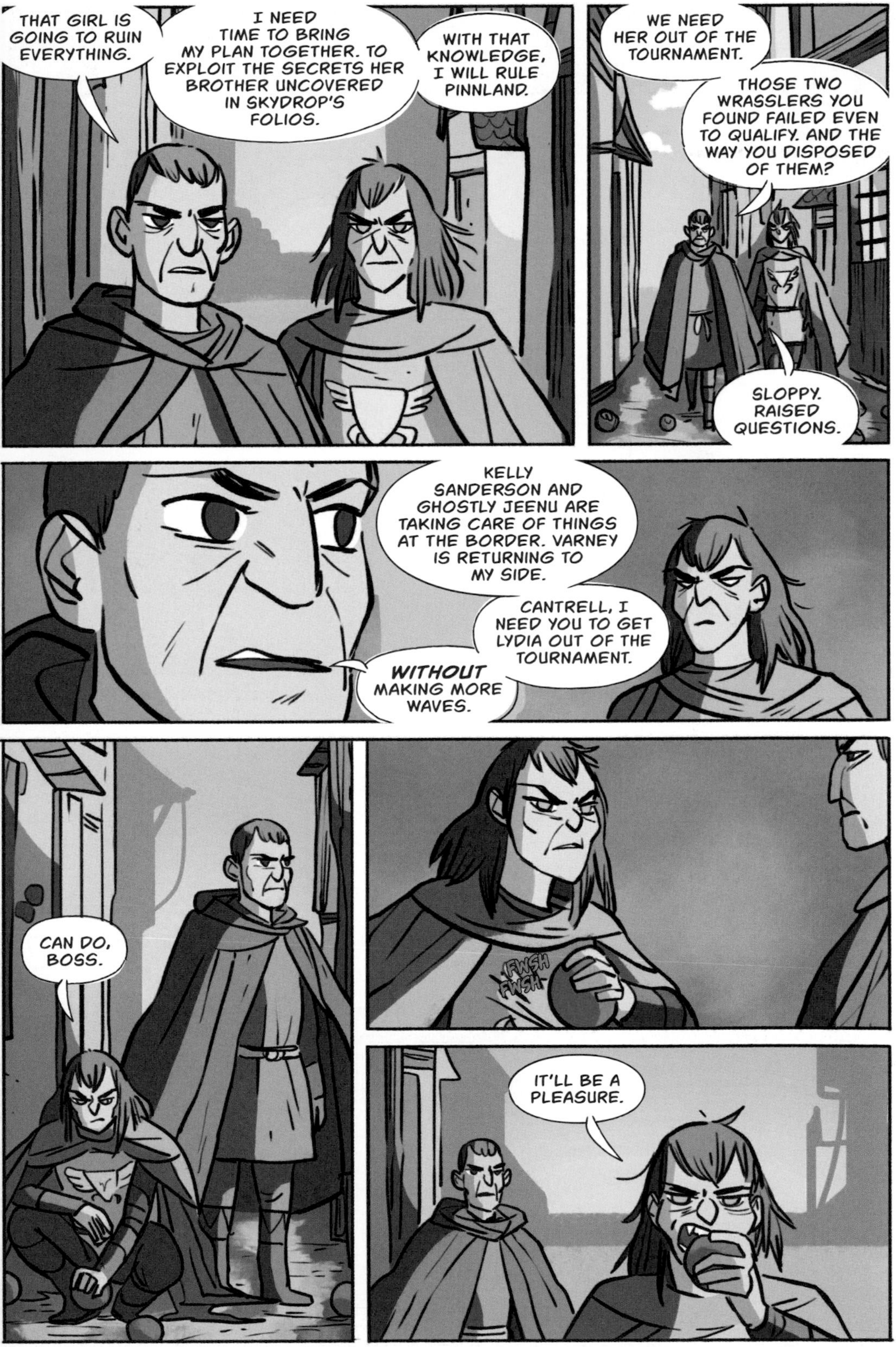
THAT GIRL IS GOING TO RUIN EVERYTHING.
I NEED TIME TO BRING MY PLAN TOGETHER. TO EXPLOIT THE SECRETS HER BROTHER UNCOVERED IN SKYDROP'S FOLIOS.
WITH THAT KNOWLEDGE, I WILL RULE PINNLAND.
WE NEED HER OUT OF THE TOURNAMENT.
THOSE TWO WRASSLERS YOU FOUND FAILED EVEN TO QUALIFY. AND THE WAY YOU DISPOSED OF THEM?
SLOPPY. RAISED QUESTIONS.
KELLY SANDERSON AND GHOSTLY JEENU ARE TAKING CARE OF THINGS AT THE BORDER. VARNEY IS RETURNING TO MY SIDE.
CANTRELL, I NEED YOU TO GET LYDIA OUT OF THE TOURNAMENT.
WITHOUT MAKING MORE WAVES.
CAN DO, BOSS.
FWSH FWSH
IT'LL BE A PLEASURE.

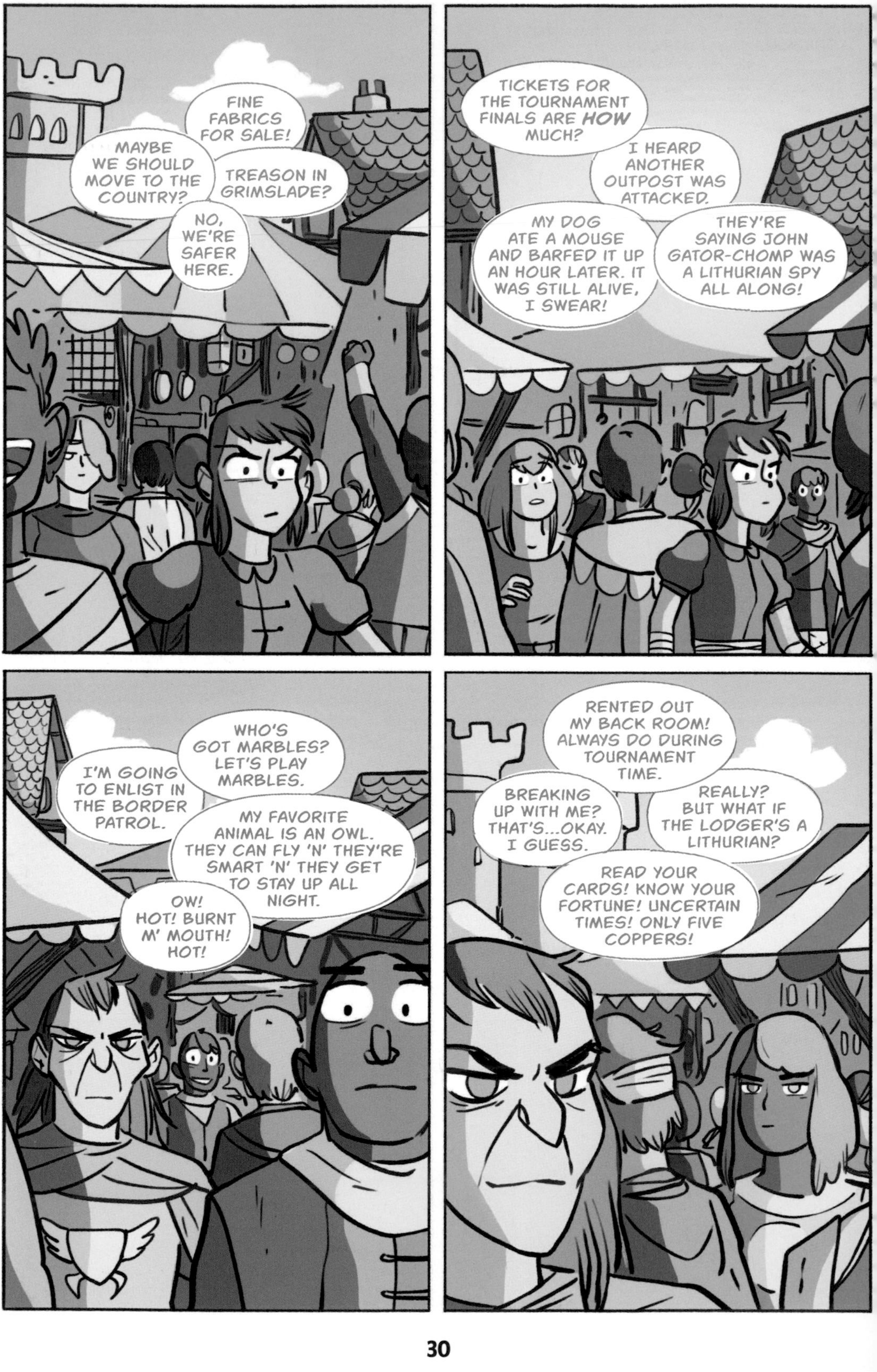
FINE FABRICS FOR SALE!
MAYBE WE SHOULD MOVE TO THE COUNTRY?
TREASON IN GRIMSLADE?
NO, WE'RE SAFER HERE.
TICKETS FOR THE TOURNAMENT FINALS ARE *HOW* MUCH?
I HEARD ANOTHER OUTPOST WAS ATTACKED.
MY DOG ATE A MOUSE AND BARFED IT UP AN HOUR LATER. IT WAS STILL ALIVE, I SWEAR!
THEY'RE SAYING JOHN GATOR-CHOMP WAS A LITHURIAN SPY ALL ALONG!
WHO'S GOT MARBLES? LET'S PLAY MARBLES.
I'M GOING TO ENLIST IN THE BORDER PATROL.
MY FAVORITE ANIMAL IS AN OWL. THEY CAN FLY 'N' THEY'RE SMART 'N' THEY GET TO STAY UP ALL NIGHT.
OW! HOT! BURNT M' MOUTH! HOT!
RENTED OUT MY BACK ROOM! ALWAYS DO DURING TOURNAMENT TIME.
BREAKING UP WITH ME? THAT'S...OKAY. I GUESS.
REALLY? BUT WHAT IF THE LODGER'S A LITHURIAN?
READ YOUR CARDS! KNOW YOUR FORTUNE! UNCERTAIN TIMES! ONLY FIVE COPPERS!

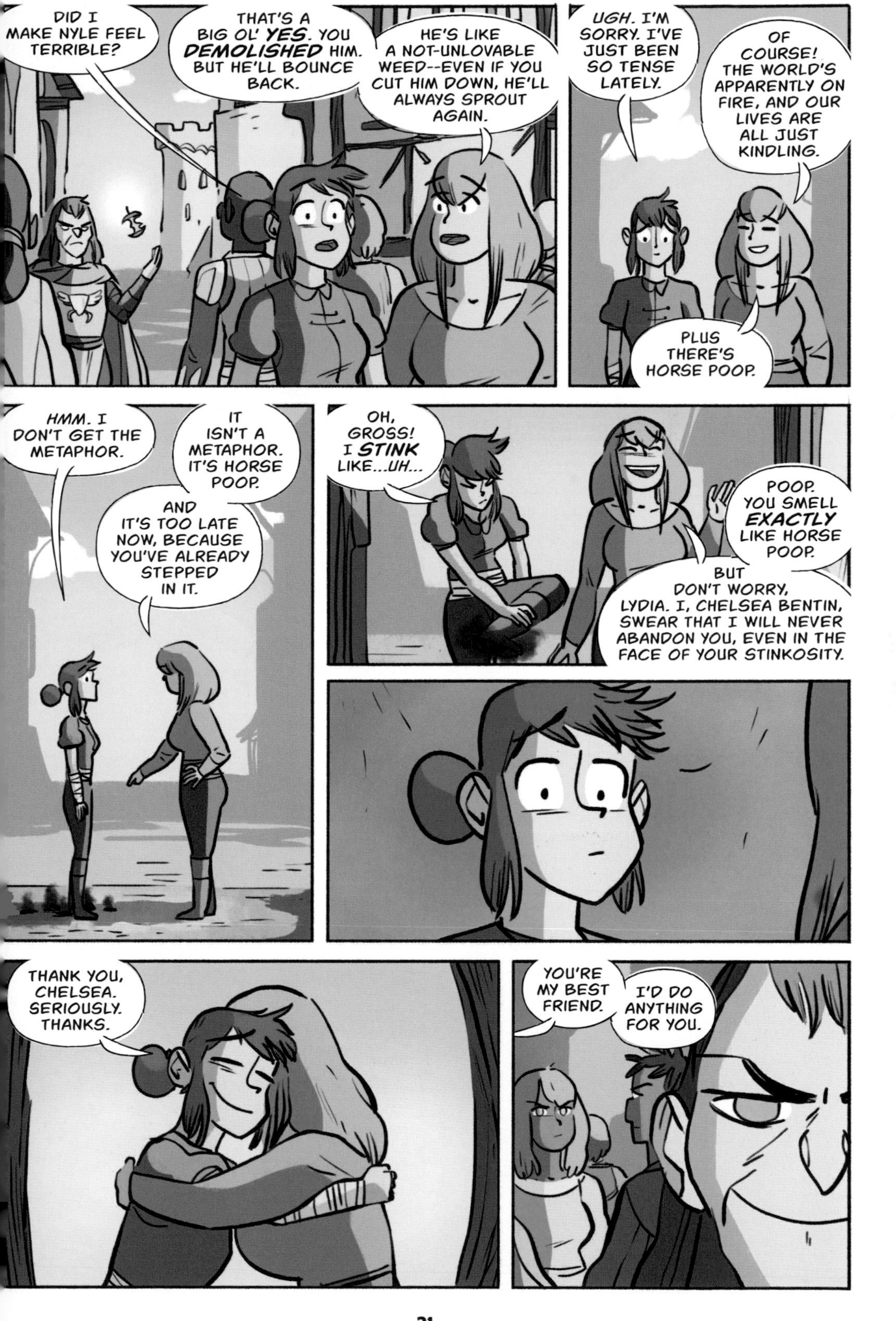
DID I MAKE NYLE FEEL TERRIBLE?
THAT'S A BIG OL' **YES**. YOU **DEMOLISHED** HIM. BUT HE'LL BOUNCE BACK.
HE'S LIKE A NOT-UNLOVABLE WEED--EVEN IF YOU CUT HIM DOWN, HE'LL ALWAYS SPROUT AGAIN.
UGH. I'M SORRY. I'VE JUST BEEN SO TENSE LATELY.
OF COURSE! THE WORLD'S APPARENTLY ON FIRE, AND OUR LIVES ARE ALL JUST KINDLING.
PLUS THERE'S HORSE POOP.
HMM. I DON'T GET THE METAPHOR.
IT ISN'T A METAPHOR. IT'S HORSE POOP.
AND IT'S TOO LATE NOW, BECAUSE YOU'VE ALREADY STEPPED IN IT.
OH, GROSS! I **STINK** LIKE...*UH*...
POOP. YOU SMELL **EXACTLY** LIKE HORSE POOP.
BUT DON'T WORRY, LYDIA. I, CHELSEA BENTIN, SWEAR THAT I WILL NEVER ABANDON YOU, EVEN IN THE FACE OF YOUR STINKOSITY.
THANK YOU, CHELSEA. SERIOUSLY. THANKS.
YOU'RE MY BEST FRIEND.
I'D DO ANYTHING FOR YOU.

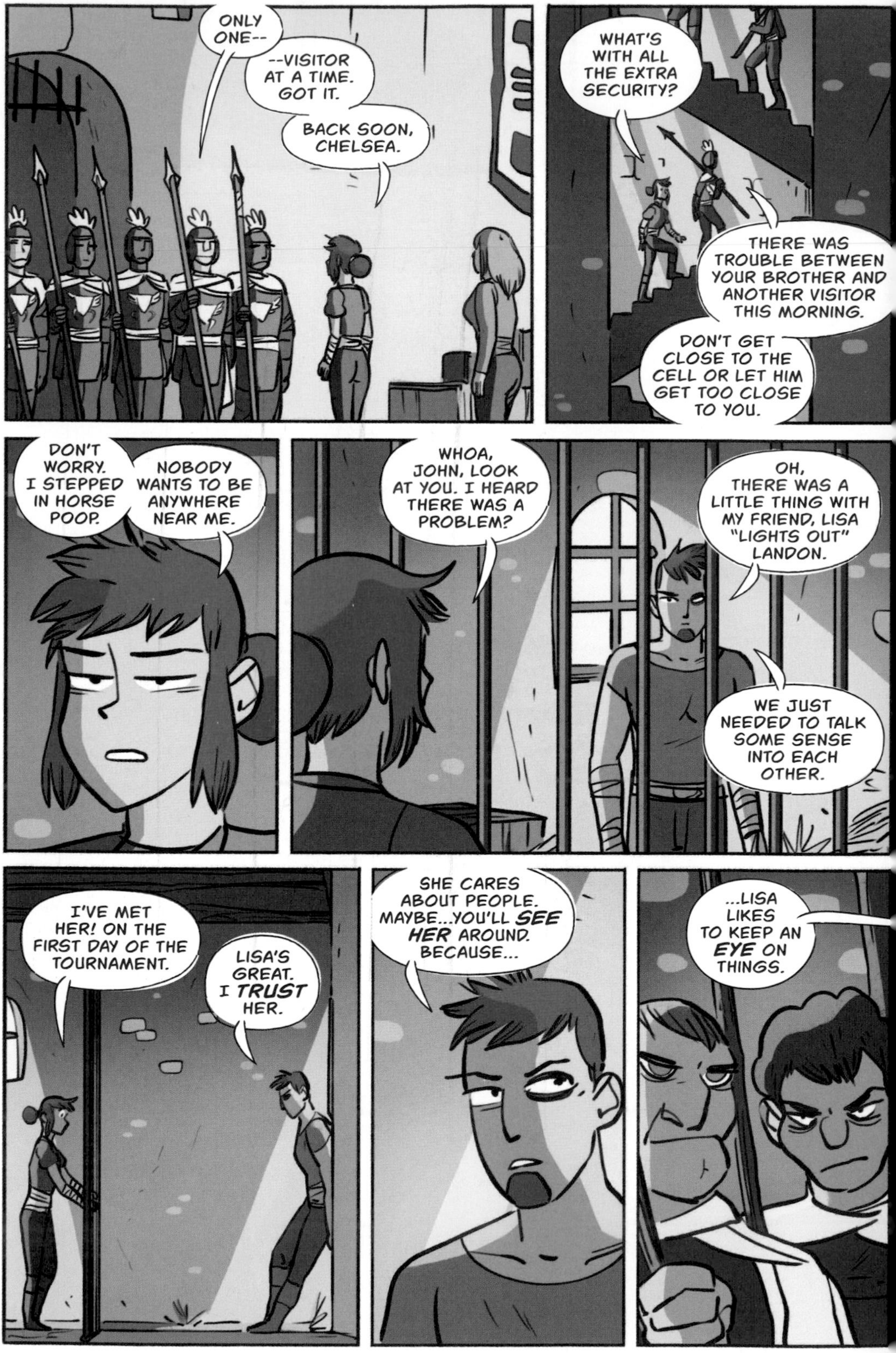
ONLY ONE--
--VISITOR AT A TIME. GOT IT.
BACK SOON, CHELSEA.
WHAT'S WITH ALL THE EXTRA SECURITY?
THERE WAS TROUBLE BETWEEN YOUR BROTHER AND ANOTHER VISITOR THIS MORNING.
DON'T GET CLOSE TO THE CELL OR LET HIM GET TOO CLOSE TO YOU.
DON'T WORRY. I STEPPED IN HORSE POOP.
NOBODY WANTS TO BE ANYWHERE NEAR ME.
WHOA, JOHN, LOOK AT YOU. I HEARD THERE WAS A PROBLEM?
OH, THERE WAS A LITTLE THING WITH MY FRIEND, LISA "LIGHTS OUT" LANDON.
WE JUST NEEDED TO TALK SOME SENSE INTO EACH OTHER.
I'VE MET HER! ON THE FIRST DAY OF THE TOURNAMENT.
LISA'S GREAT. I TRUST HER.
SHE CARES ABOUT PEOPLE. MAYBE...YOU'LL SEE HER AROUND. BECAUSE...
...LISA LIKES TO KEEP AN EYE ON THINGS.

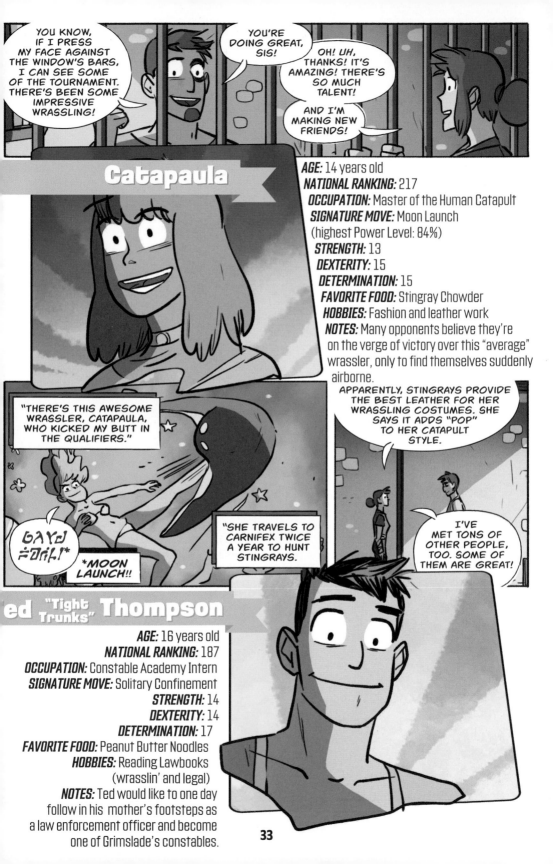

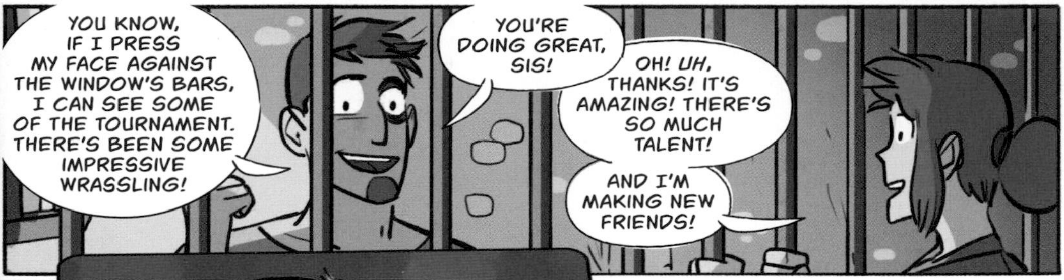
YOU KNOW, IF I PRESS MY FACE AGAINST THE WINDOW'S BARS, I CAN SEE SOME OF THE TOURNAMENT. THERE'S BEEN SOME IMPRESSIVE WRASSLING!
YOU'RE DOING GREAT, SIS!
OH! UH, THANKS! IT'S AMAZING! THERE'S SO MUCH TALENT!
AND I'M MAKING NEW FRIENDS!

Catapaula

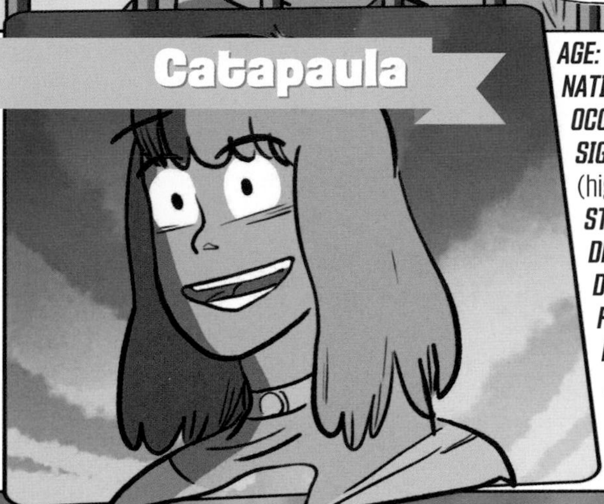

AGE: 14 years old
NATIONAL RANKING: 217
OCCUPATION: Master of the Human Catapult
SIGNATURE MOVE: Moon Launch (highest Power Level: 84%)
STRENGTH: 13
DEXTERITY: 15
DETERMINATION: 15
FAVORITE FOOD: Stingray Chowder
HOBBIES: Fashion and leather work
NOTES: Many opponents believe they're on the verge of victory over this "average" wrassler, only to find themselves suddenly airborne.

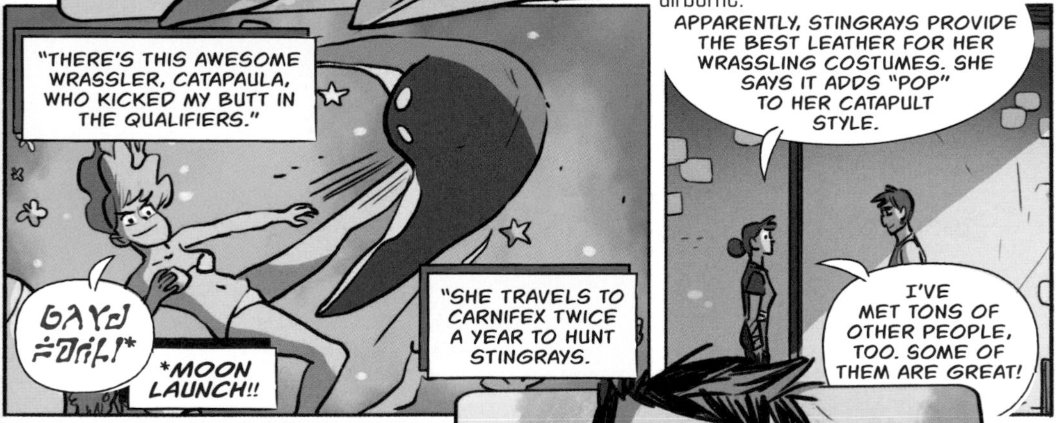
"THERE'S THIS AWESOME WRASSLER, CATAPAULA, WHO KICKED MY BUTT IN THE QUALIFIERS."
*MOON LAUNCH!!
"SHE TRAVELS TO CARNIFEX TWICE A YEAR TO HUNT STINGRAYS.
APPARENTLY, STINGRAYS PROVIDE THE BEST LEATHER FOR HER WRASSLING COSTUMES. SHE SAYS IT ADDS "POP" TO HER CATAPULT STYLE.
I'VE MET TONS OF OTHER PEOPLE, TOO. SOME OF THEM ARE GREAT!

ed "Tight Trunks" Thompson

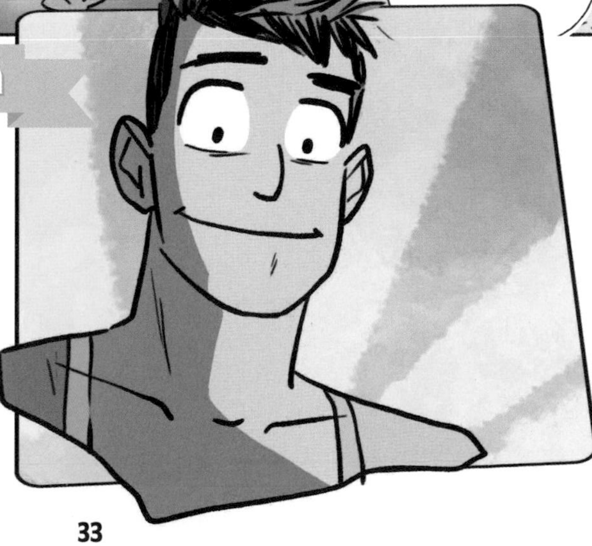

AGE: 16 years old
NATIONAL RANKING: 187
OCCUPATION: Constable Academy Intern
SIGNATURE MOVE: Solitary Confinement
STRENGTH: 14
DEXTERITY: 14
DETERMINATION: 17
FAVORITE FOOD: Peanut Butter Noodles
HOBBIES: Reading Lawbooks (wrasslin' and legal)
NOTES: Ted would like to one day follow in his mother's footsteps as a law enforcement officer and become one of Grimslade's constables.

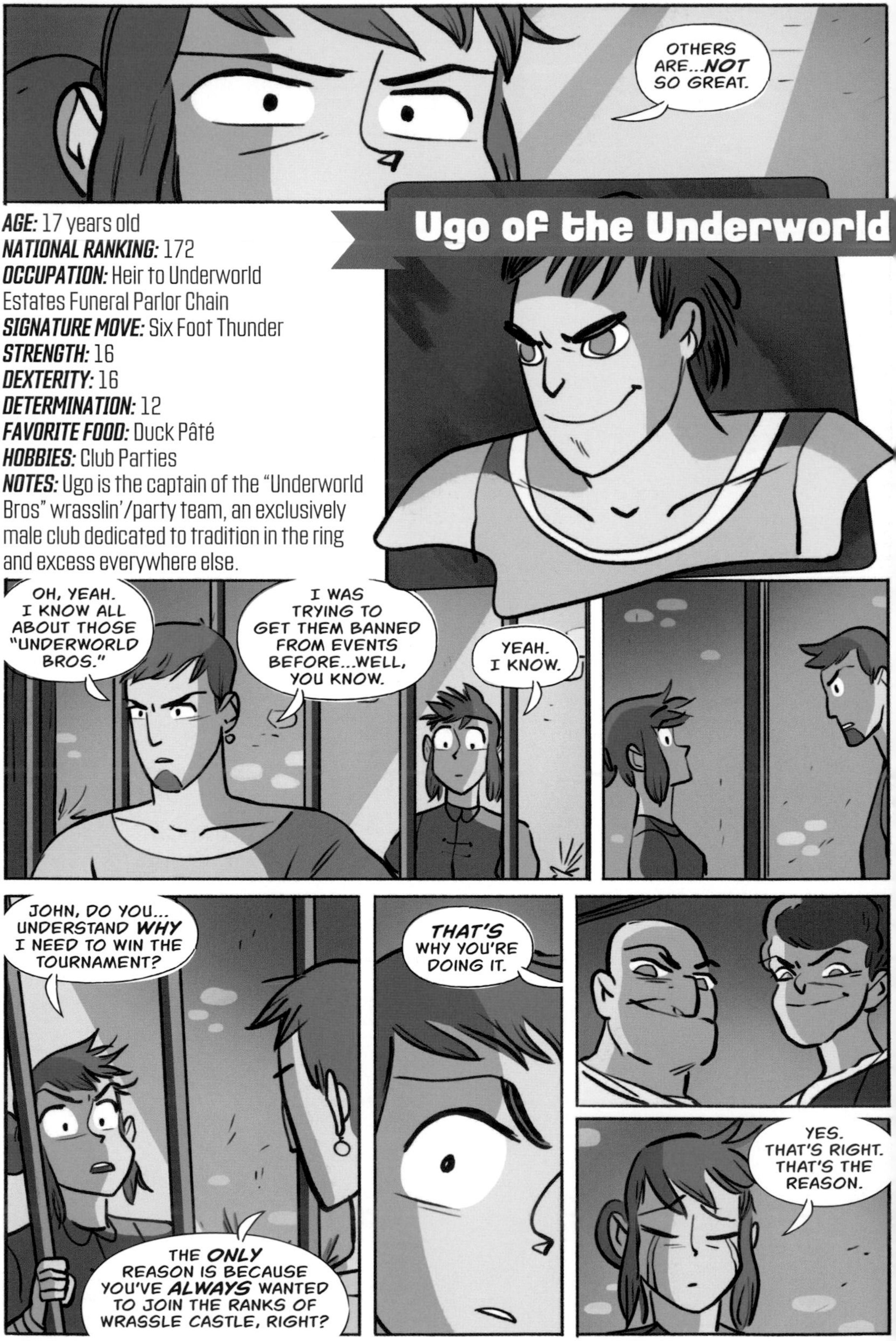

OTHERS ARE...NOT SO GREAT.
Ugo of the Underworld
AGE: 17 years old
NATIONAL RANKING: 172
OCCUPATION: Heir to Underworld Estates Funeral Parlor Chain
SIGNATURE MOVE: Six Foot Thunder
STRENGTH: 16
DEXTERITY: 16
DETERMINATION: 12
FAVORITE FOOD: Duck Pâté
HOBBIES: Club Parties
NOTES: Ugo is the captain of the "Underworld Bros" wrasslin'/party team, an exclusively male club dedicated to tradition in the ring and excess everywhere else.
OH, YEAH. I KNOW ALL ABOUT THOSE "UNDERWORLD BROS."
I WAS TRYING TO GET THEM BANNED FROM EVENTS BEFORE...WELL, YOU KNOW.
YEAH. I KNOW.
JOHN, DO YOU... UNDERSTAND WHY I NEED TO WIN THE TOURNAMENT?
THE ONLY REASON IS BECAUSE YOU'VE ALWAYS WANTED TO JOIN THE RANKS OF WRASSLE CASTLE, RIGHT?
THAT'S WHY YOU'RE DOING IT.
YES. THAT'S RIGHT. THAT'S THE REASON.

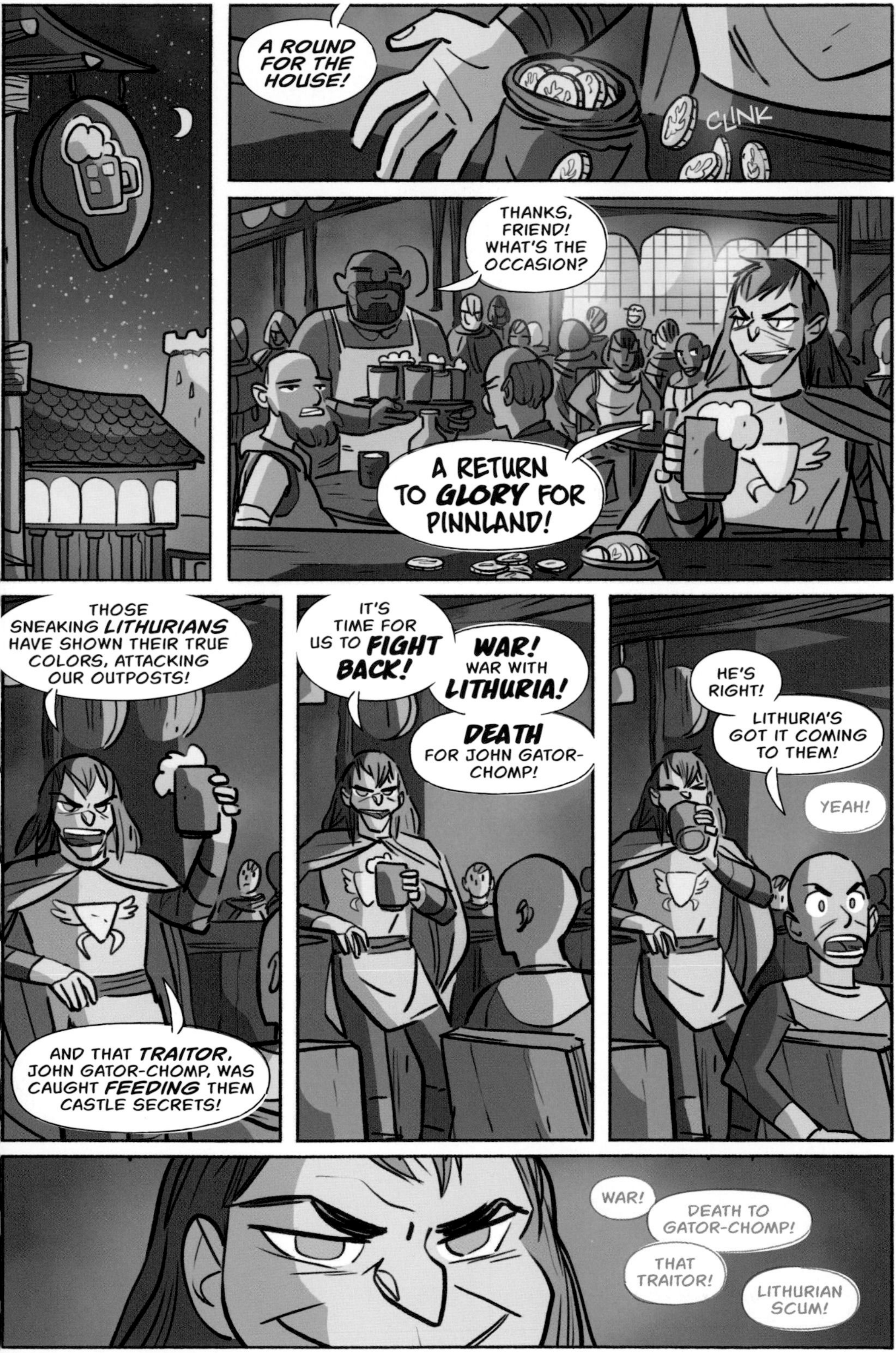
A ROUND FOR THE HOUSE!
CLINK
THANKS, FRIEND! WHAT'S THE OCCASION?
A RETURN TO GLORY FOR PINNLAND!
THOSE SNEAKING LITHURIANS HAVE SHOWN THEIR TRUE COLORS, ATTACKING OUR OUTPOSTS!
AND THAT TRAITOR, JOHN GATOR-CHOMP, WAS CAUGHT FEEDING THEM CASTLE SECRETS!
IT'S TIME FOR US TO FIGHT BACK!
WAR! WAR WITH LITHURIA!
DEATH FOR JOHN GATOR-CHOMP!
HE'S RIGHT!
LITHURIA'S GOT IT COMING TO THEM!
YEAH!
WAR!
DEATH TO GATOR-CHOMP!
THAT TRAITOR!
LITHURIAN SCUM!

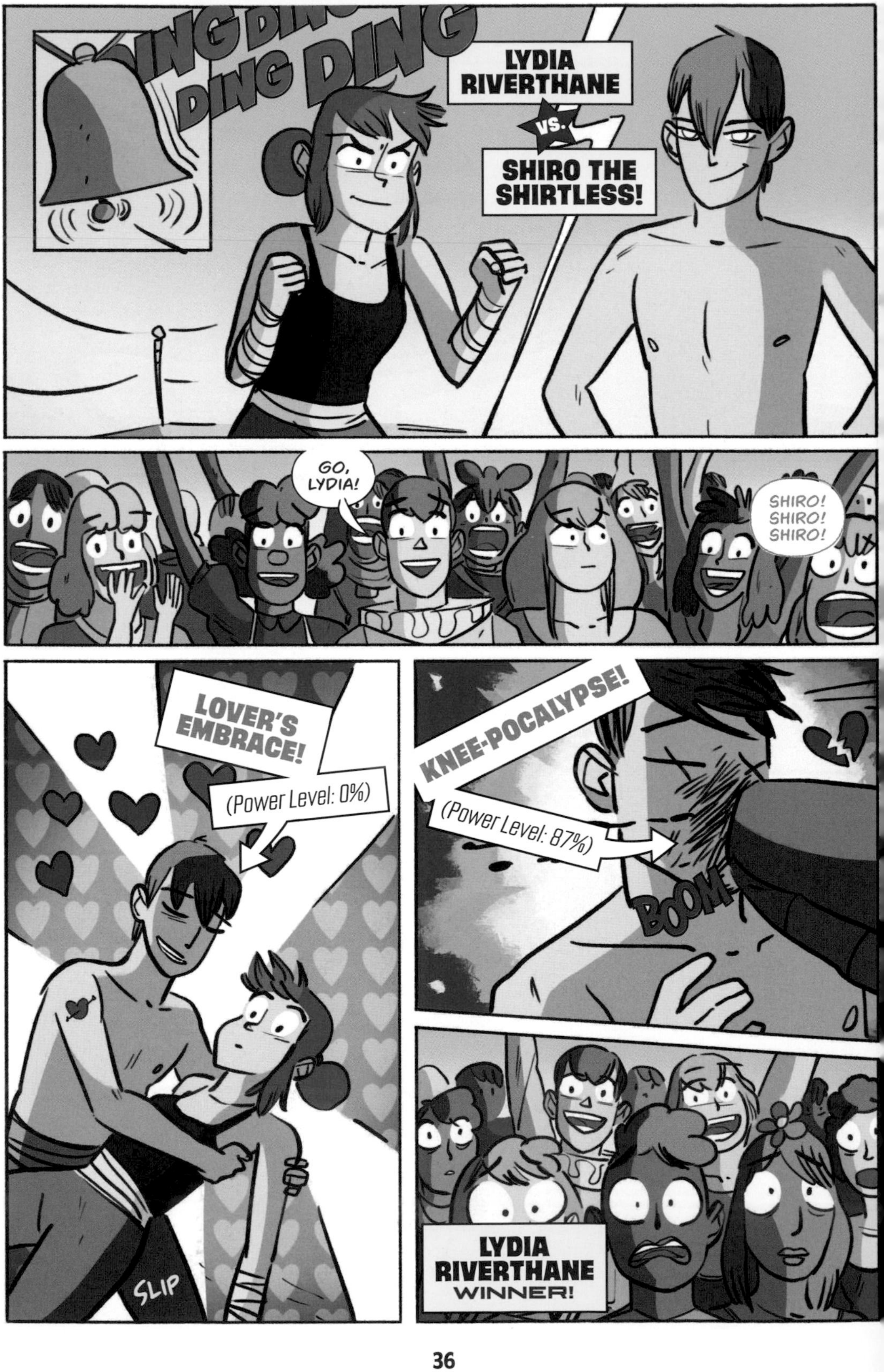
DING DING
DING DING
LYDIA RIVERTHANE
VS.
SHIRO THE SHIRTLESS!
GO, LYDIA!
SHIRO! SHIRO! SHIRO!
LOVER'S EMBRACE!
(Power Level: 0%)
SLIP
KNEE-POCALYPSE!
(Power Level: 87%)
BOOM
LYDIA RIVERTHANE
WINNER!

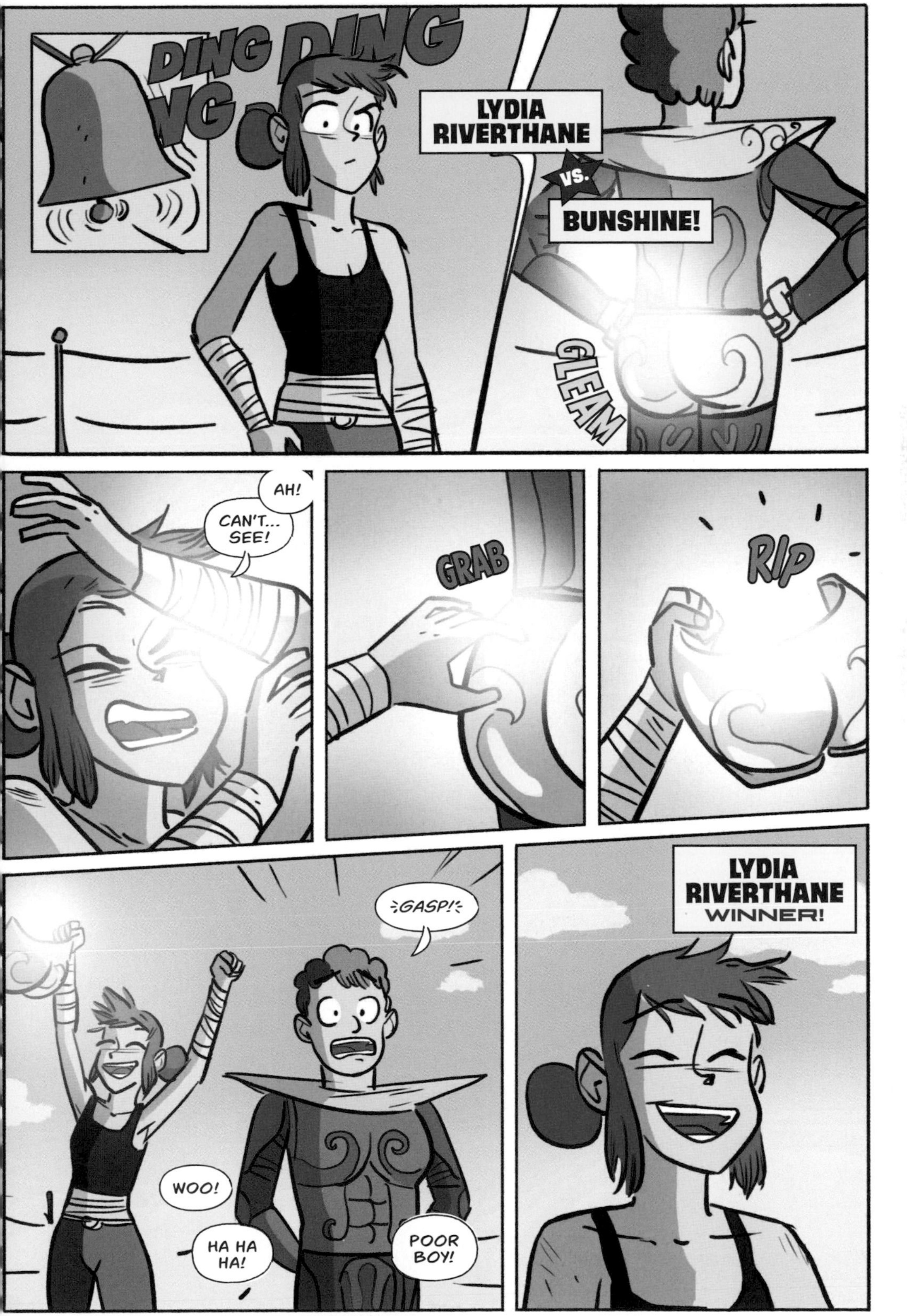
DING DING
NG
LYDIA RIVERTHANE
VS.
BUNSHINE!
GLEAM
AH!
CAN'T... SEE!
GRAB
RIP
:GASP!:
WOO!
HA HA HA!
POOR BOY!
LYDIA RIVERTHANE
WINNER!

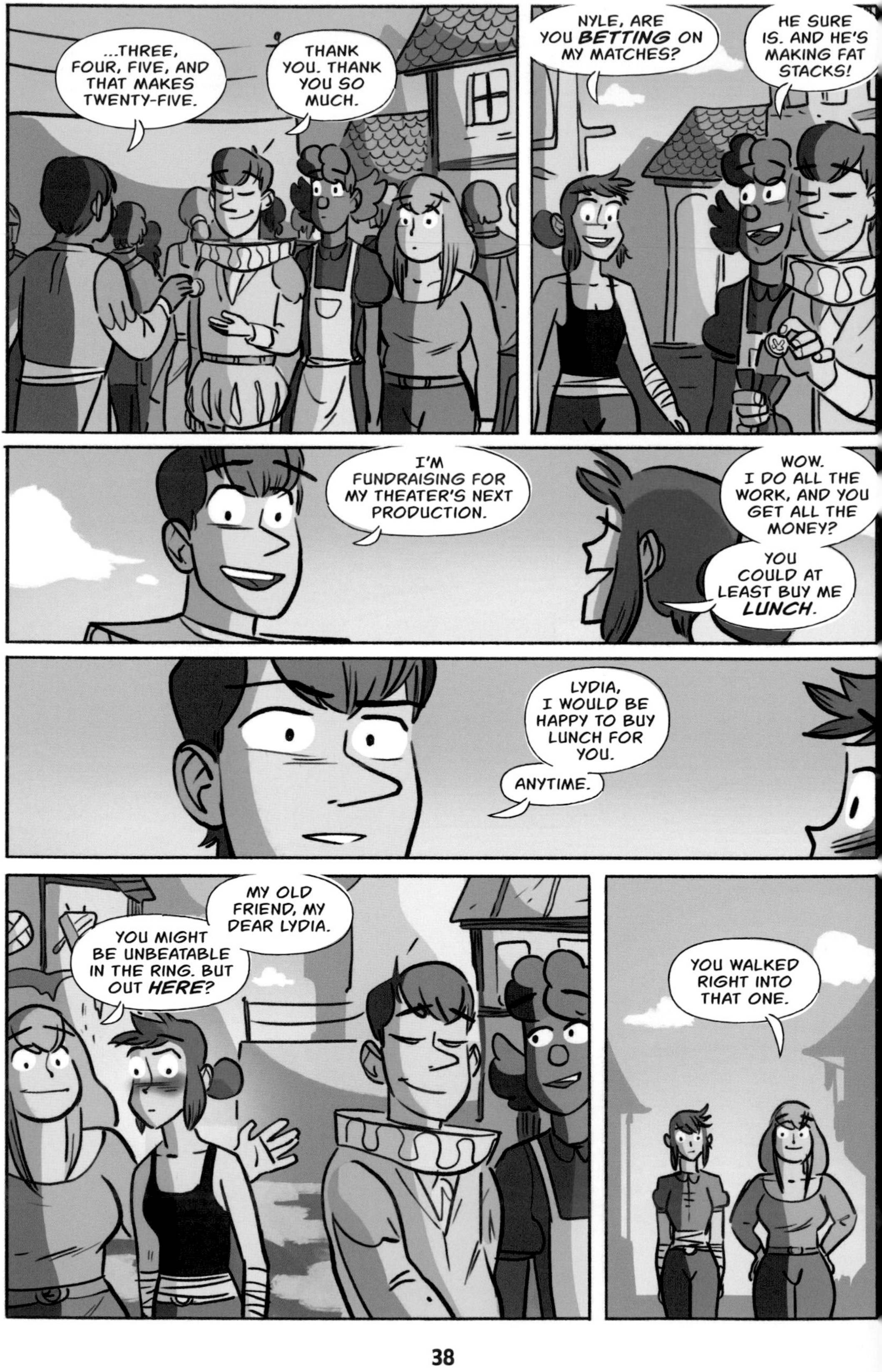
...THREE, FOUR, FIVE, AND THAT MAKES TWENTY-FIVE.
THANK YOU. THANK YOU SO MUCH.
NYLE, ARE YOU BETTING ON MY MATCHES?
HE SURE IS. AND HE'S MAKING FAT STACKS!
I'M FUNDRAISING FOR MY THEATER'S NEXT PRODUCTION.
WOW. I DO ALL THE WORK, AND YOU GET ALL THE MONEY?
YOU COULD AT LEAST BUY ME LUNCH.
LYDIA, I WOULD BE HAPPY TO BUY LUNCH FOR YOU.
ANYTIME.
MY OLD FRIEND, MY DEAR LYDIA.
YOU MIGHT BE UNBEATABLE IN THE RING. BUT OUT HERE?
YOU WALKED RIGHT INTO THAT ONE.

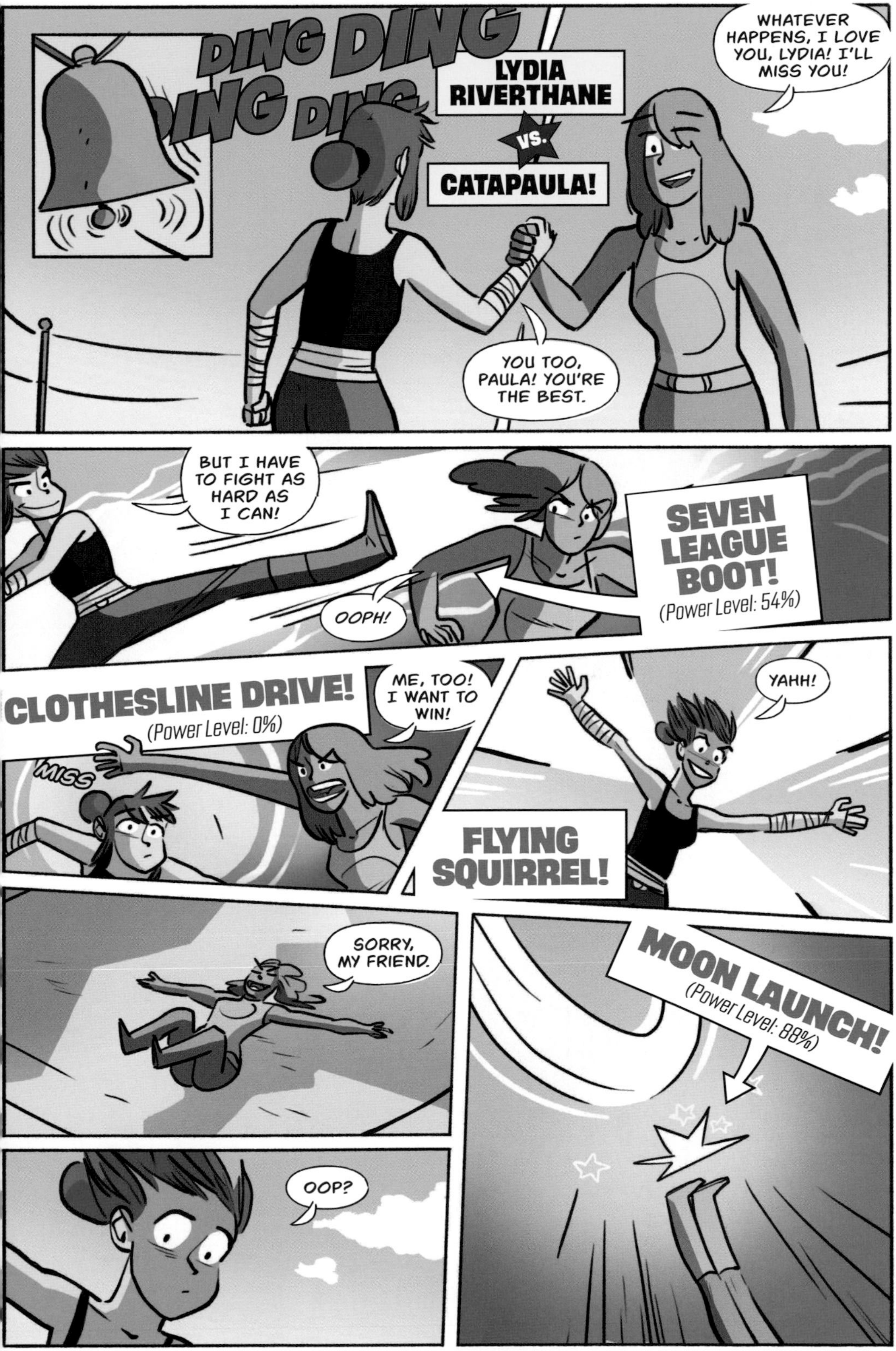
DING DING
DING DING
LYDIA RIVERTHANE
VS.
CATAPAULA!
WHATEVER HAPPENS, I LOVE YOU, LYDIA! I'LL MISS YOU!
YOU TOO, PAULA! YOU'RE THE BEST.
BUT I HAVE TO FIGHT AS HARD AS I CAN!
SEVEN LEAGUE BOOT!
(Power Level: 54%)
OOPH!
CLOTHESLINE DRIVE!
(Power Level: 0%)
ME, TOO! I WANT TO WIN!
MISS
YAHH!
FLYING SQUIRREL!
SORRY, MY FRIEND.
MOON LAUNCH!
(Power Level: 88%)
OOP?

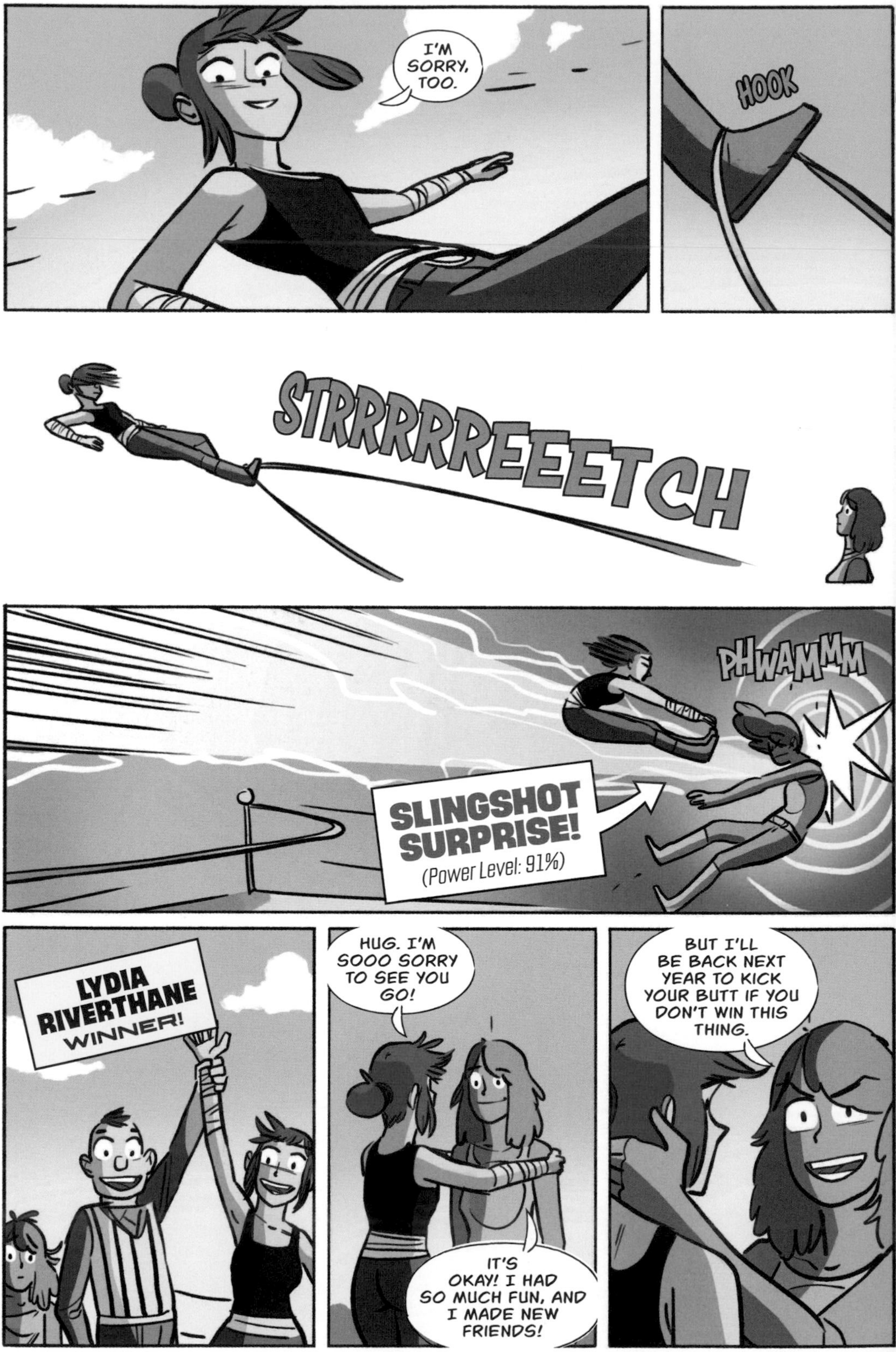
I'M SORRY, TOO.
HOOK
STRRRRRREEEETCH
PHWAMMM
SLINGSHOT SURPRISE!
(Power Level: 91%)
LYDIA RIVERTHANE WINNER!
HUG. I'M SOOO SORRY TO SEE YOU GO!
IT'S OKAY! I HAD SO MUCH FUN, AND I MADE NEW FRIENDS!
BUT I'LL BE BACK NEXT YEAR TO KICK YOUR BUTT IF YOU DON'T WIN THIS THING.

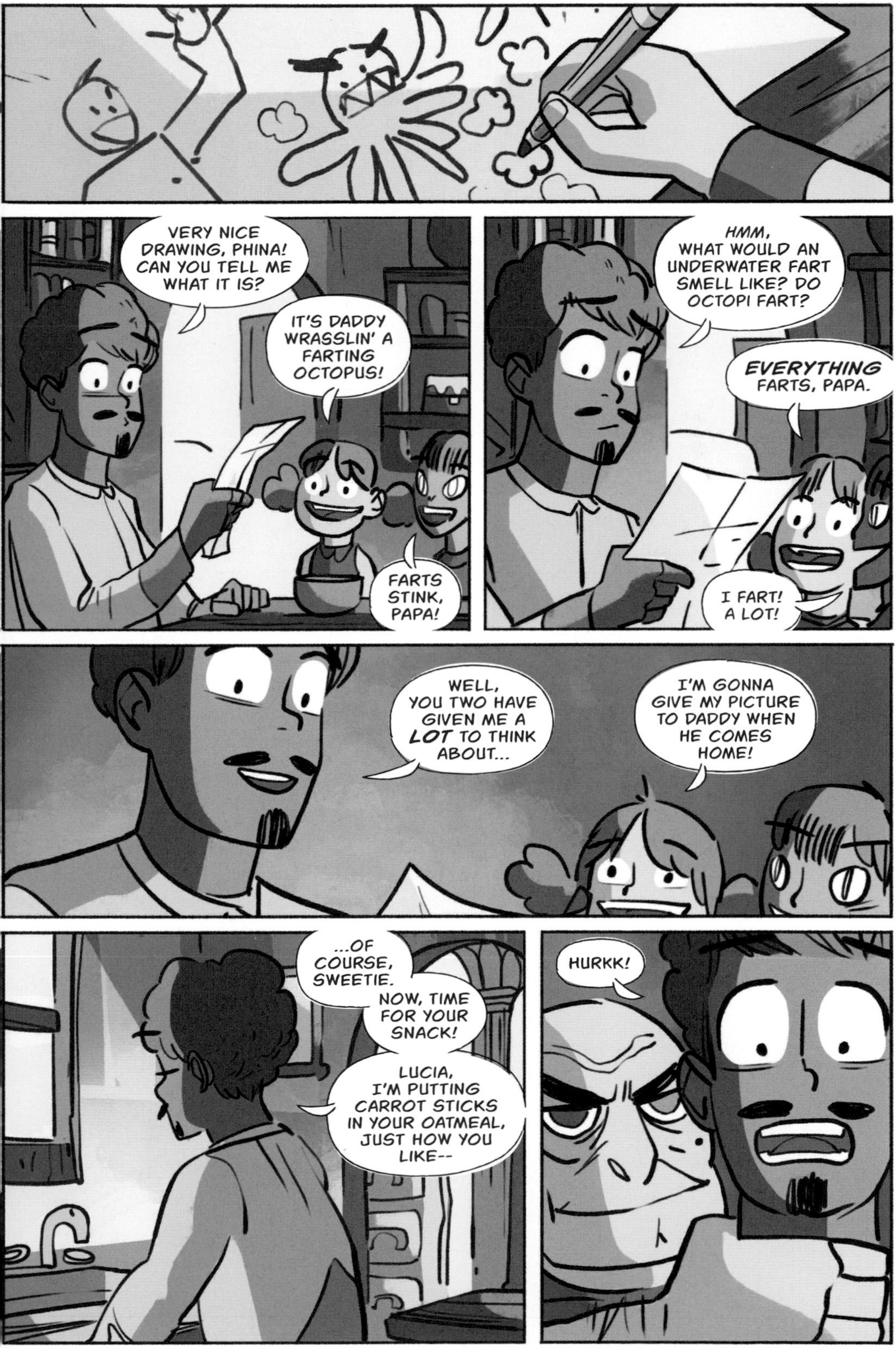
VERY NICE DRAWING, PHINA! CAN YOU TELL ME WHAT IT IS?
IT'S DADDY WRASSLIN' A FARTING OCTOPUS!
FARTS STINK, PAPA!
HMM, WHAT WOULD AN UNDERWATER FART SMELL LIKE? DO OCTOPI FART?
EVERYTHING FARTS, PAPA.
I FART! A LOT!
WELL, YOU TWO HAVE GIVEN ME A LOT TO THINK ABOUT...
I'M GONNA GIVE MY PICTURE TO DADDY WHEN HE COMES HOME!
...OF COURSE, SWEETIE.
NOW, TIME FOR YOUR SNACK!
LUCIA, I'M PUTTING CARROT STICKS IN YOUR OATMEAL, JUST HOW YOU LIKE--
HURKK!

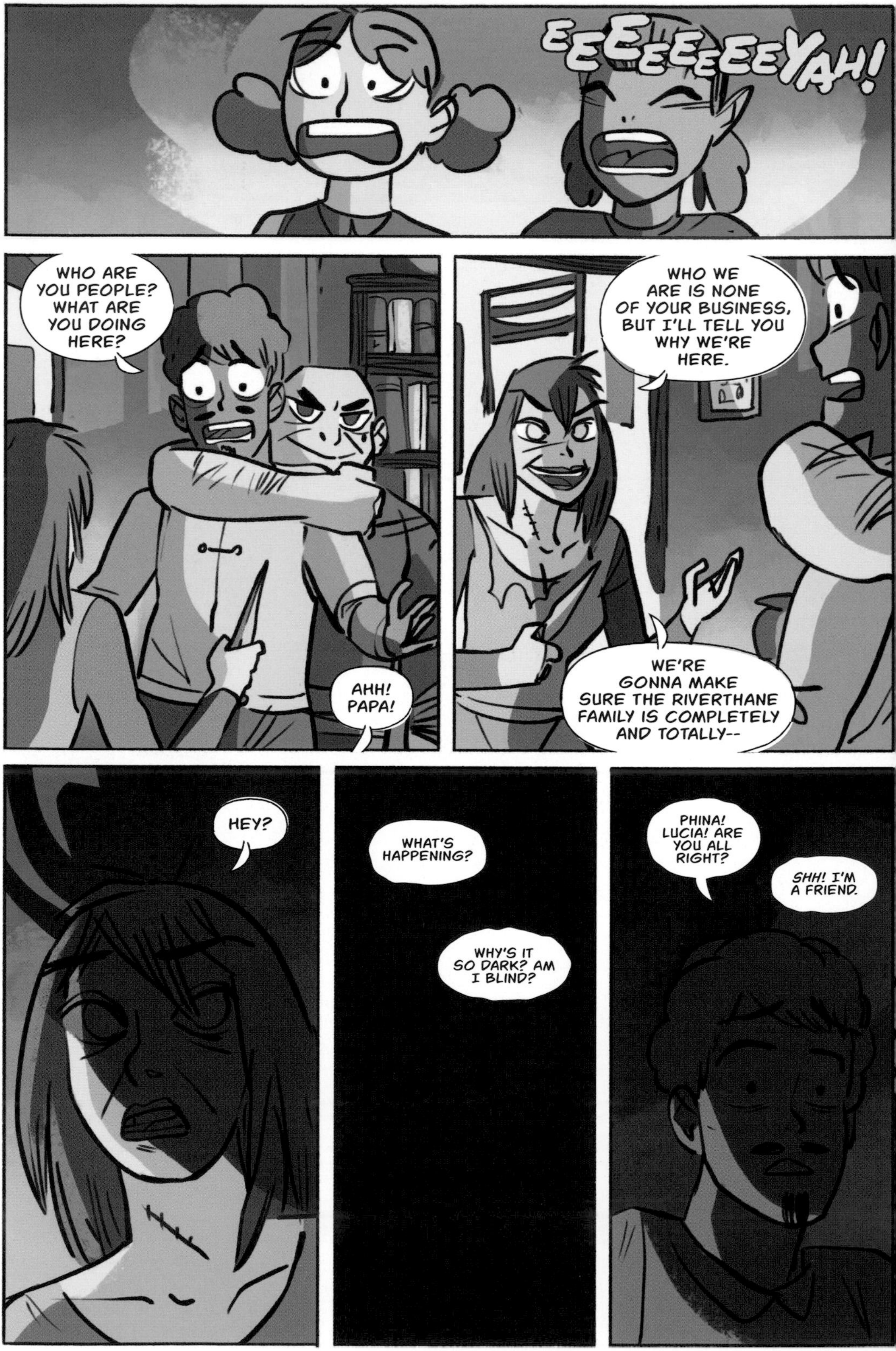
EEEEEEEEEYAH!
WHO ARE YOU PEOPLE? WHAT ARE YOU DOING HERE?
AHH! PAPA!
WHO WE ARE IS NONE OF YOUR BUSINESS, BUT I'LL TELL YOU WHY WE'RE HERE.
WE'RE GONNA MAKE SURE THE RIVERTHANE FAMILY IS COMPLETELY AND TOTALLY--
HEY?
WHAT'S HAPPENING?
WHY'S IT SO DARK? AM I BLIND?
PHINA! LUCIA! ARE YOU ALL RIGHT?
SHH! I'M A FRIEND.

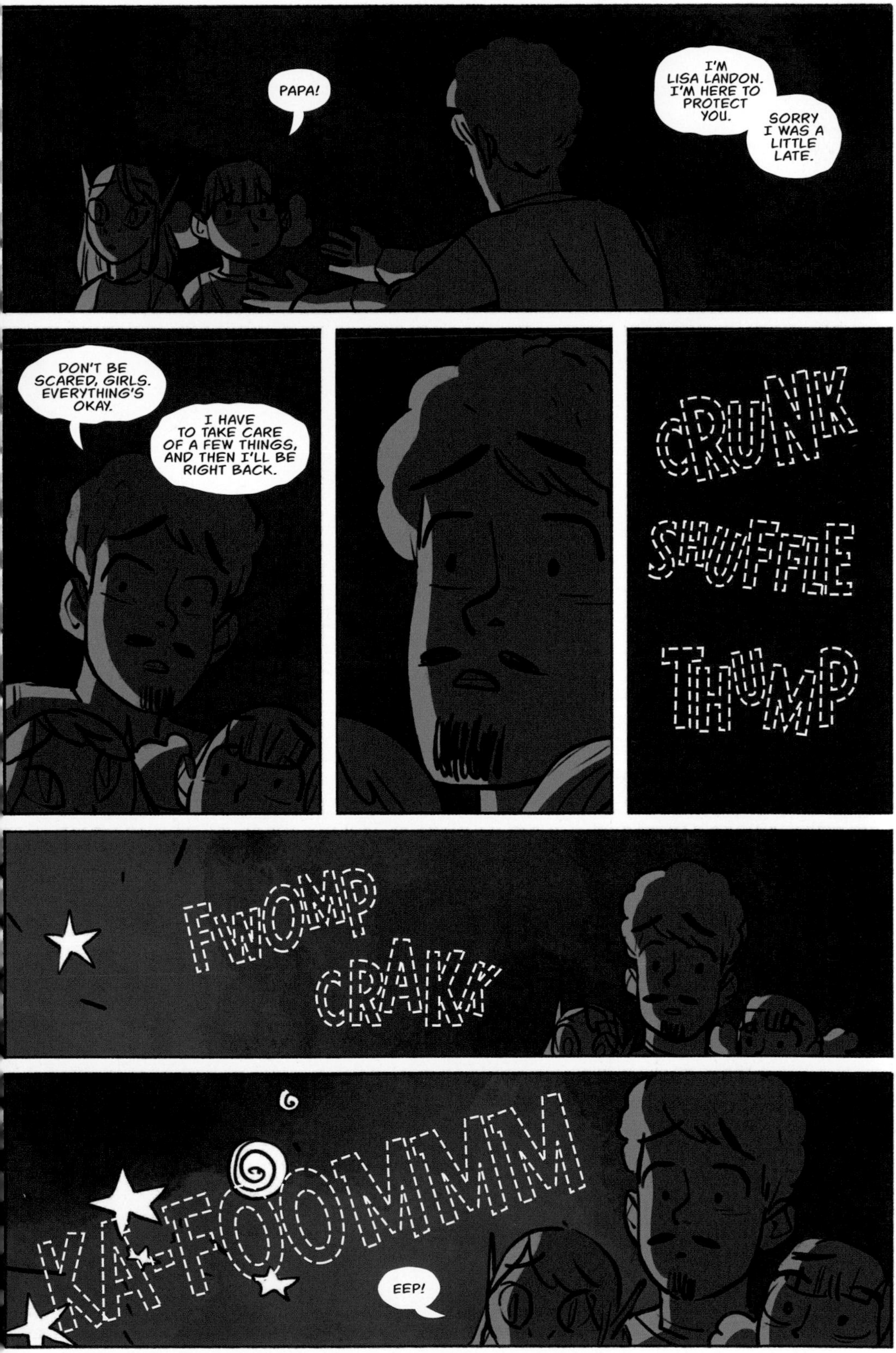
PAPA!
I'M LISA LANDON. I'M HERE TO PROTECT YOU.
SORRY I WAS A LITTLE LATE.
DON'T BE SCARED, GIRLS. EVERYTHING'S OKAY.
I HAVE TO TAKE CARE OF A FEW THINGS, AND THEN I'LL BE RIGHT BACK.
CRUNK
SHUFFLE
THUMP
FWOMP
CRAKK
KA-FOOOMMMM
EEP!

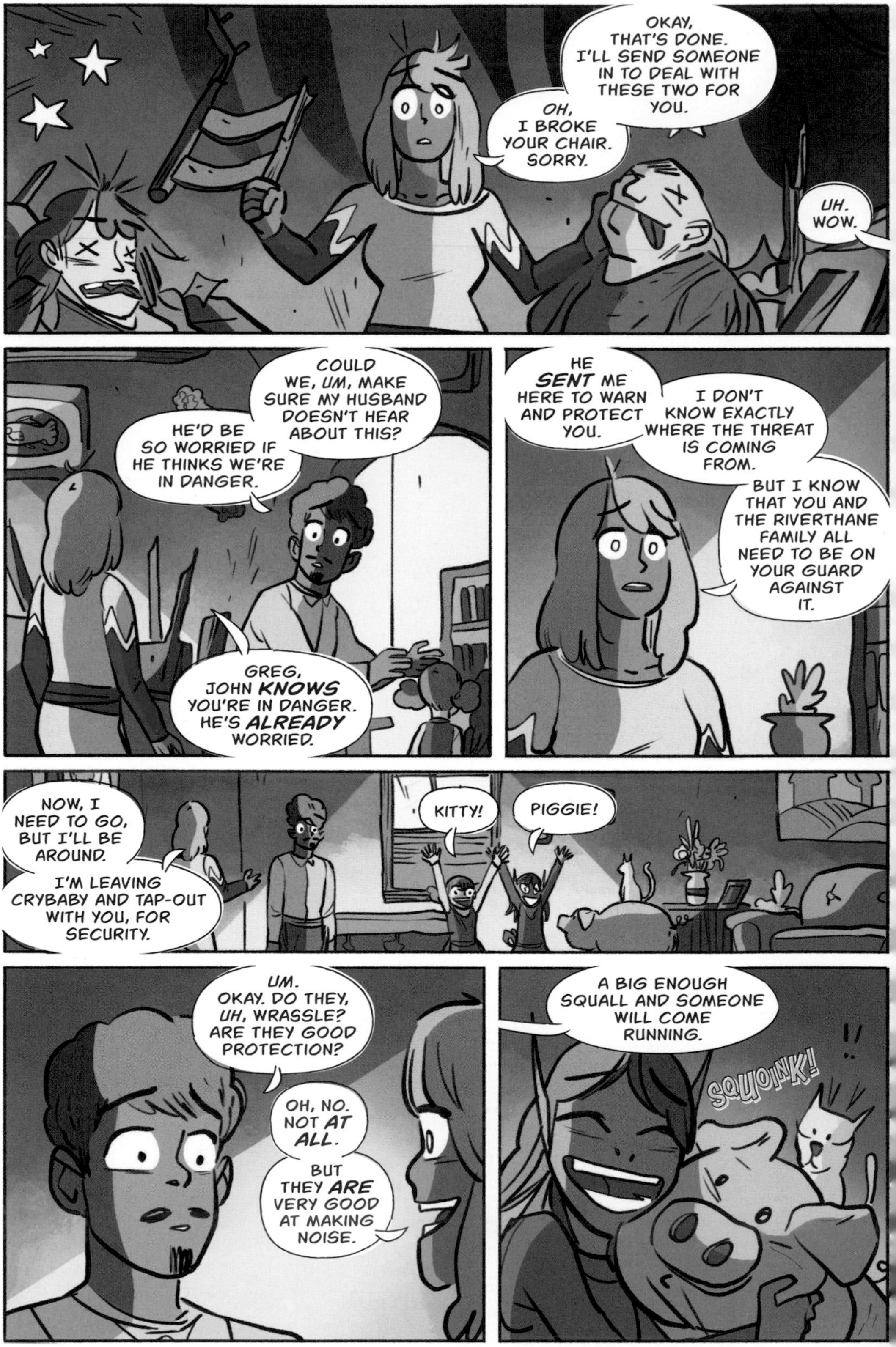
OKAY, THAT'S DONE. I'LL SEND SOMEONE IN TO DEAL WITH THESE TWO FOR YOU.
OH, I BROKE YOUR CHAIR. SORRY.
UH. WOW.
COULD WE, UM, MAKE SURE MY HUSBAND DOESN'T HEAR ABOUT THIS?
HE'D BE SO WORRIED IF HE THINKS WE'RE IN DANGER.
GREG, JOHN KNOWS YOU'RE IN DANGER. HE'S ALREADY WORRIED.
HE SENT ME HERE TO WARN AND PROTECT YOU.
I DON'T KNOW EXACTLY WHERE THE THREAT IS COMING FROM.
BUT I KNOW THAT YOU AND THE RIVERTHANE FAMILY ALL NEED TO BE ON YOUR GUARD AGAINST IT.
NOW, I NEED TO GO, BUT I'LL BE AROUND.
I'M LEAVING CRYBABY AND TAP-OUT WITH YOU, FOR SECURITY.
KITTY!
PIGGIE!
UM. OKAY. DO THEY, UH, WRASSLE? ARE THEY GOOD PROTECTION?
OH, NO. NOT AT ALL.
BUT THEY ARE VERY GOOD AT MAKING NOISE.
A BIG ENOUGH SQUALL AND SOMEONE WILL COME RUNNING.
SQUOINK!
!!

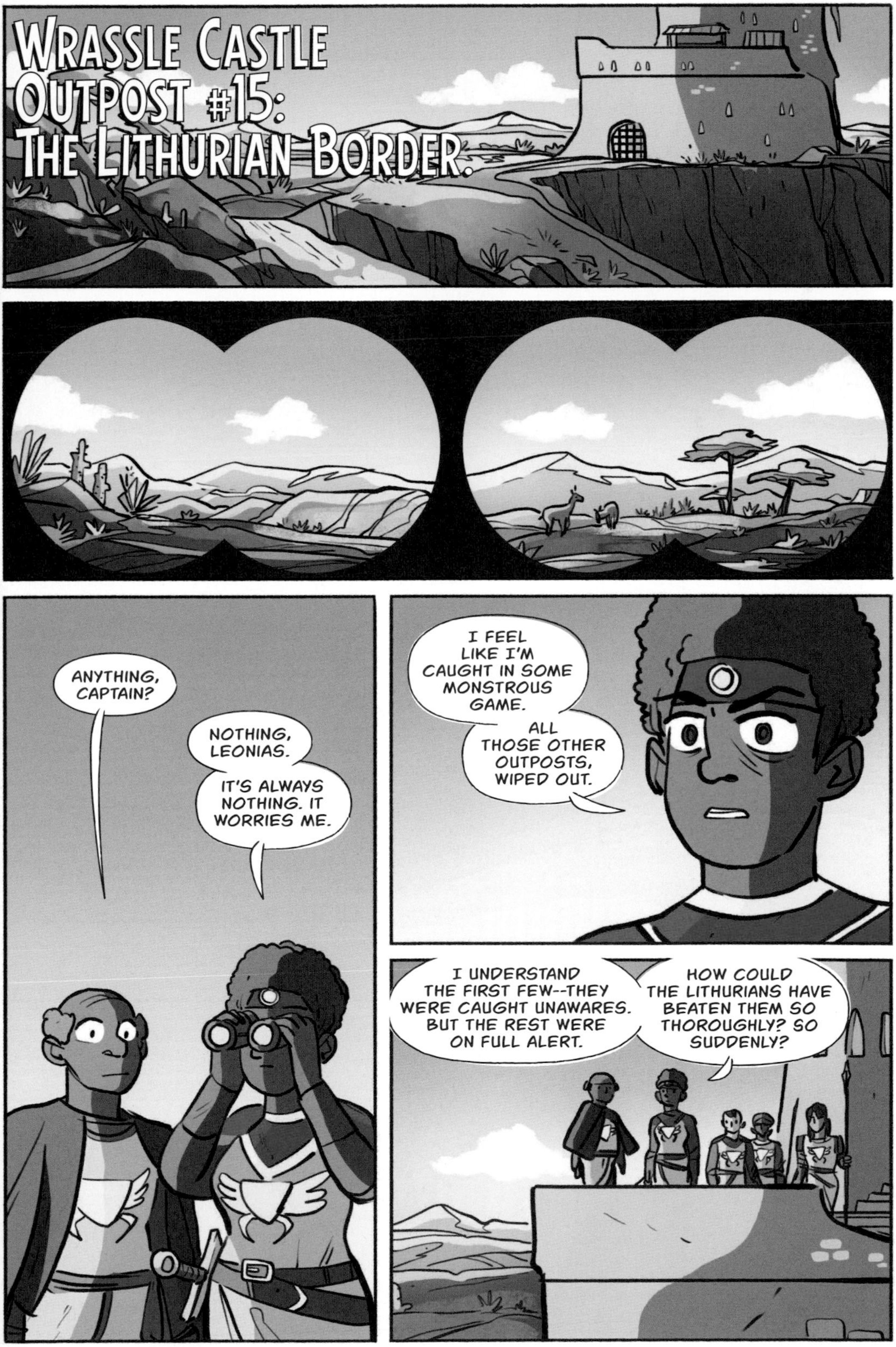
WRASSLE CASTLE OUTPOST #15: THE LITHURIAN BORDER.
ANYTHING, CAPTAIN?
NOTHING, LEONIAS.
IT'S ALWAYS NOTHING. IT WORRIES ME.
I FEEL LIKE I'M CAUGHT IN SOME MONSTROUS GAME.
ALL THOSE OTHER OUTPOSTS, WIPED OUT.
I UNDERSTAND THE FIRST FEW--THEY WERE CAUGHT UNAWARES. BUT THE REST WERE ON FULL ALERT.
HOW COULD THE LITHURIANS HAVE BEATEN THEM SO THOROUGHLY? SO SUDDENLY?

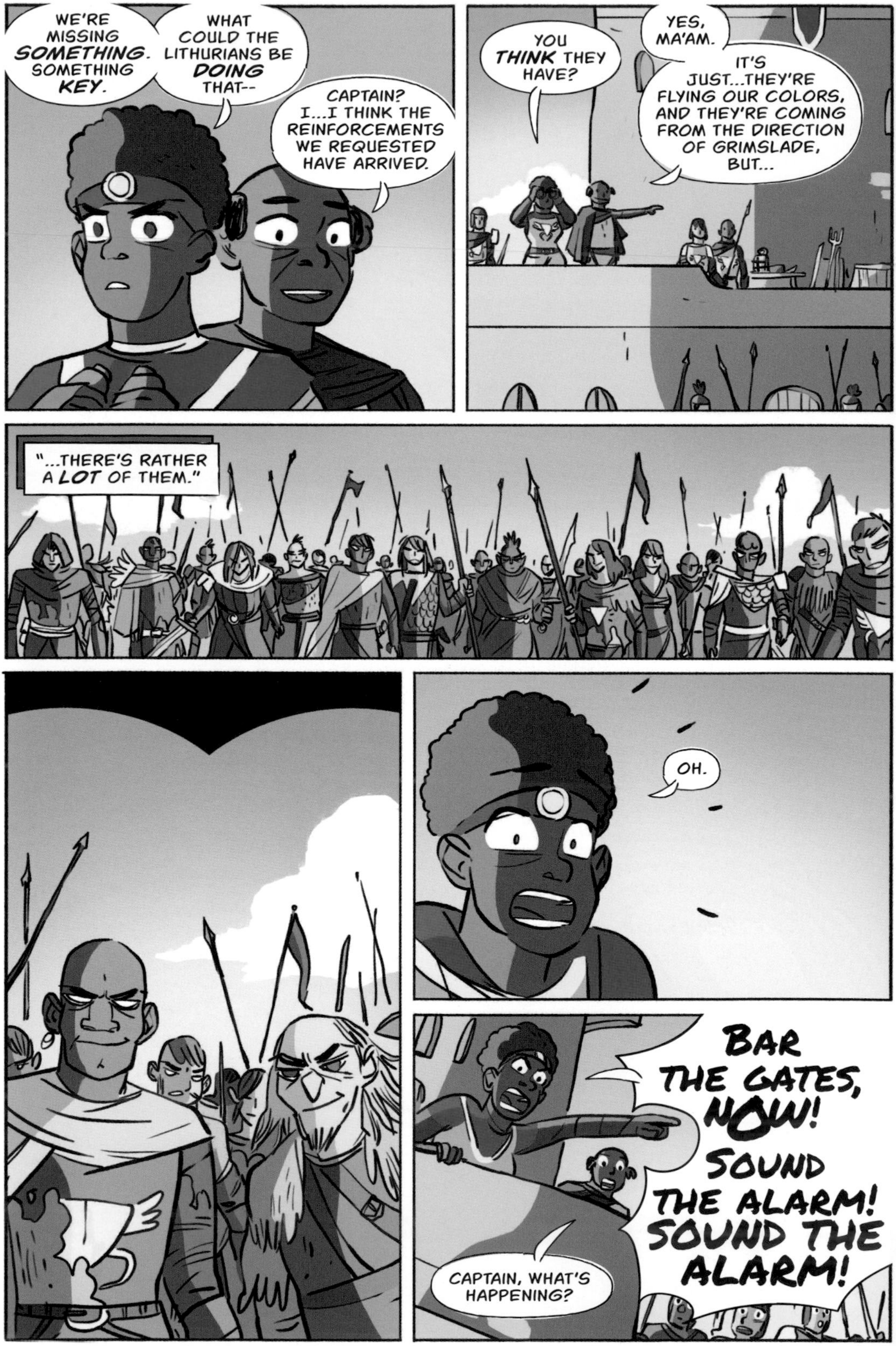
WE'RE MISSING SOMETHING. SOMETHING KEY.
WHAT COULD THE LITHURIANS BE DOING THAT--
CAPTAIN? I...I THINK THE REINFORCEMENTS WE REQUESTED HAVE ARRIVED.
YOU THINK THEY HAVE?
YES, MA'AM.
IT'S JUST...THEY'RE FLYING OUR COLORS, AND THEY'RE COMING FROM THE DIRECTION OF GRIMSLADE, BUT...
"...THERE'S RATHER A LOT OF THEM."
OH.
BAR THE GATES, NOW! SOUND THE ALARM! SOUND THE ALARM!
CAPTAIN, WHAT'S HAPPENING?

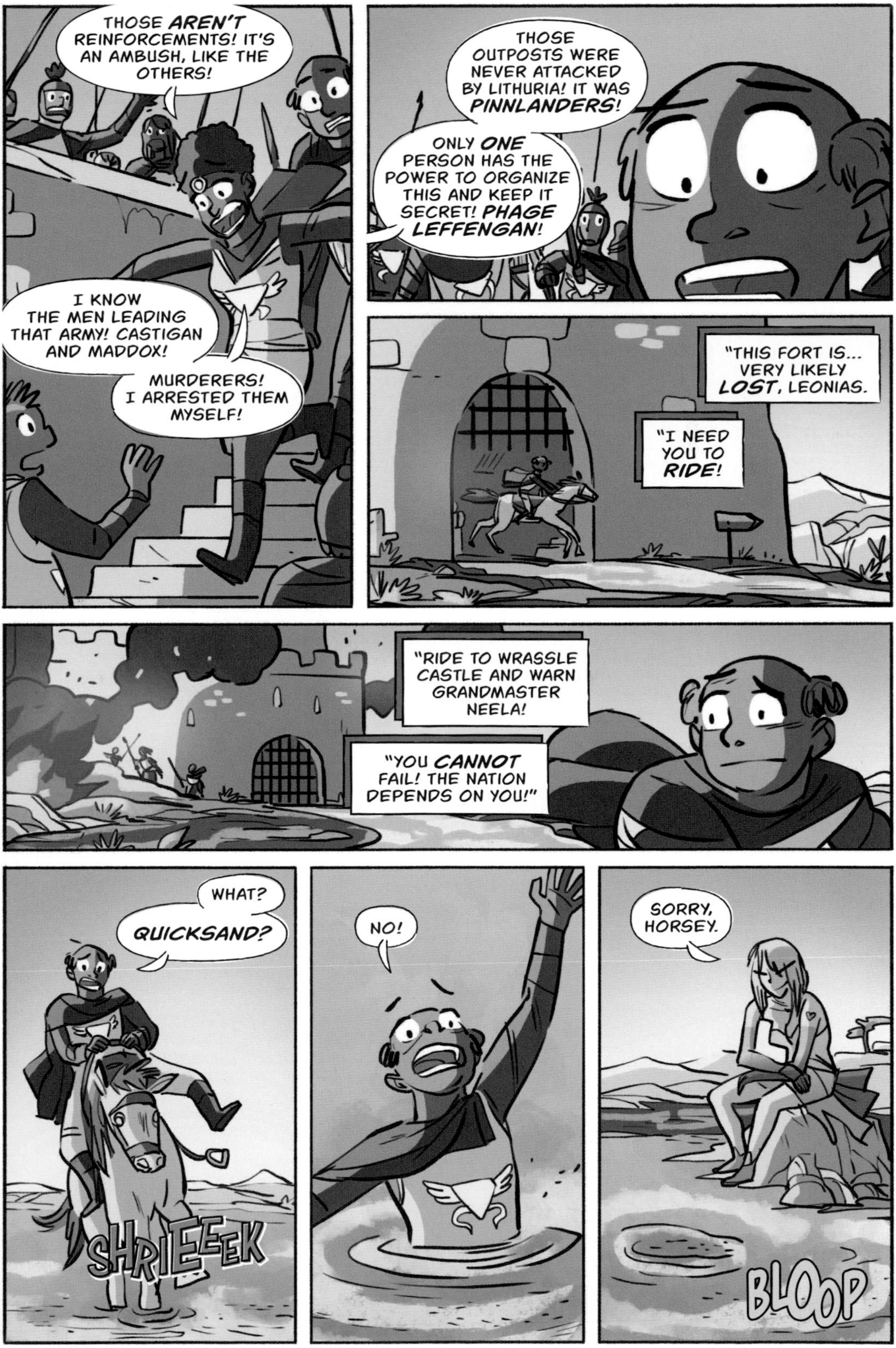
THOSE AREN'T REINFORCEMENTS! IT'S AN AMBUSH, LIKE THE OTHERS!
I KNOW THE MEN LEADING THAT ARMY! CASTIGAN AND MADDOX!
MURDERERS! I ARRESTED THEM MYSELF!
THOSE OUTPOSTS WERE NEVER ATTACKED BY LITHURIA! IT WAS PINNLANDERS!
ONLY ONE PERSON HAS THE POWER TO ORGANIZE THIS AND KEEP IT SECRET! PHAGE LEFFENGAN!
"THIS FORT IS... VERY LIKELY LOST, LEONIAS.
"I NEED YOU TO RIDE!
"RIDE TO WRASSLE CASTLE AND WARN GRANDMASTER NEELA!
"YOU CANNOT FAIL! THE NATION DEPENDS ON YOU!"
WHAT? QUICKSAND?
SHRIEEEK
NO!
SORRY, HORSEY.
BLOOP

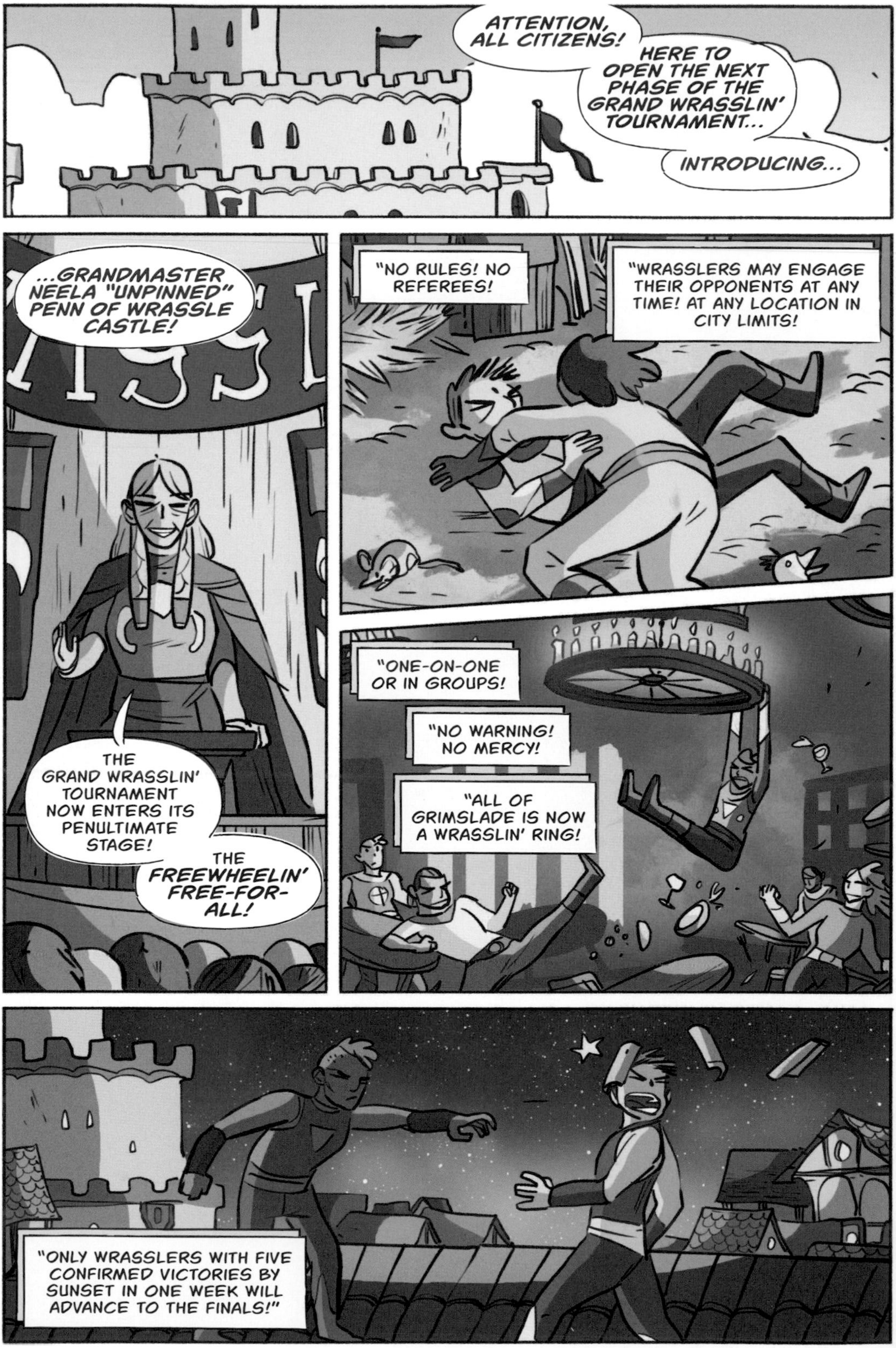
ATTENTION, ALL CITIZENS!
HERE TO OPEN THE NEXT PHASE OF THE GRAND WRASSLIN' TOURNAMENT...
INTRODUCING...
...GRANDMASTER NEELA "UNPINNED" PENN OF WRASSLE CASTLE!
THE GRAND WRASSLIN' TOURNAMENT NOW ENTERS ITS PENULTIMATE STAGE!
THE *FREEWHEELIN' FREE-FOR-ALL!*
"NO RULES! NO REFEREES!
"WRASSLERS MAY ENGAGE THEIR OPPONENTS AT ANY TIME! AT ANY LOCATION IN CITY LIMITS!
"ONE-ON-ONE OR IN GROUPS!
"NO WARNING! NO MERCY!
"ALL OF GRIMSLADE IS NOW A WRASSLIN' RING!
"ONLY WRASSLERS WITH FIVE CONFIRMED VICTORIES BY SUNSET IN ONE WEEK WILL ADVANCE TO THE FINALS!"

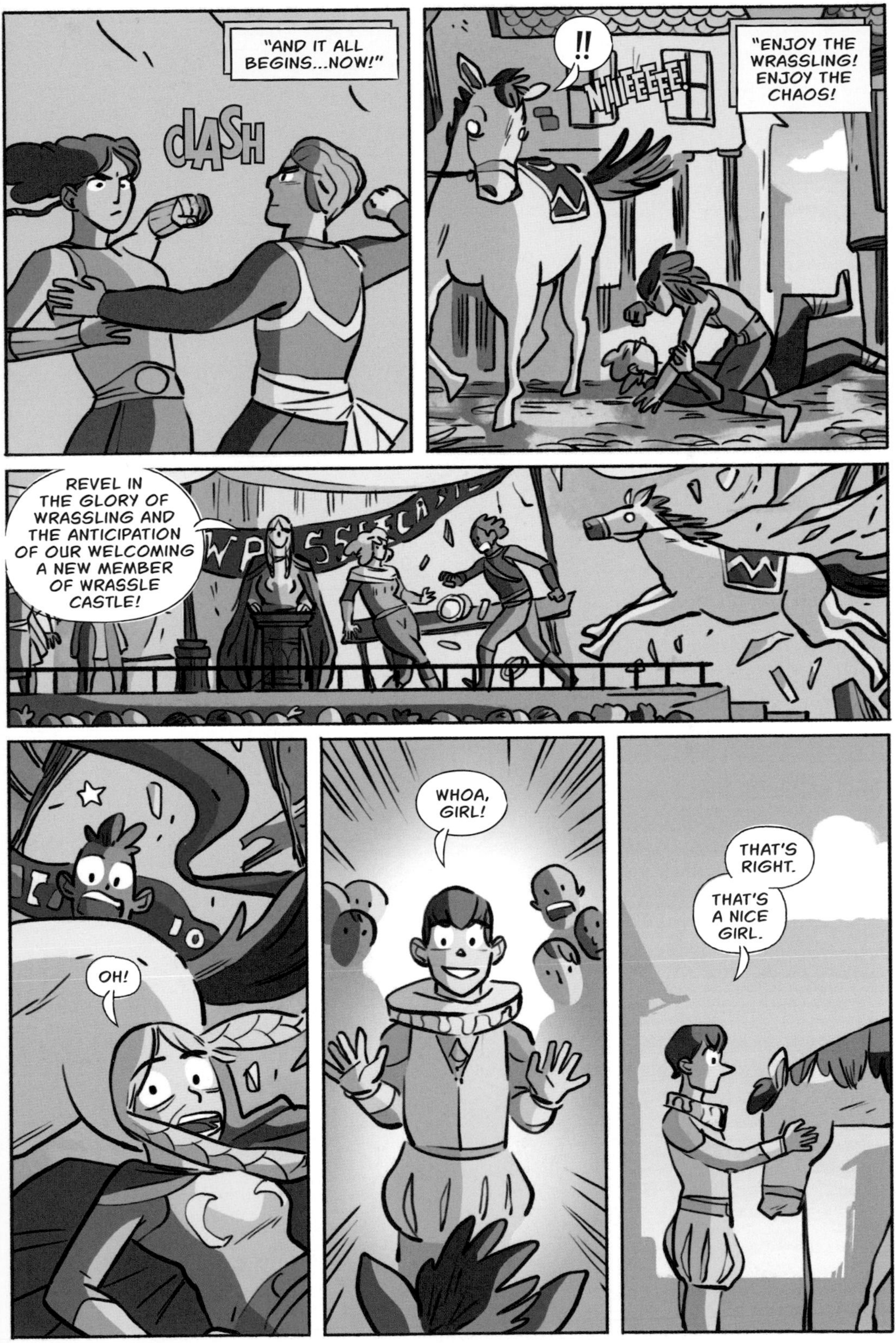
"AND IT ALL BEGINS...NOW!"
CLASH
!!
NIIEEEEE!
"ENJOY THE WRASSLING! ENJOY THE CHAOS!
REVEL IN THE GLORY OF WRASSLING AND THE ANTICIPATION OF OUR WELCOMING A NEW MEMBER OF WRASSLE CASTLE!
OH!
WHOA, GIRL!
THAT'S RIGHT.
THAT'S A NICE GIRL.

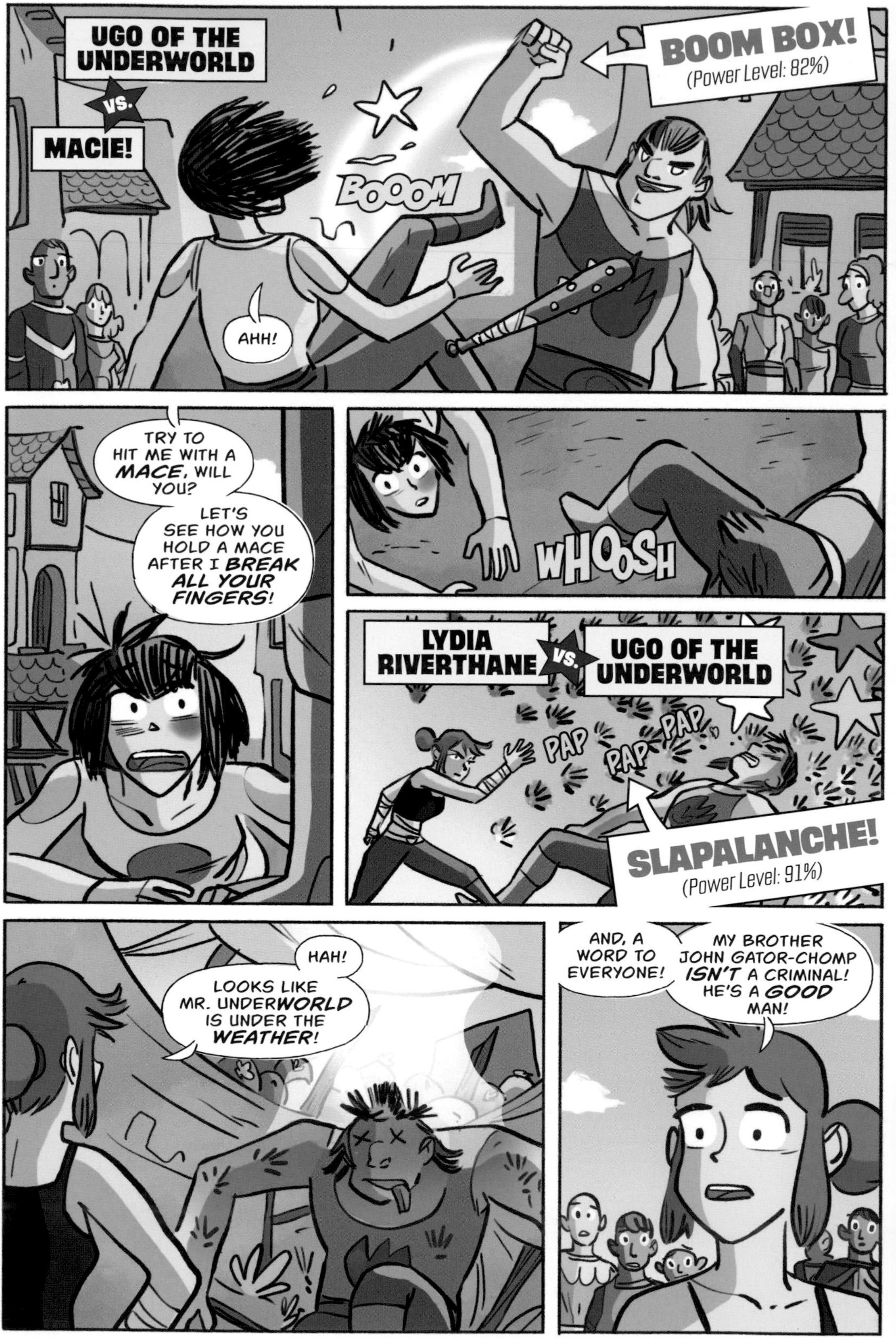
UGO OF THE UNDERWORLD
VS.
MACIE!
BOOM BOX!
(Power Level: 82%)
BOOOM
AHH!
TRY TO HIT ME WITH A *MACE*, WILL YOU?
LET'S SEE HOW YOU HOLD A MACE AFTER I ***BREAK ALL YOUR FINGERS***!
WHOOSH
LYDIA RIVERTHANE
VS.
UGO OF THE UNDERWORLD
PAP
PAP
PAP
SLAPALANCHE!
(Power Level: 91%)
HAH!
LOOKS LIKE MR. UNDER***WORLD*** IS UNDER THE ***WEATHER***!
AND, A WORD TO EVERYONE!
MY BROTHER JOHN GATOR-CHOMP ***ISN'T*** A CRIMINAL! HE'S A ***GOOD*** MAN!

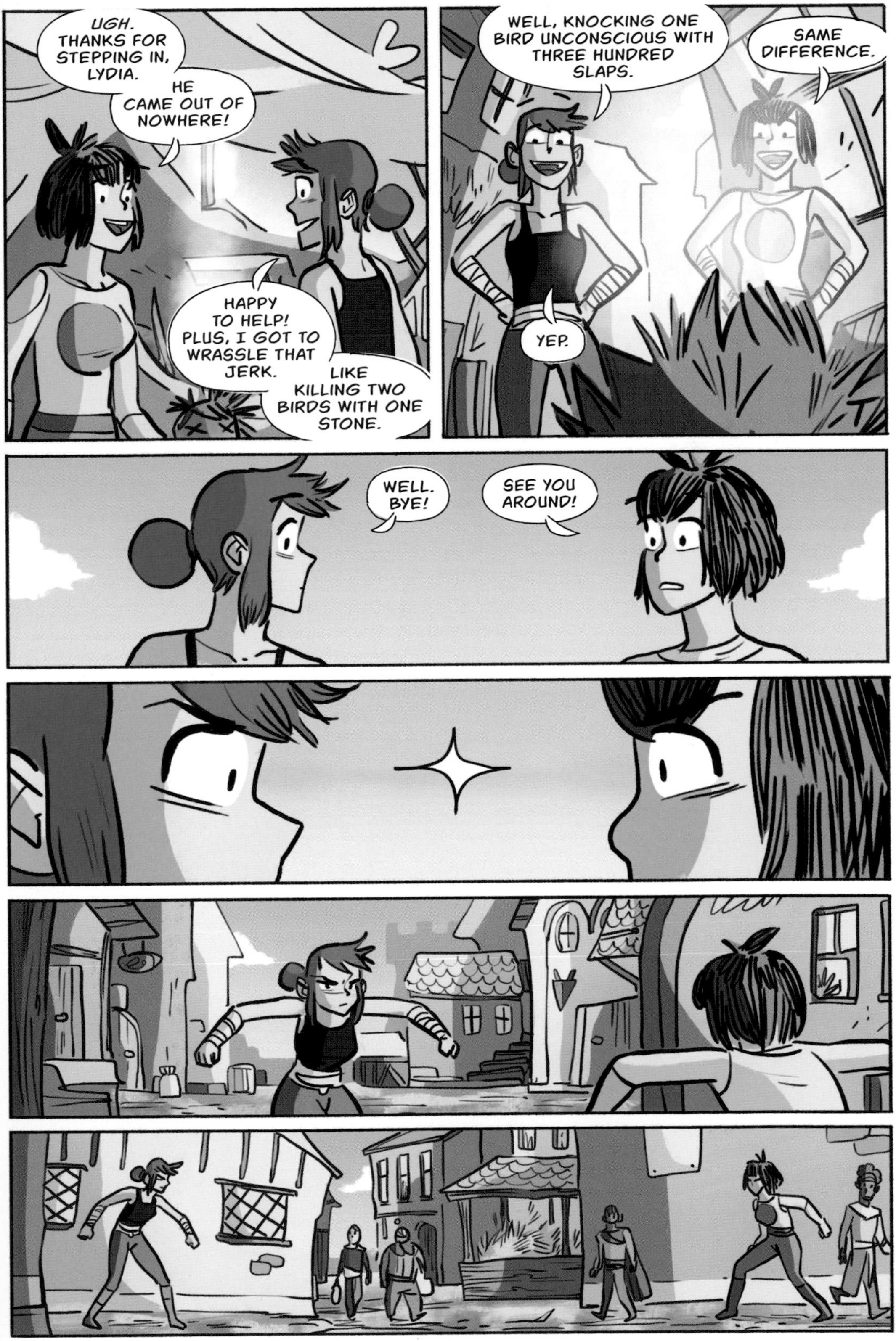
UGH. THANKS FOR STEPPING IN, LYDIA.
HE CAME OUT OF NOWHERE!
HAPPY TO HELP! PLUS, I GOT TO WRASSLE THAT JERK.
LIKE KILLING TWO BIRDS WITH ONE STONE.
WELL, KNOCKING ONE BIRD UNCONSCIOUS WITH THREE HUNDRED SLAPS.
SAME DIFFERENCE.
YEP.
WELL. BYE!
SEE YOU AROUND!

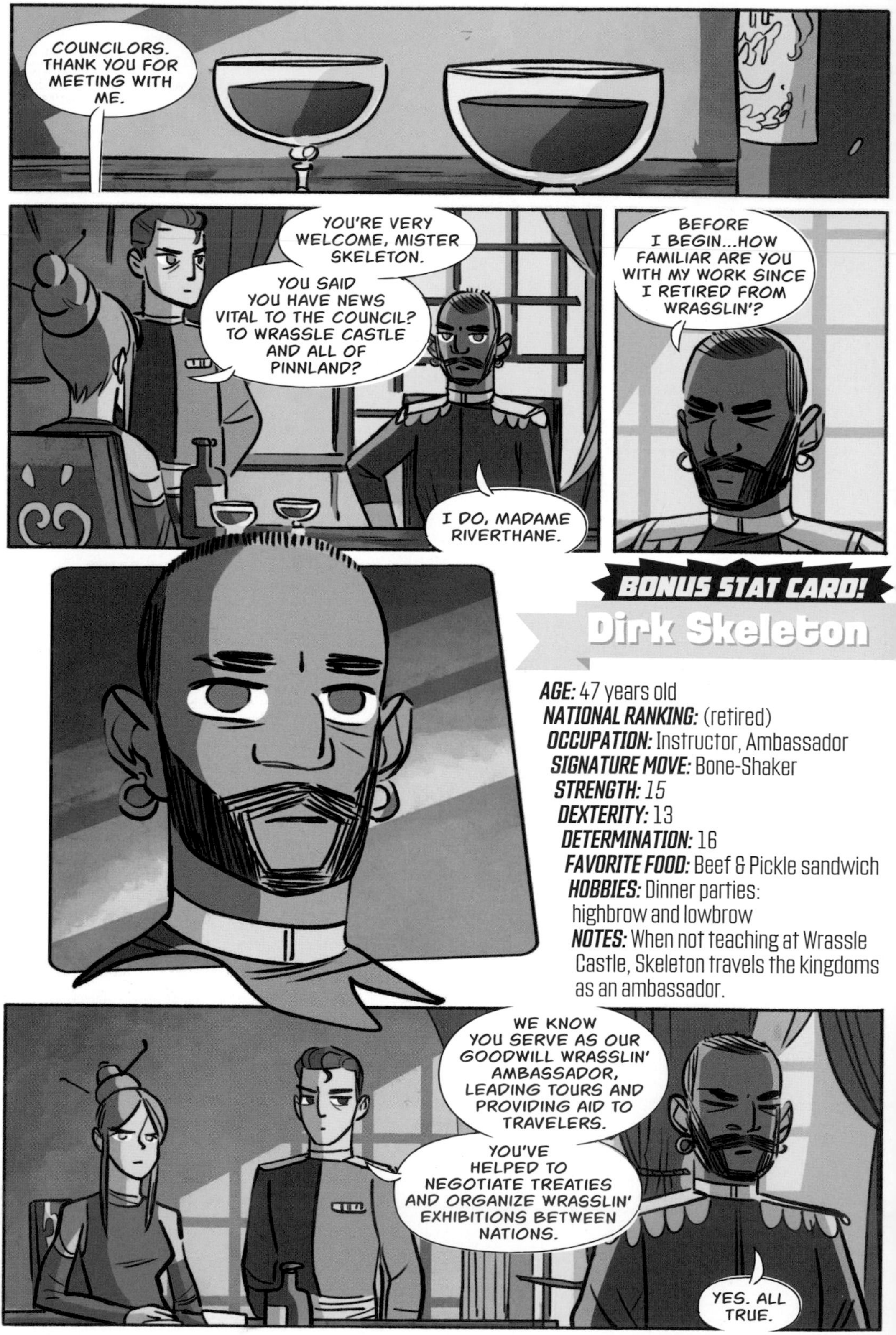
COUNCILORS. THANK YOU FOR MEETING WITH ME.
YOU'RE VERY WELCOME, MISTER SKELETON.
YOU SAID YOU HAVE NEWS VITAL TO THE COUNCIL? TO WRASSLE CASTLE AND ALL OF PINNLAND?
I DO, MADAME RIVERTHANE.
BEFORE I BEGIN...HOW FAMILIAR ARE YOU WITH MY WORK SINCE I RETIRED FROM WRASSLIN'?
BONUS STAT CARD!
Dirk Skeleton
AGE: 47 years old
NATIONAL RANKING: (retired)
OCCUPATION: Instructor, Ambassador
SIGNATURE MOVE: Bone-Shaker
STRENGTH: 15
DEXTERITY: 13
DETERMINATION: 16
FAVORITE FOOD: Beef & Pickle sandwich
HOBBIES: Dinner parties: highbrow and lowbrow
NOTES: When not teaching at Wrassle Castle, Skeleton travels the kingdoms as an ambassador.
WE KNOW YOU SERVE AS OUR GOODWILL WRASSLIN' AMBASSADOR, LEADING TOURS AND PROVIDING AID TO TRAVELERS.
YOU'VE HELPED TO NEGOTIATE TREATIES AND ORGANIZE WRASSLIN' EXHIBITIONS BETWEEN NATIONS.
YES. ALL TRUE.

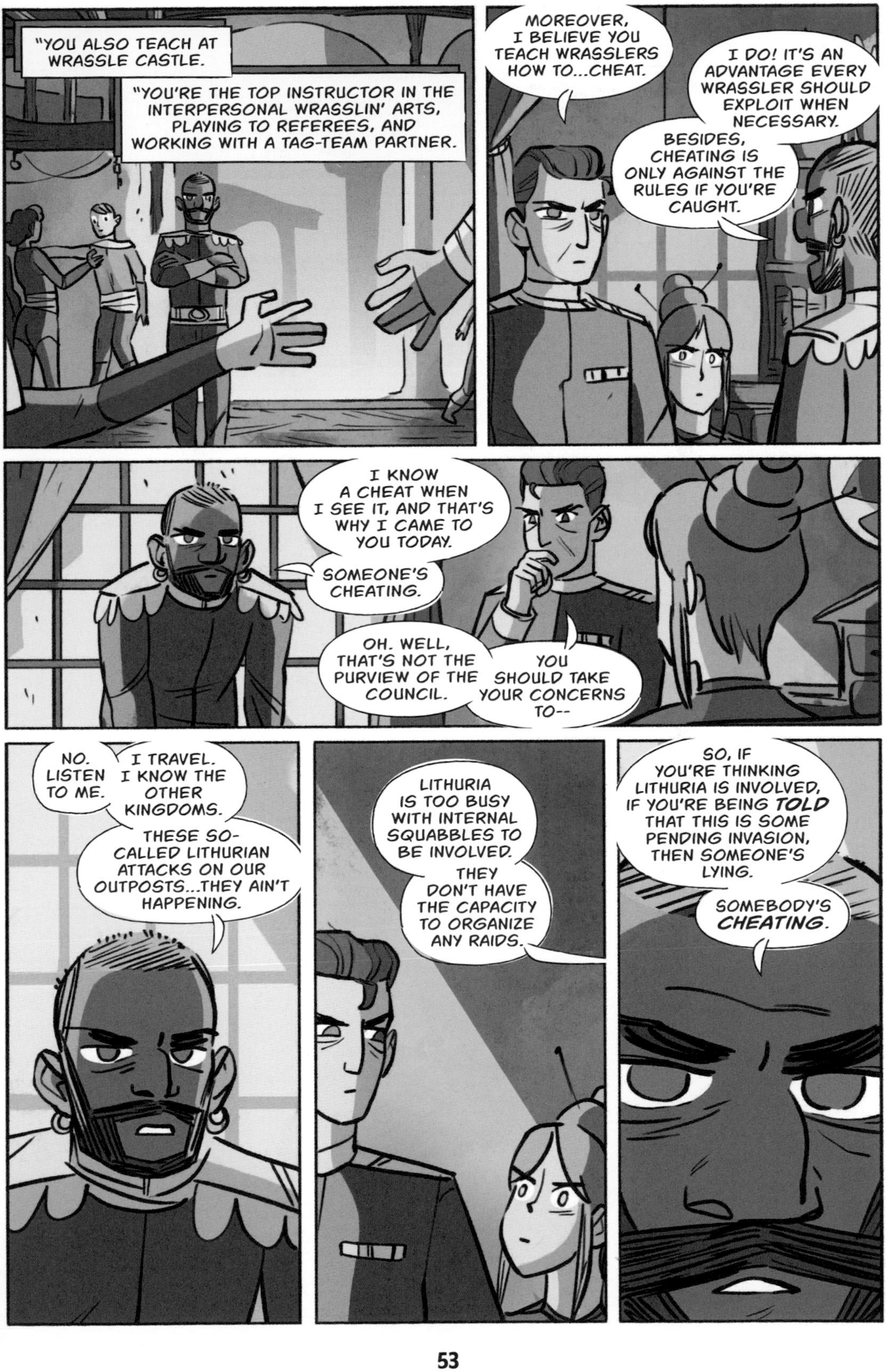
"YOU ALSO TEACH AT WRASSLE CASTLE.
"YOU'RE THE TOP INSTRUCTOR IN THE INTERPERSONAL WRASSLIN' ARTS, PLAYING TO REFEREES, AND WORKING WITH A TAG-TEAM PARTNER.
MOREOVER, I BELIEVE YOU TEACH WRASSLERS HOW TO...CHEAT.
I DO! IT'S AN ADVANTAGE EVERY WRASSLER SHOULD EXPLOIT WHEN NECESSARY.
BESIDES, CHEATING IS ONLY AGAINST THE RULES IF YOU'RE CAUGHT.
I KNOW A CHEAT WHEN I SEE IT, AND THAT'S WHY I CAME TO YOU TODAY.
SOMEONE'S CHEATING.
OH. WELL, THAT'S NOT THE PURVIEW OF THE COUNCIL.
YOU SHOULD TAKE YOUR CONCERNS TO--
NO. LISTEN TO ME.
I TRAVEL. I KNOW THE OTHER KINGDOMS.
THESE SO-CALLED LITHURIAN ATTACKS ON OUR OUTPOSTS...THEY AIN'T HAPPENING.
LITHURIA IS TOO BUSY WITH INTERNAL SQUABBLES TO BE INVOLVED.
THEY DON'T HAVE THE CAPACITY TO ORGANIZE ANY RAIDS.
SO, IF YOU'RE THINKING LITHURIA IS INVOLVED, IF YOU'RE BEING ***TOLD*** THAT THIS IS SOME PENDING INVASION, THEN SOMEONE'S LYING.
SOMEBODY'S ***CHEATING.***

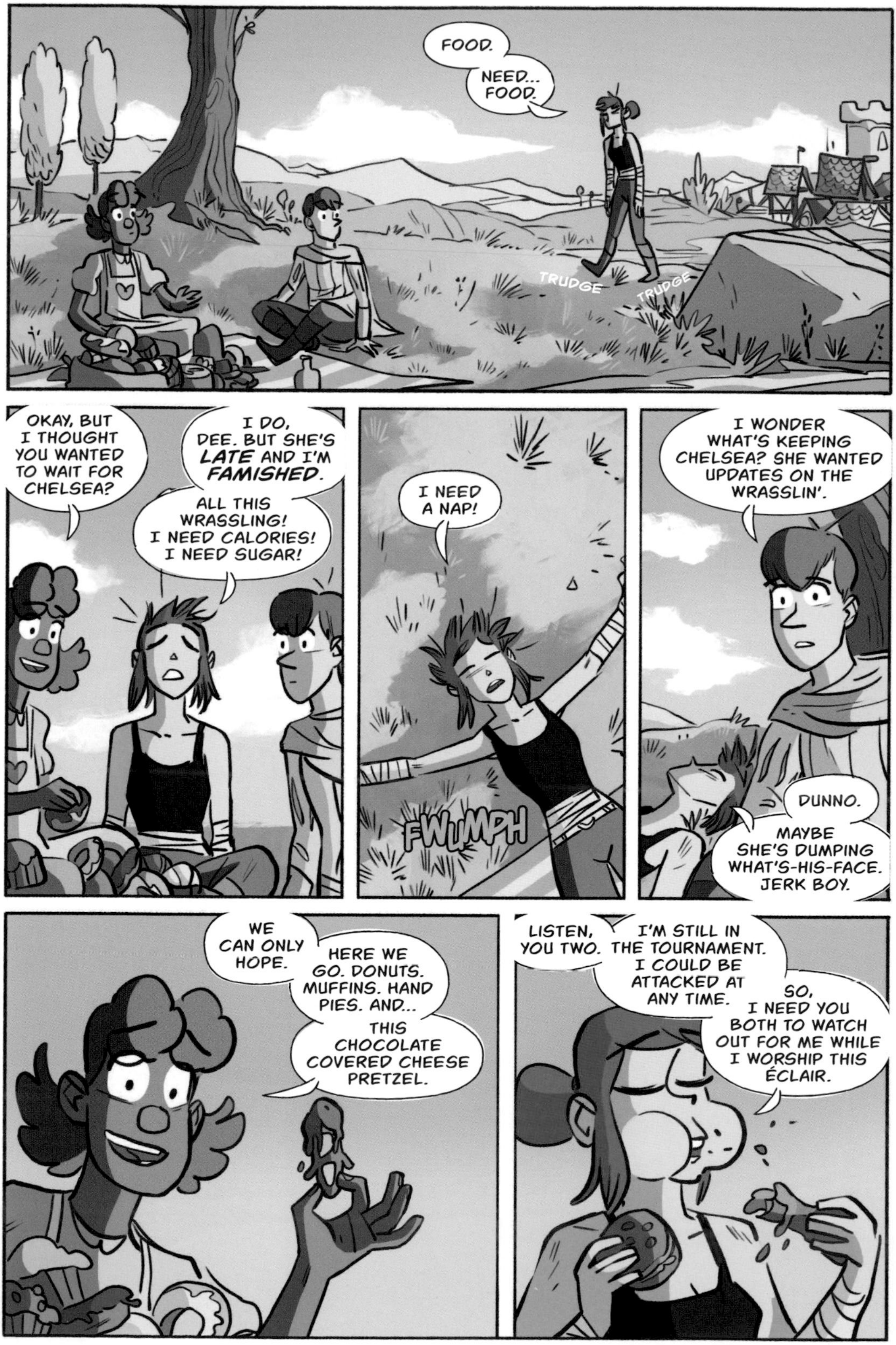
FOOD.
NEED... FOOD.
TRUDGE
TRUDGE
OKAY, BUT I THOUGHT YOU WANTED TO WAIT FOR CHELSEA?
I DO, DEE. BUT SHE'S *LATE* AND I'M ***FAMISHED***.
ALL THIS WRASSLING! I NEED CALORIES! I NEED SUGAR!
I NEED A NAP!
FWUMPH
I WONDER WHAT'S KEEPING CHELSEA? SHE WANTED UPDATES ON THE WRASSLIN'.
DUNNO.
MAYBE SHE'S DUMPING WHAT'S-HIS-FACE. JERK BOY.
WE CAN ONLY HOPE.
HERE WE GO. DONUTS. MUFFINS. HAND PIES. AND...
THIS CHOCOLATE COVERED CHEESE PRETZEL.
LISTEN, YOU TWO.
I'M STILL IN THE TOURNAMENT. I COULD BE ATTACKED AT ANY TIME.
SO, I NEED YOU BOTH TO WATCH OUT FOR ME WHILE I WORSHIP THIS ÉCLAIR.

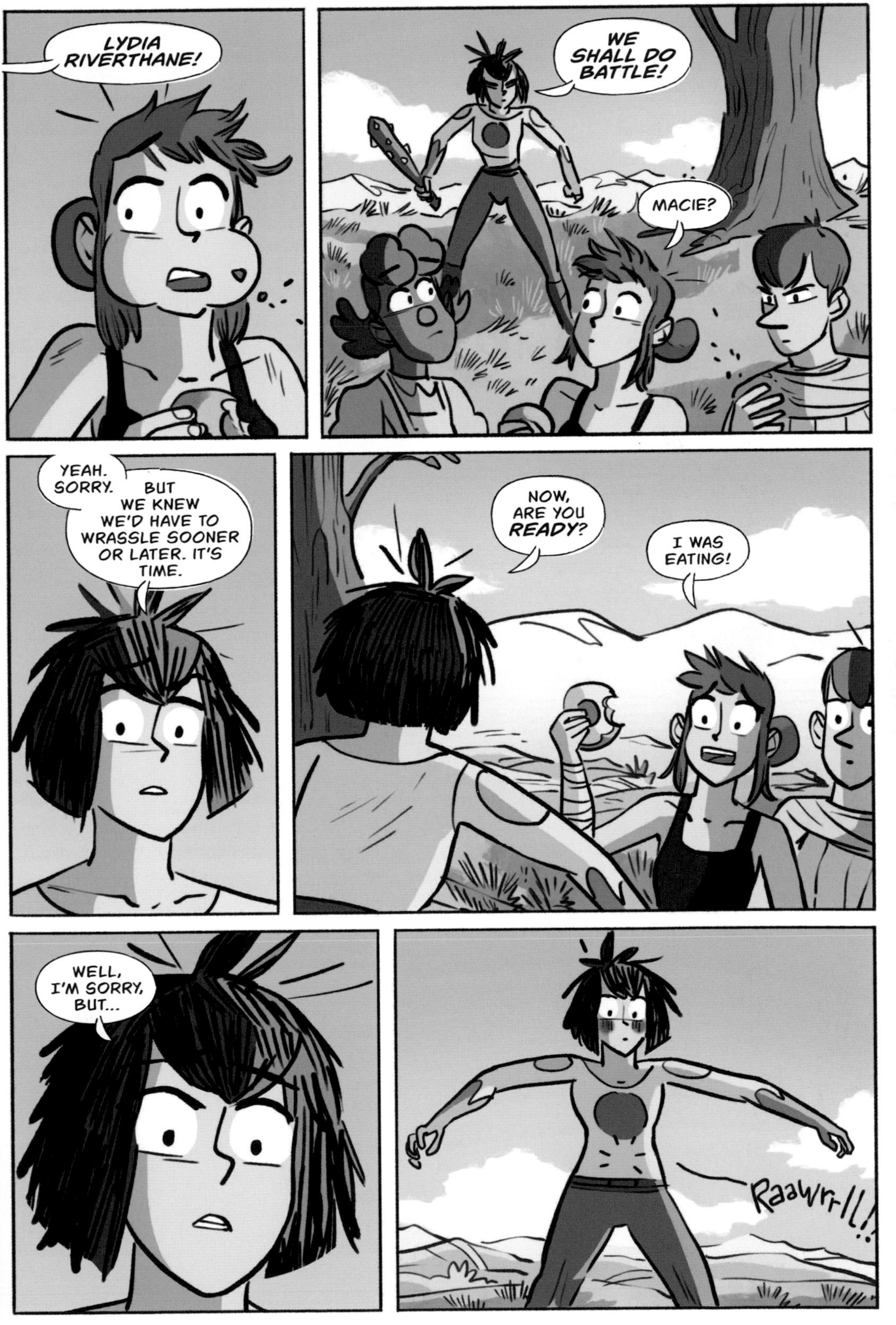
LYDIA RIVERTHANE!
WE SHALL DO BATTLE!
MACIE?
YEAH. SORRY.
BUT WE KNEW WE'D HAVE TO WRASSLE SOONER OR LATER. IT'S TIME.
NOW, ARE YOU *READY*?
I WAS EATING!
WELL, I'M SORRY, BUT...
Raawrrll!!

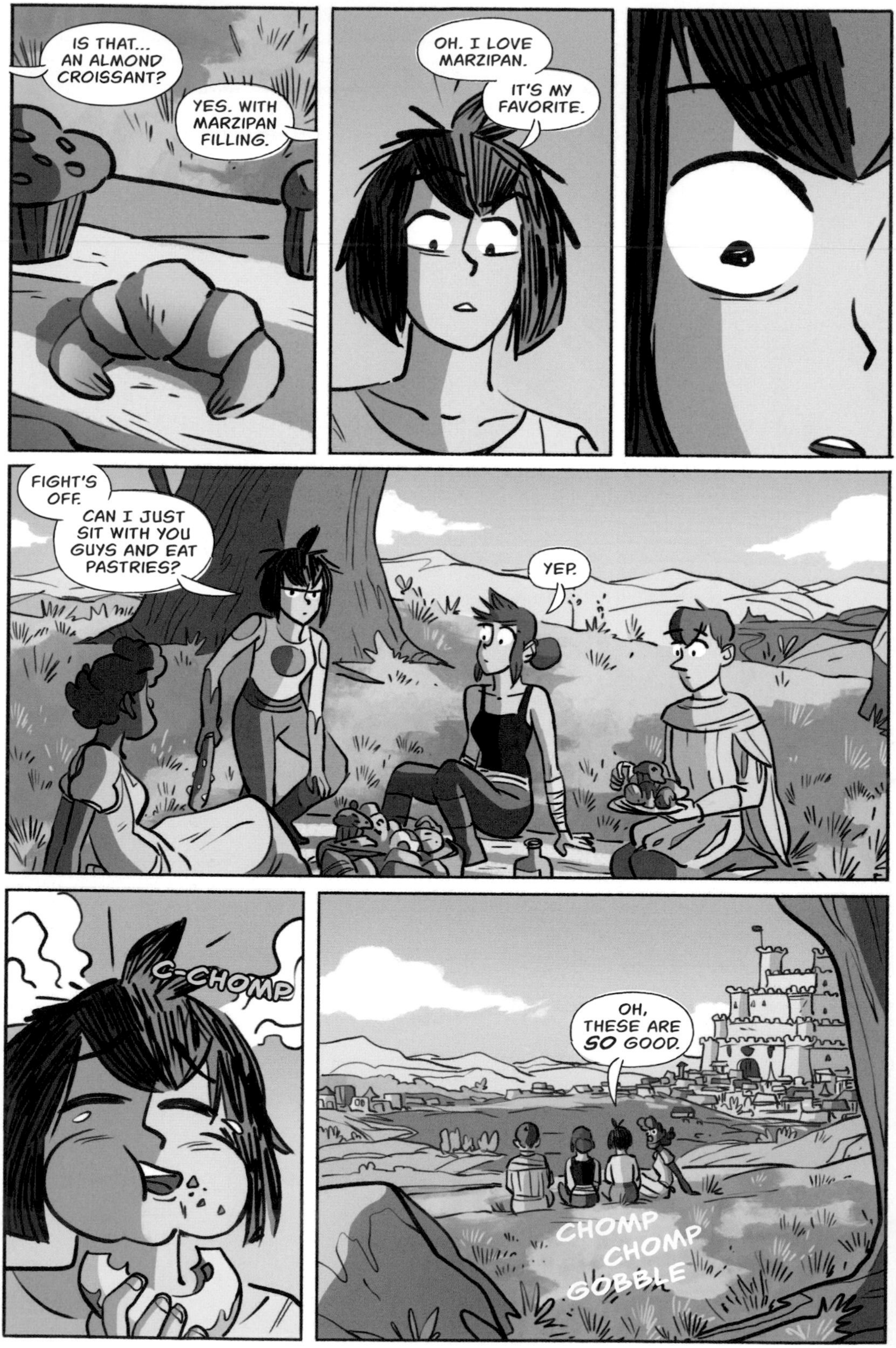
IS THAT... AN ALMOND CROISSANT?
YES. WITH MARZIPAN FILLING.
OH. I LOVE MARZIPAN.
IT'S MY FAVORITE.
FIGHT'S OFF.
CAN I JUST SIT WITH YOU GUYS AND EAT PASTRIES?
YEP.
C-CHOMP
OH, THESE ARE SO GOOD.
CHOMP
CHOMP
GOBBLE

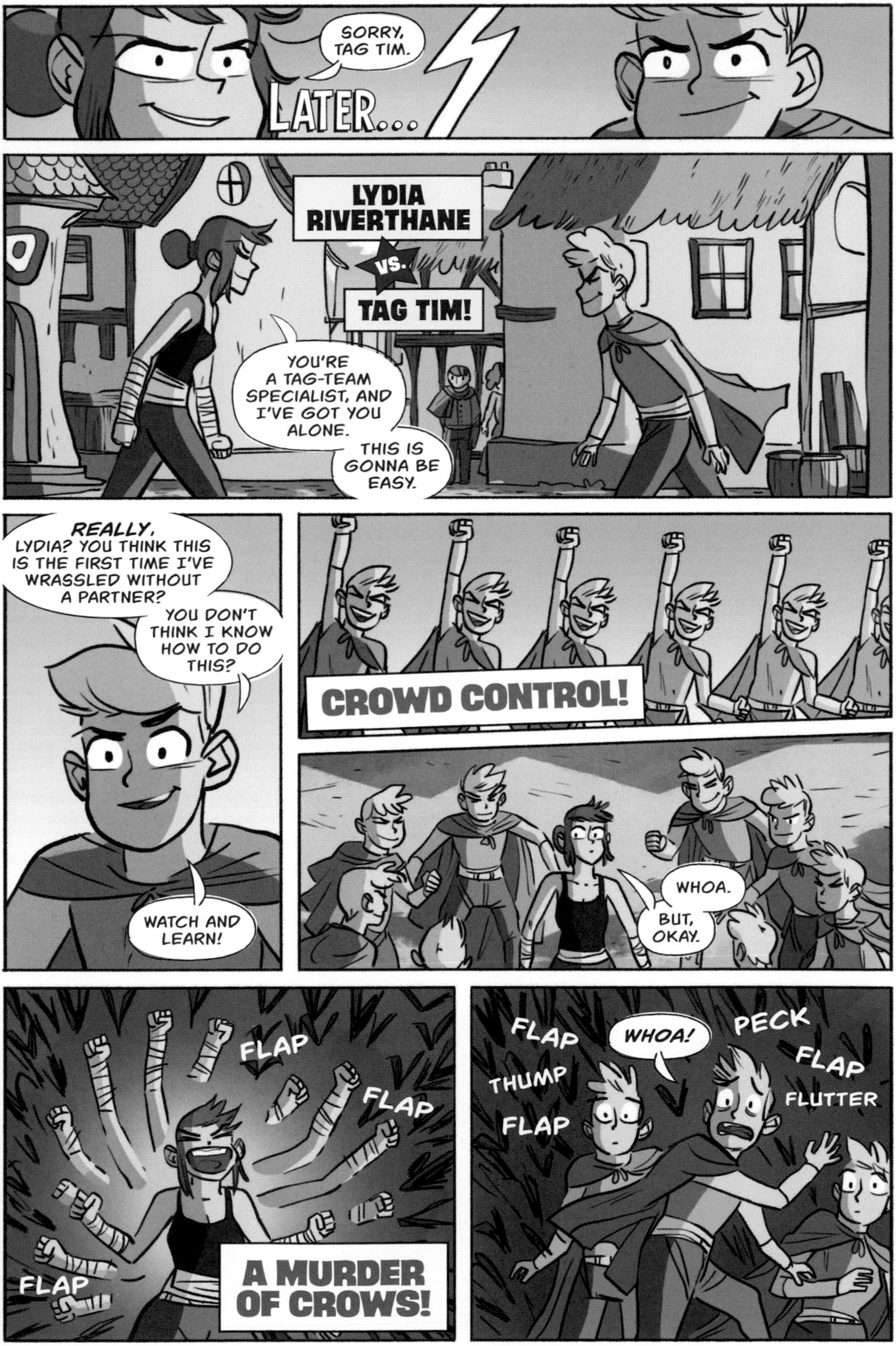
SORRY, TAG TIM.
LATER...
LYDIA RIVERTHANE
VS.
TAG TIM!
YOU'RE A TAG-TEAM SPECIALIST, AND I'VE GOT YOU ALONE.
THIS IS GONNA BE EASY.
REALLY, LYDIA? YOU THINK THIS IS THE FIRST TIME I'VE WRASSLED WITHOUT A PARTNER?
YOU DON'T THINK I KNOW HOW TO DO THIS?
WATCH AND LEARN!
CROWD CONTROL!
WHOA.
BUT, OKAY.
FLAP
FLAP
FLAP
A MURDER OF CROWS!
FLAP
WHOA!
PECK
THUMP
FLAP
FLAP
FLUTTER

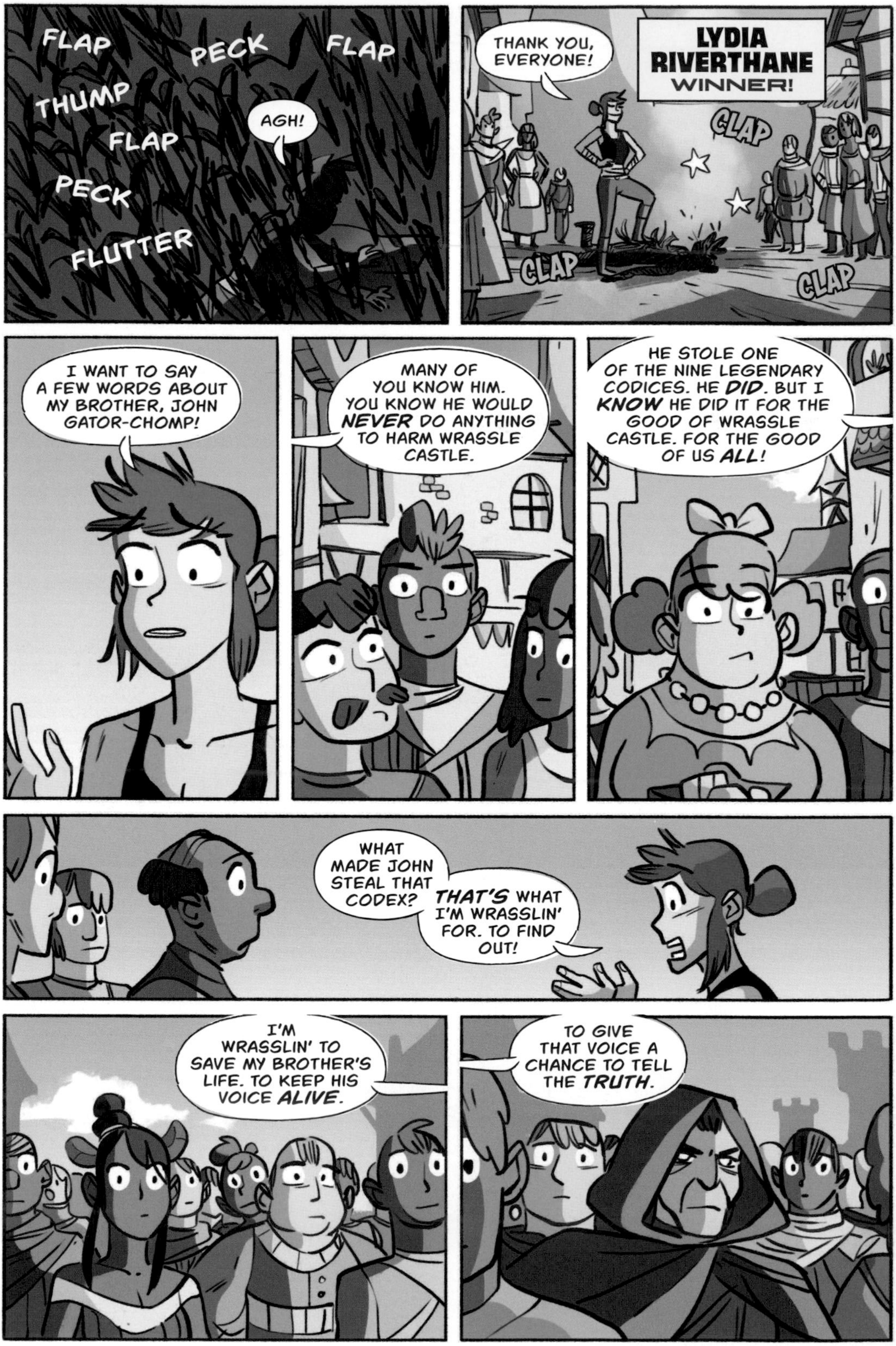
FLAP
PECK
FLAP
THUMP
AGH!
FLAP
PECK
FLUTTER
THANK YOU, EVERYONE!
LYDIA RIVERTHANE WINNER!
CLAP
CLAP
CLAP
I WANT TO SAY A FEW WORDS ABOUT MY BROTHER, JOHN GATOR-CHOMP!
MANY OF YOU KNOW HIM. YOU KNOW HE WOULD NEVER DO ANYTHING TO HARM WRASSLE CASTLE.
HE STOLE ONE OF THE NINE LEGENDARY CODICES. HE DID. BUT I KNOW HE DID IT FOR THE GOOD OF WRASSLE CASTLE. FOR THE GOOD OF US ALL!
WHAT MADE JOHN STEAL THAT CODEX?
THAT'S WHAT I'M WRASSLIN' FOR. TO FIND OUT!
I'M WRASSLIN' TO SAVE MY BROTHER'S LIFE. TO KEEP HIS VOICE ALIVE.
TO GIVE THAT VOICE A CHANCE TO TELL THE TRUTH.

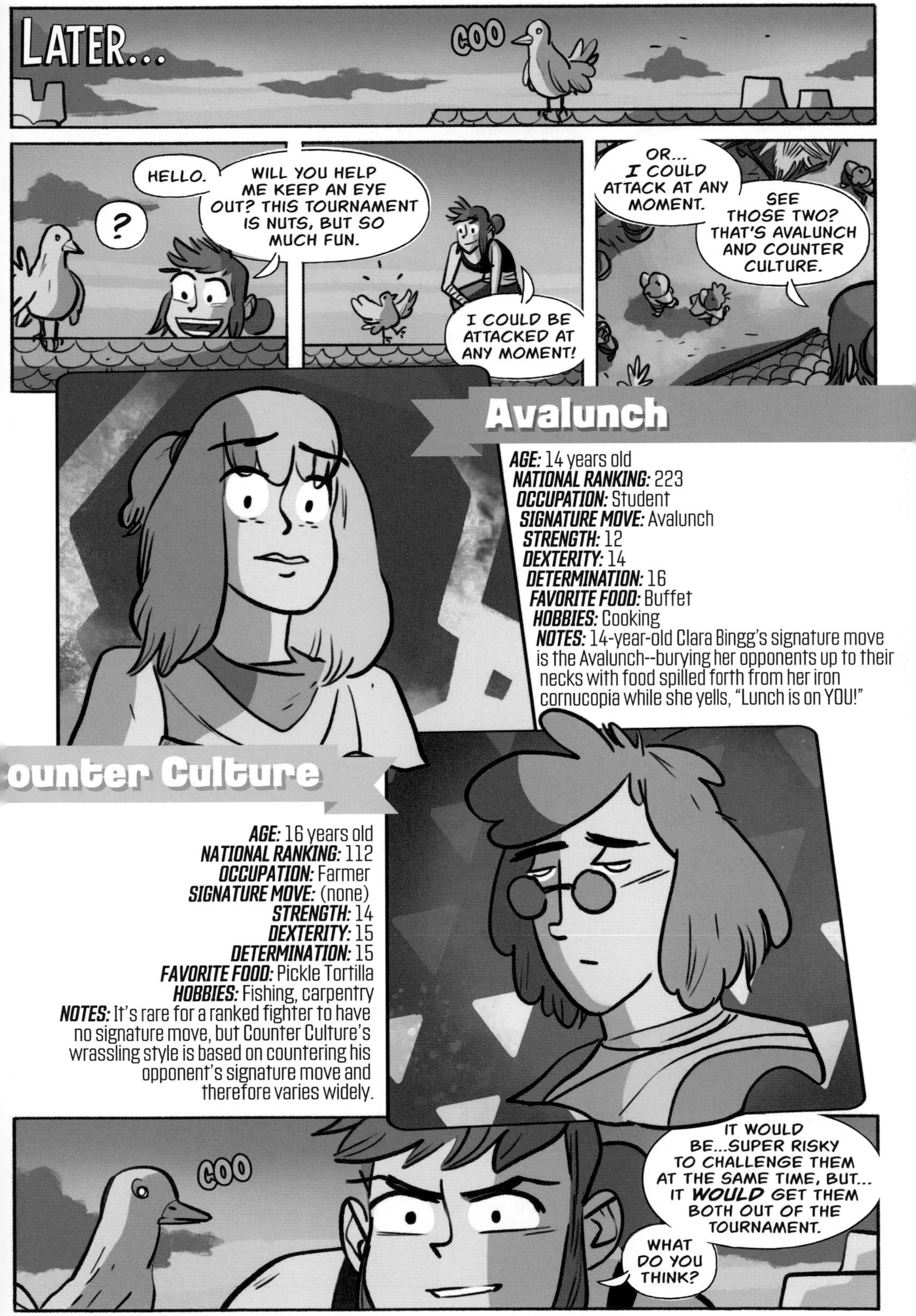
LATER...
COO
HELLO.
?
WILL YOU HELP ME KEEP AN EYE OUT? THIS TOURNAMENT IS NUTS, BUT SO MUCH FUN.
I COULD BE ATTACKED AT ANY MOMENT!
OR... I COULD ATTACK AT ANY MOMENT.
SEE THOSE TWO? THAT'S AVALUNCH AND COUNTER CULTURE.
Avalunch
AGE: 14 years old
NATIONAL RANKING: 223
OCCUPATION: Student
SIGNATURE MOVE: Avalunch
STRENGTH: 12
DEXTERITY: 14
DETERMINATION: 16
FAVORITE FOOD: Buffet
HOBBIES: Cooking
NOTES: 14-year-old Clara Bingg's signature move is the Avalunch--burying her opponents up to their necks with food spilled forth from her iron cornucopia while she yells, "Lunch is on YOU!"
ounter Culture
AGE: 16 years old
NATIONAL RANKING: 112
OCCUPATION: Farmer
SIGNATURE MOVE: (none)
STRENGTH: 14
DEXTERITY: 15
DETERMINATION: 15
FAVORITE FOOD: Pickle Tortilla
HOBBIES: Fishing, carpentry
NOTES: It's rare for a ranked fighter to have no signature move, but Counter Culture's wrassling style is based on countering his opponent's signature move and therefore varies widely.
COO
IT WOULD BE...SUPER RISKY TO CHALLENGE THEM AT THE SAME TIME, BUT... IT WOULD GET THEM BOTH OUT OF THE TOURNAMENT.
WHAT DO YOU THINK?

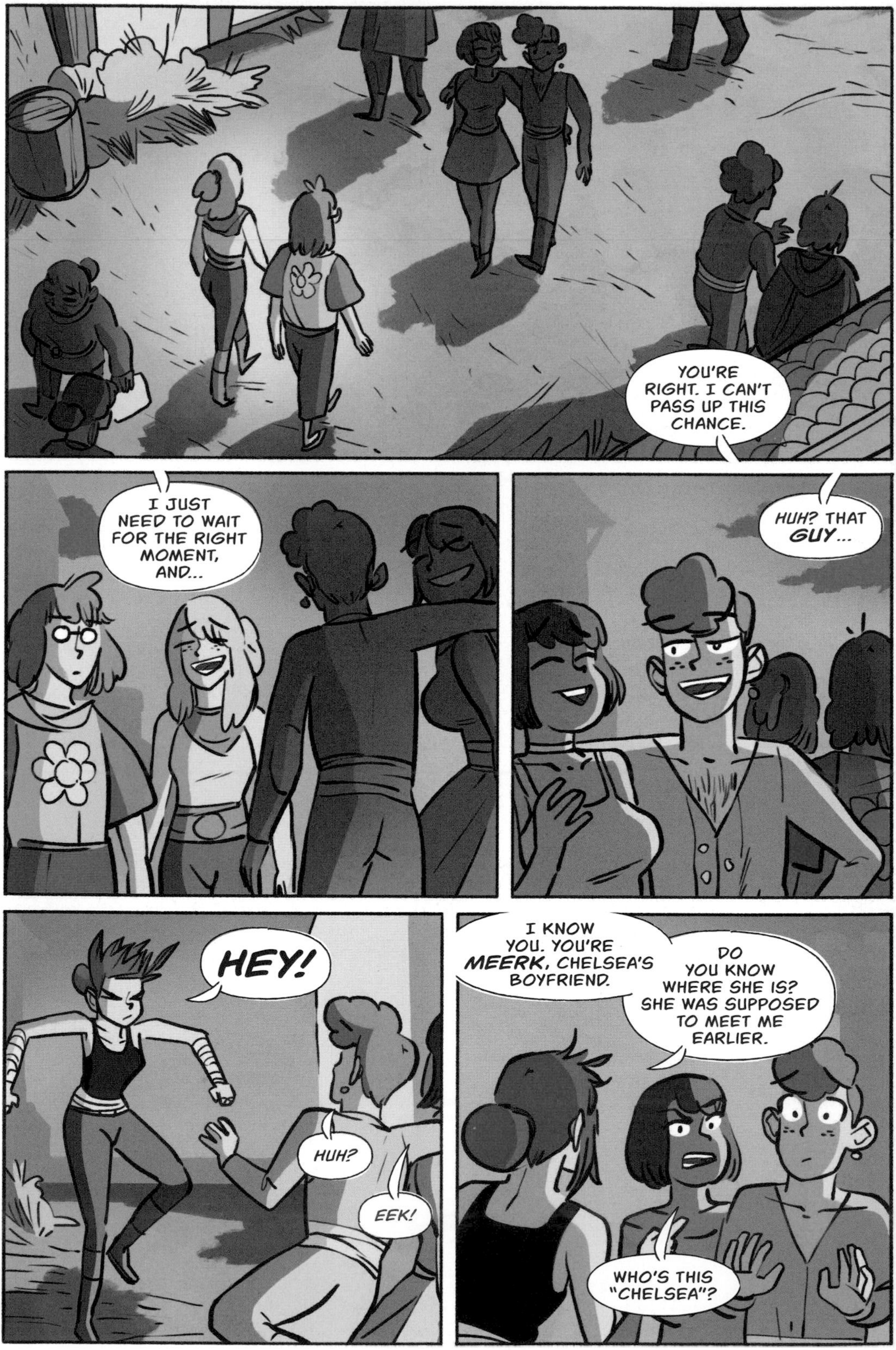
YOU'RE RIGHT. I CAN'T PASS UP THIS CHANCE.
I JUST NEED TO WAIT FOR THE RIGHT MOMENT, AND...
HUH? THAT GUY...
HEY!
HUH?
EEK!
I KNOW YOU. YOU'RE MEERK, CHELSEA'S BOYFRIEND.
DO YOU KNOW WHERE SHE IS? SHE WAS SUPPOSED TO MEET ME EARLIER.
WHO'S THIS "CHELSEA"?

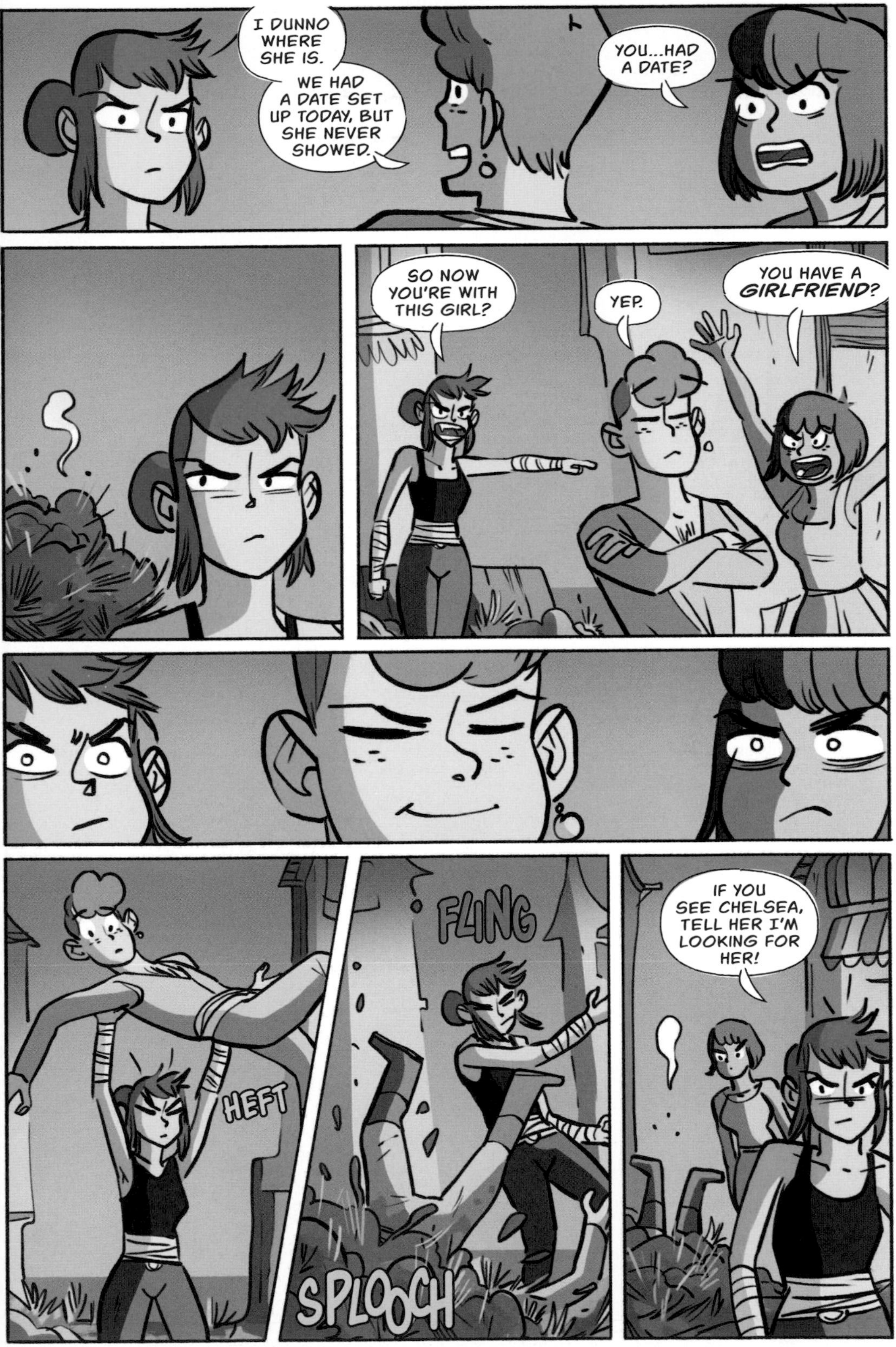
I DUNNO WHERE SHE IS.
WE HAD A DATE SET UP TODAY, BUT SHE NEVER SHOWED.
YOU...HAD A DATE?
SO NOW YOU'RE WITH THIS GIRL?
YEP.
YOU HAVE A GIRLFRIEND?
HEFT
FLING
SPLOOCH
IF YOU SEE CHELSEA, TELL HER I'M LOOKING FOR HER!

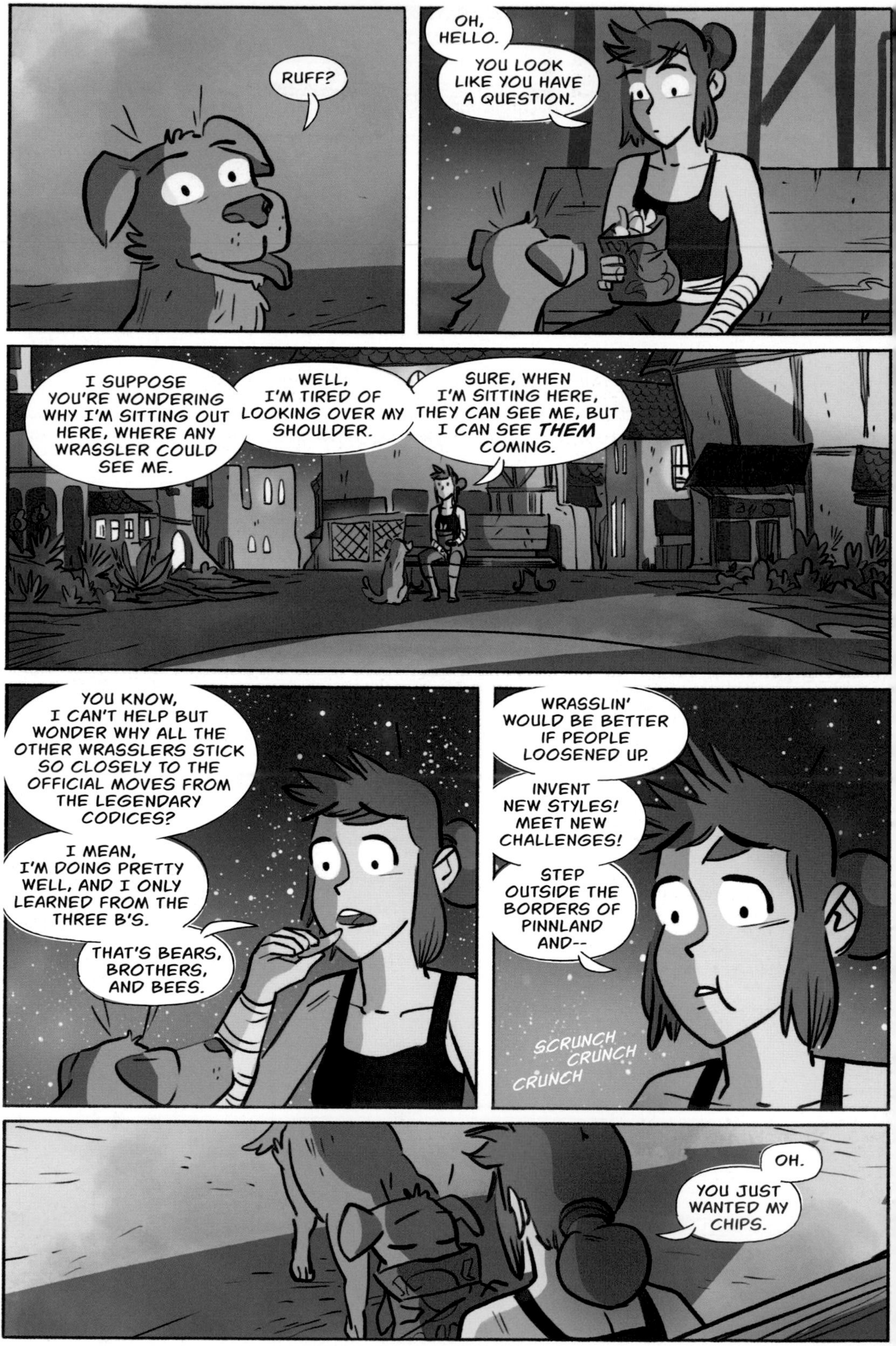
RUFF?
OH, HELLO.
YOU LOOK LIKE YOU HAVE A QUESTION.
I SUPPOSE YOU'RE WONDERING WHY I'M SITTING OUT HERE, WHERE ANY WRASSLER COULD SEE ME.
WELL, I'M TIRED OF LOOKING OVER MY SHOULDER.
SURE, WHEN I'M SITTING HERE, THEY CAN SEE ME, BUT I CAN SEE THEM COMING.
YOU KNOW, I CAN'T HELP BUT WONDER WHY ALL THE OTHER WRASSLERS STICK SO CLOSELY TO THE OFFICIAL MOVES FROM THE LEGENDARY CODICES?
I MEAN, I'M DOING PRETTY WELL, AND I ONLY LEARNED FROM THE THREE B'S.
THAT'S BEARS, BROTHERS, AND BEES.
WRASSLIN' WOULD BE BETTER IF PEOPLE LOOSENED UP.
INVENT NEW STYLES! MEET NEW CHALLENGES!
STEP OUTSIDE THE BORDERS OF PINNLAND AND--
SCRUNCH CRUNCH CRUNCH
OH.
YOU JUST WANTED MY CHIPS.

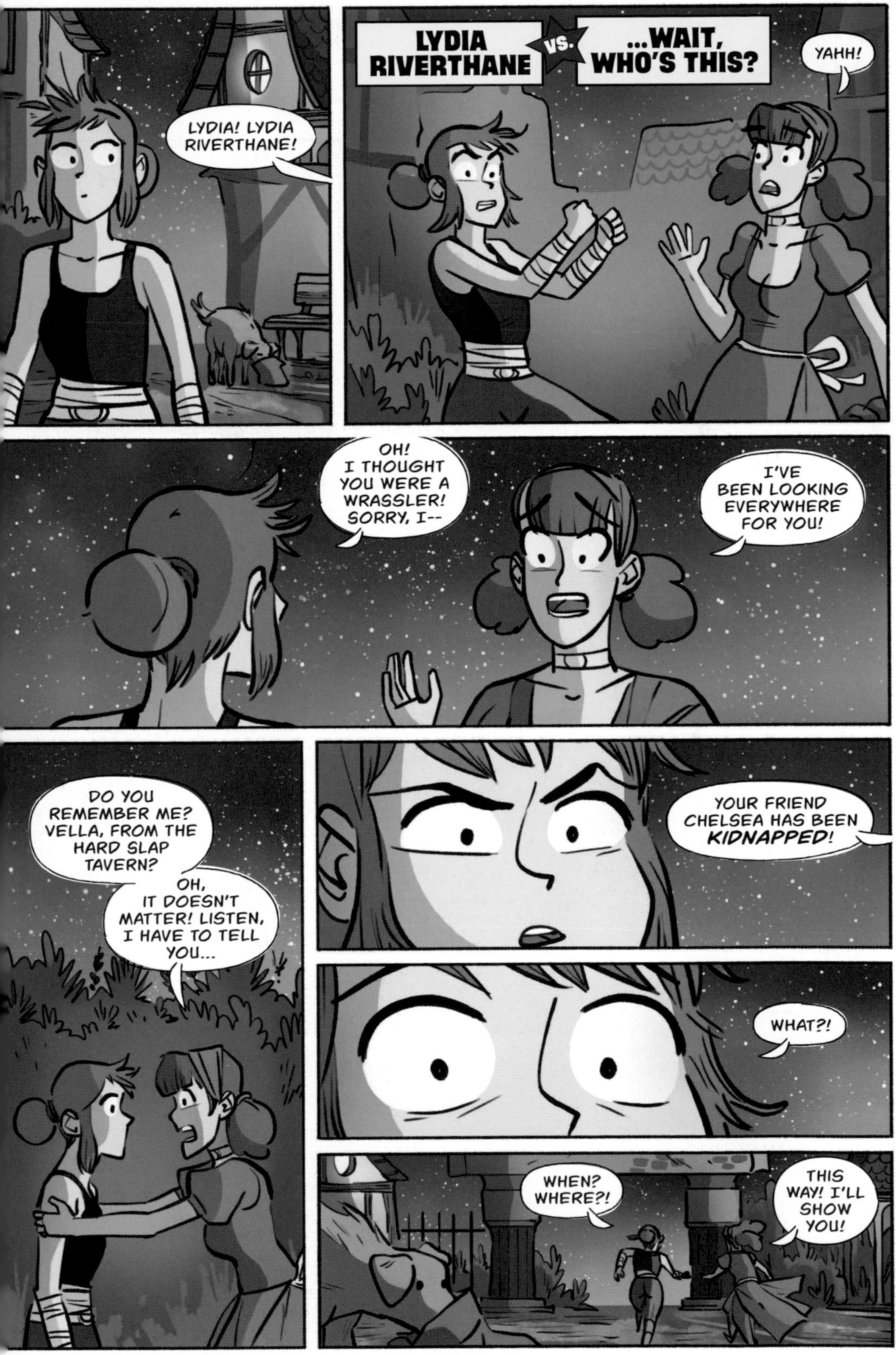
LYDIA! LYDIA RIVERTHANE!
LYDIA RIVERTHANE
VS.
...WAIT, WHO'S THIS?
YAHH!
OH! I THOUGHT YOU WERE A WRASSLER! SORRY, I--
I'VE BEEN LOOKING EVERYWHERE FOR YOU!
DO YOU REMEMBER ME? VELLA, FROM THE HARD SLAP TAVERN?
OH, IT DOESN'T MATTER! LISTEN, I HAVE TO TELL YOU...
YOUR FRIEND CHELSEA HAS BEEN KIDNAPPED!
WHAT?!
WHEN? WHERE?!
THIS WAY! I'LL SHOW YOU!

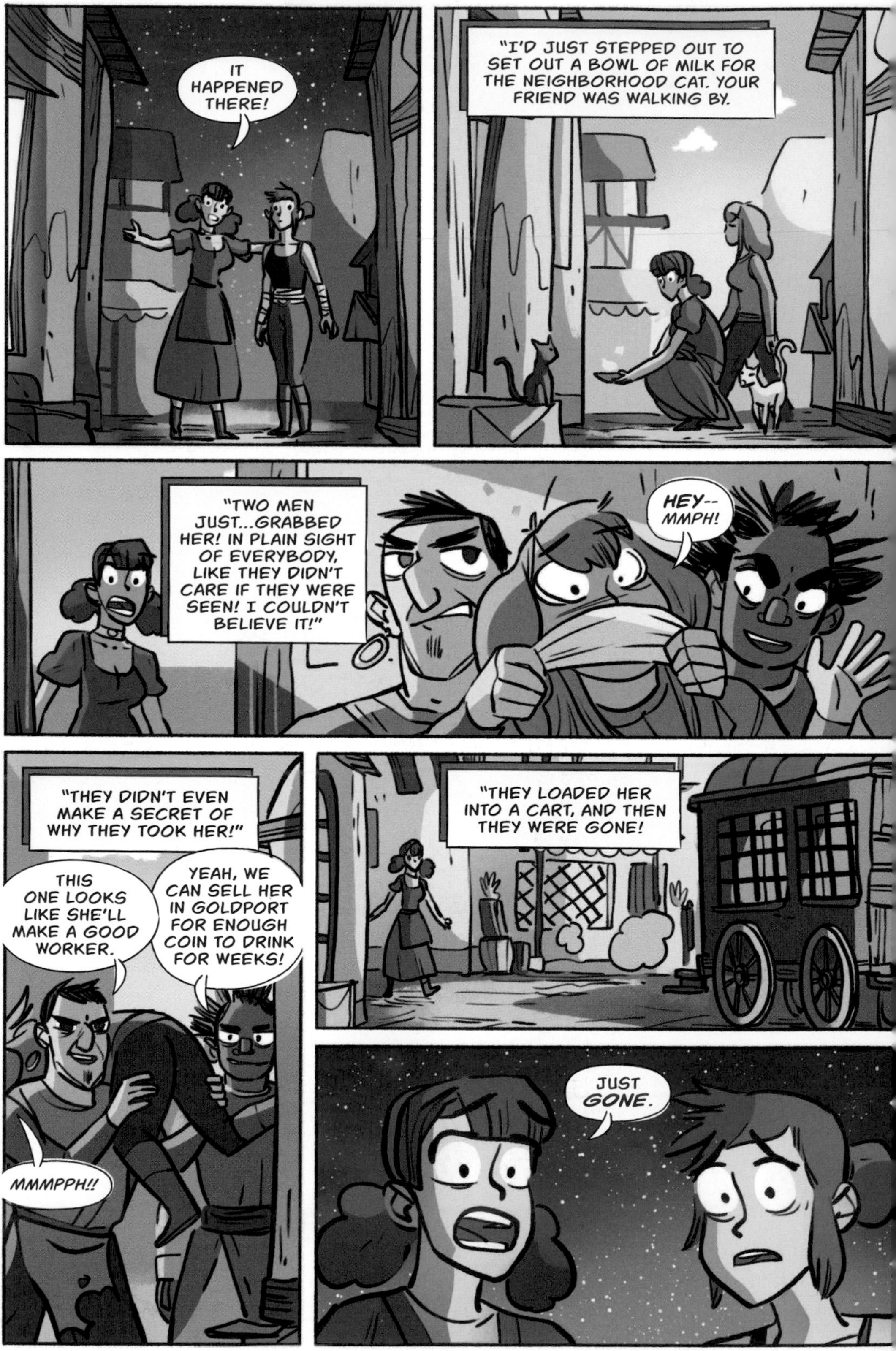
IT HAPPENED THERE!
"I'D JUST STEPPED OUT TO SET OUT A BOWL OF MILK FOR THE NEIGHBORHOOD CAT. YOUR FRIEND WAS WALKING BY.
"TWO MEN JUST...GRABBED HER! IN PLAIN SIGHT OF EVERYBODY, LIKE THEY DIDN'T CARE IF THEY WERE SEEN! I COULDN'T BELIEVE IT!"
HEY-- MMPH!
"THEY DIDN'T EVEN MAKE A SECRET OF WHY THEY TOOK HER!"
THIS ONE LOOKS LIKE SHE'LL MAKE A GOOD WORKER.
YEAH, WE CAN SELL HER IN GOLDPORT FOR ENOUGH COIN TO DRINK FOR WEEKS!
MMMPPH!!
"THEY LOADED HER INTO A CART, AND THEN THEY WERE GONE!
JUST GONE.

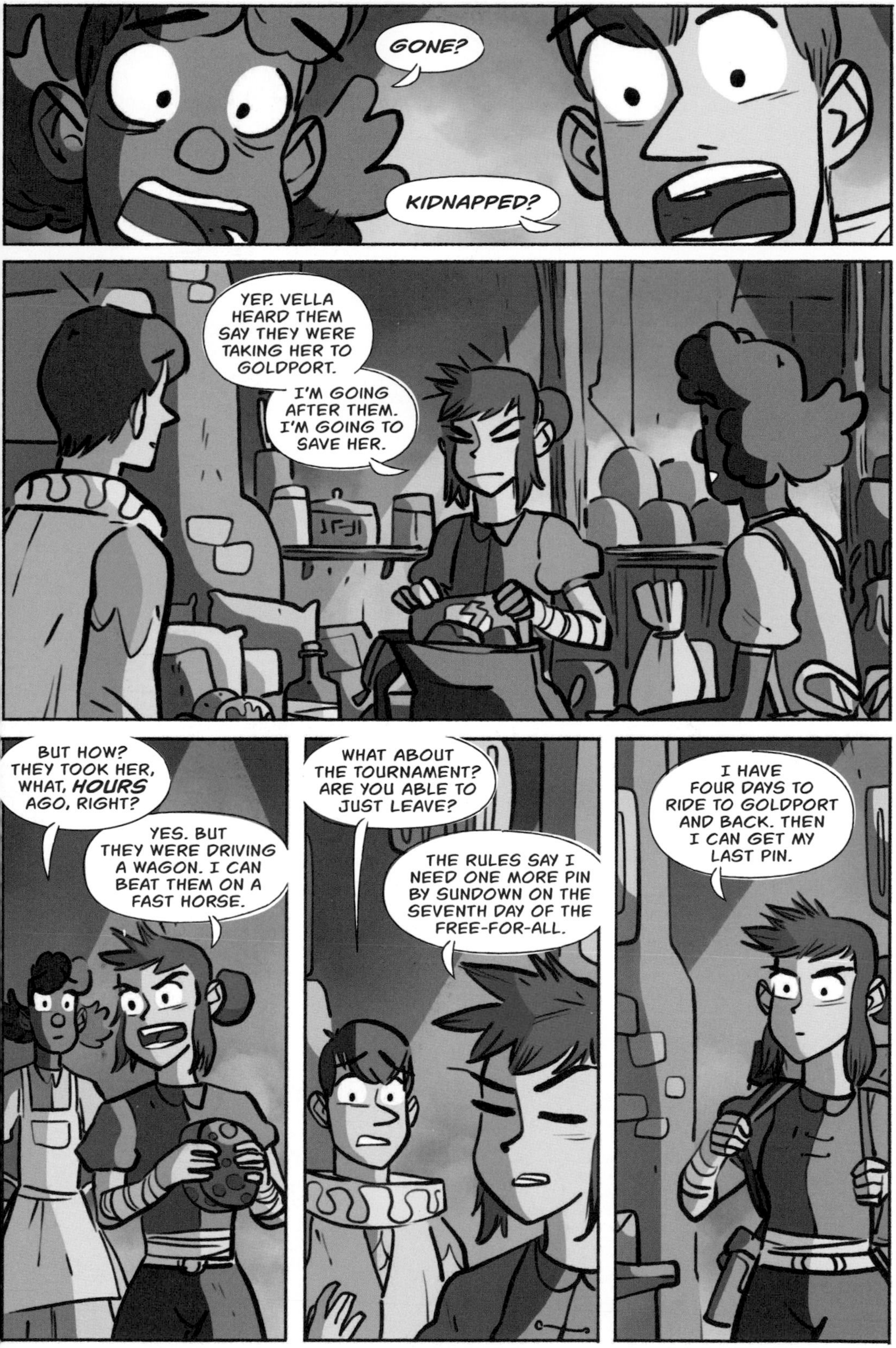
GONE?
KIDNAPPED?
YEP. VELLA HEARD THEM SAY THEY WERE TAKING HER TO GOLDPORT.
I'M GOING AFTER THEM. I'M GOING TO SAVE HER.
BUT HOW? THEY TOOK HER, WHAT, **HOURS** AGO, RIGHT?
YES. BUT THEY WERE DRIVING A WAGON. I CAN BEAT THEM ON A FAST HORSE.
WHAT ABOUT THE TOURNAMENT? ARE YOU ABLE TO JUST LEAVE?
THE RULES SAY I NEED ONE MORE PIN BY SUNDOWN ON THE SEVENTH DAY OF THE FREE-FOR-ALL.
I HAVE FOUR DAYS TO RIDE TO GOLDPORT AND BACK. THEN I CAN GET MY LAST PIN.

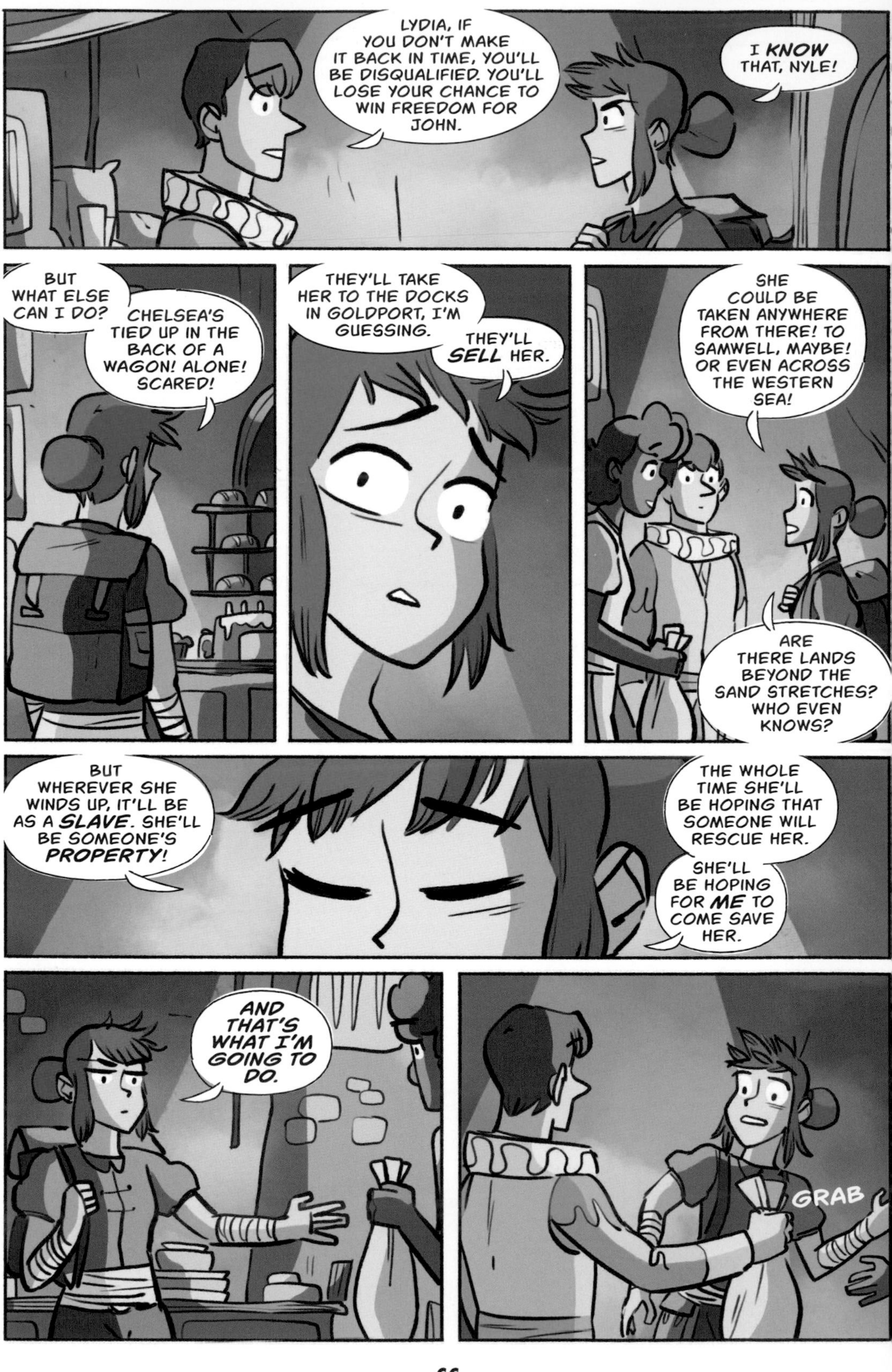
LYDIA, IF YOU DON'T MAKE IT BACK IN TIME, YOU'LL BE DISQUALIFIED. YOU'LL LOSE YOUR CHANCE TO WIN FREEDOM FOR JOHN.
I KNOW THAT, NYLE!
BUT WHAT ELSE CAN I DO?
CHELSEA'S TIED UP IN THE BACK OF A WAGON! ALONE! SCARED!
THEY'LL TAKE HER TO THE DOCKS IN GOLDPORT, I'M GUESSING.
THEY'LL SELL HER.
SHE COULD BE TAKEN ANYWHERE FROM THERE! TO SAMWELL, MAYBE! OR EVEN ACROSS THE WESTERN SEA!
ARE THERE LANDS BEYOND THE SAND STRETCHES? WHO EVEN KNOWS?
BUT WHEREVER SHE WINDS UP, IT'LL BE AS A SLAVE. SHE'LL BE SOMEONE'S PROPERTY!
THE WHOLE TIME SHE'LL BE HOPING THAT SOMEONE WILL RESCUE HER.
SHE'LL BE HOPING FOR ME TO COME SAVE HER.
AND THAT'S WHAT I'M GOING TO DO.
GRAB

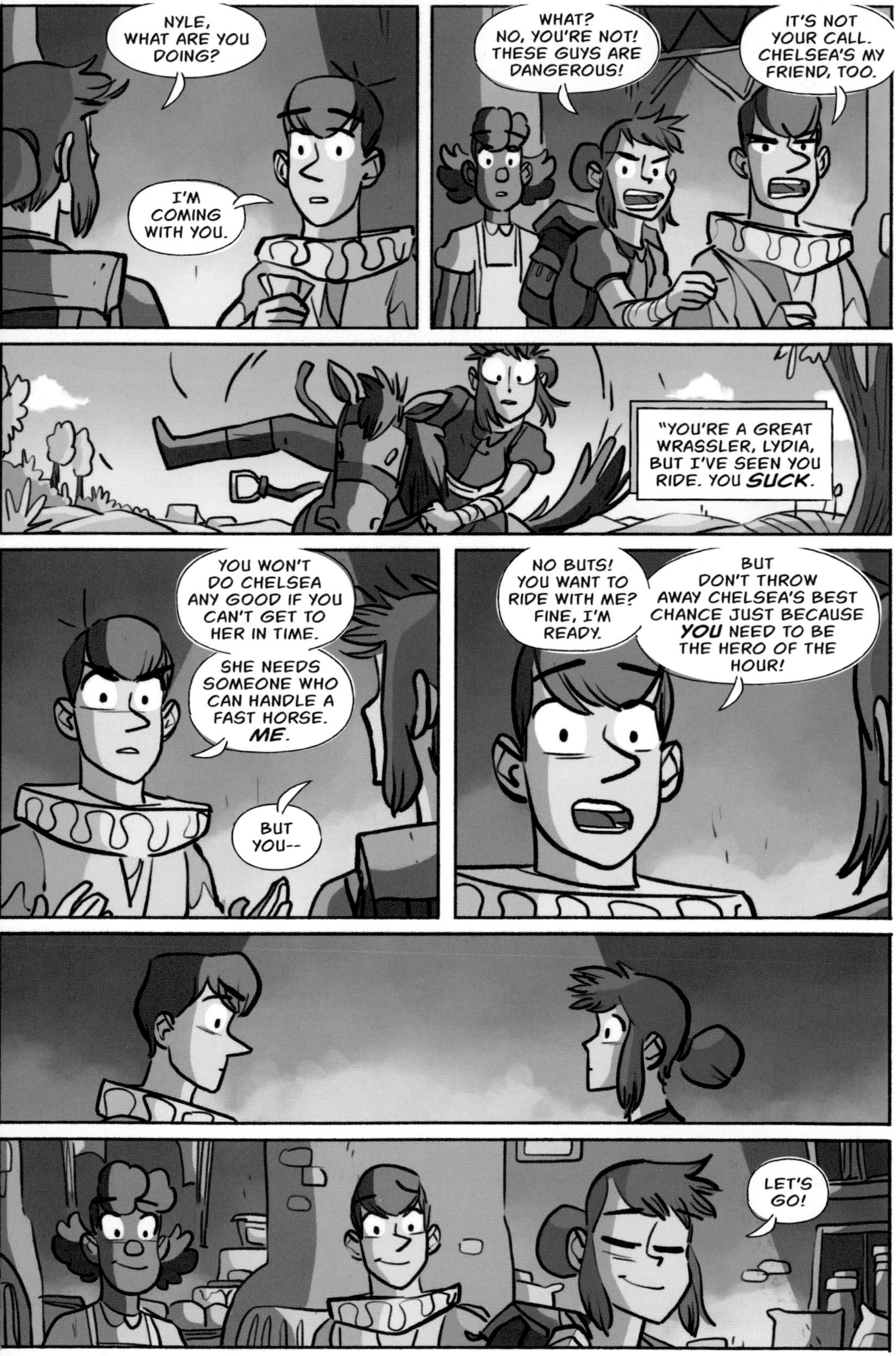
NYLE, WHAT ARE YOU DOING?
I'M COMING WITH YOU.
WHAT? NO, YOU'RE NOT! THESE GUYS ARE DANGEROUS!
IT'S NOT YOUR CALL. CHELSEA'S MY FRIEND, TOO.
"YOU'RE A GREAT WRASSLER, LYDIA, BUT I'VE SEEN YOU RIDE. YOU SUCK.
YOU WON'T DO CHELSEA ANY GOOD IF YOU CAN'T GET TO HER IN TIME.
SHE NEEDS SOMEONE WHO CAN HANDLE A FAST HORSE. ME.
BUT YOU--
NO BUTS! YOU WANT TO RIDE WITH ME? FINE, I'M READY.
BUT DON'T THROW AWAY CHELSEA'S BEST CHANCE JUST BECAUSE YOU NEED TO BE THE HERO OF THE HOUR!
LET'S GO!

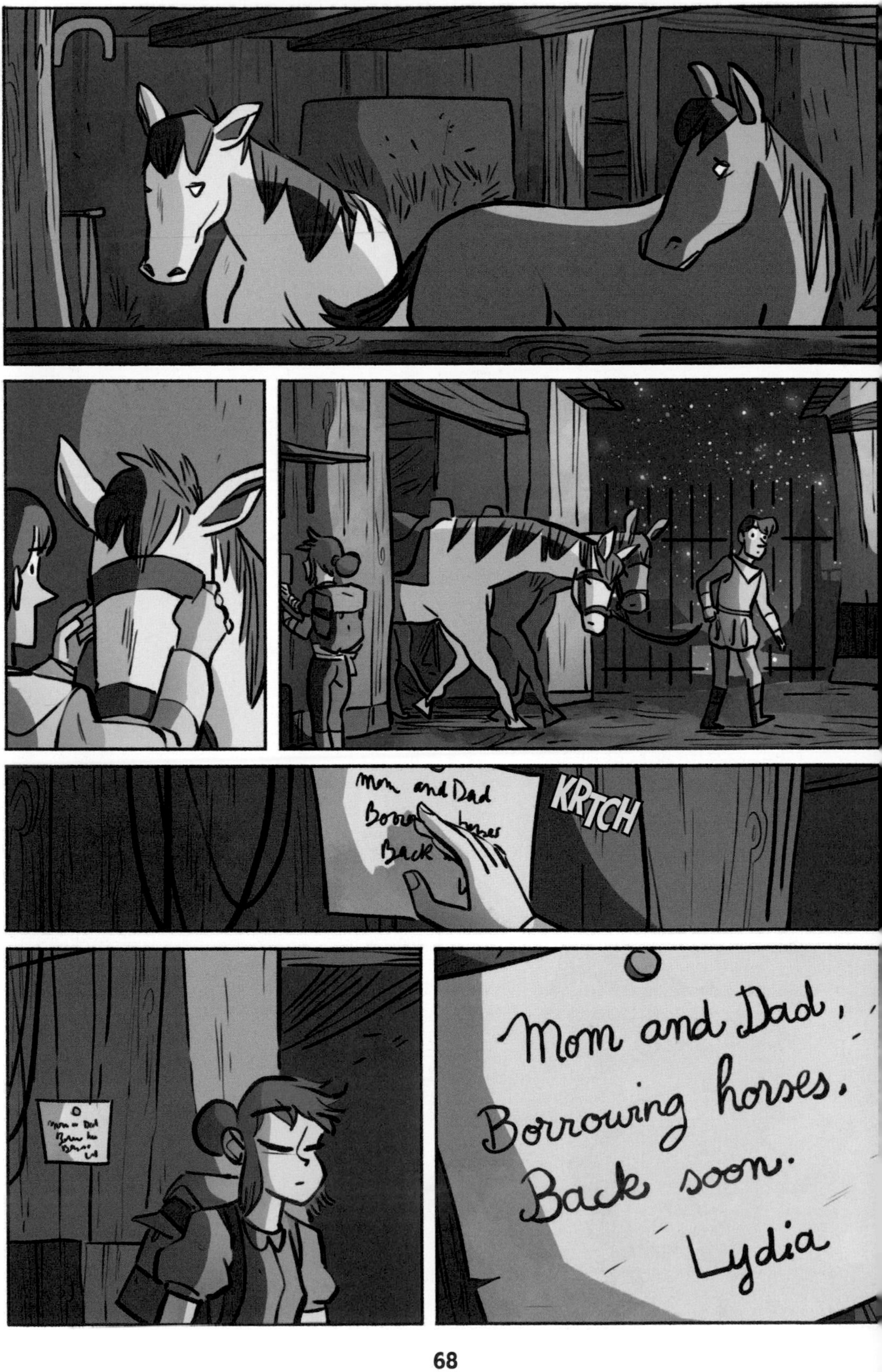
KRTCH
Mom and Dad,
Borrowing horses.
Back soon.
Lydia

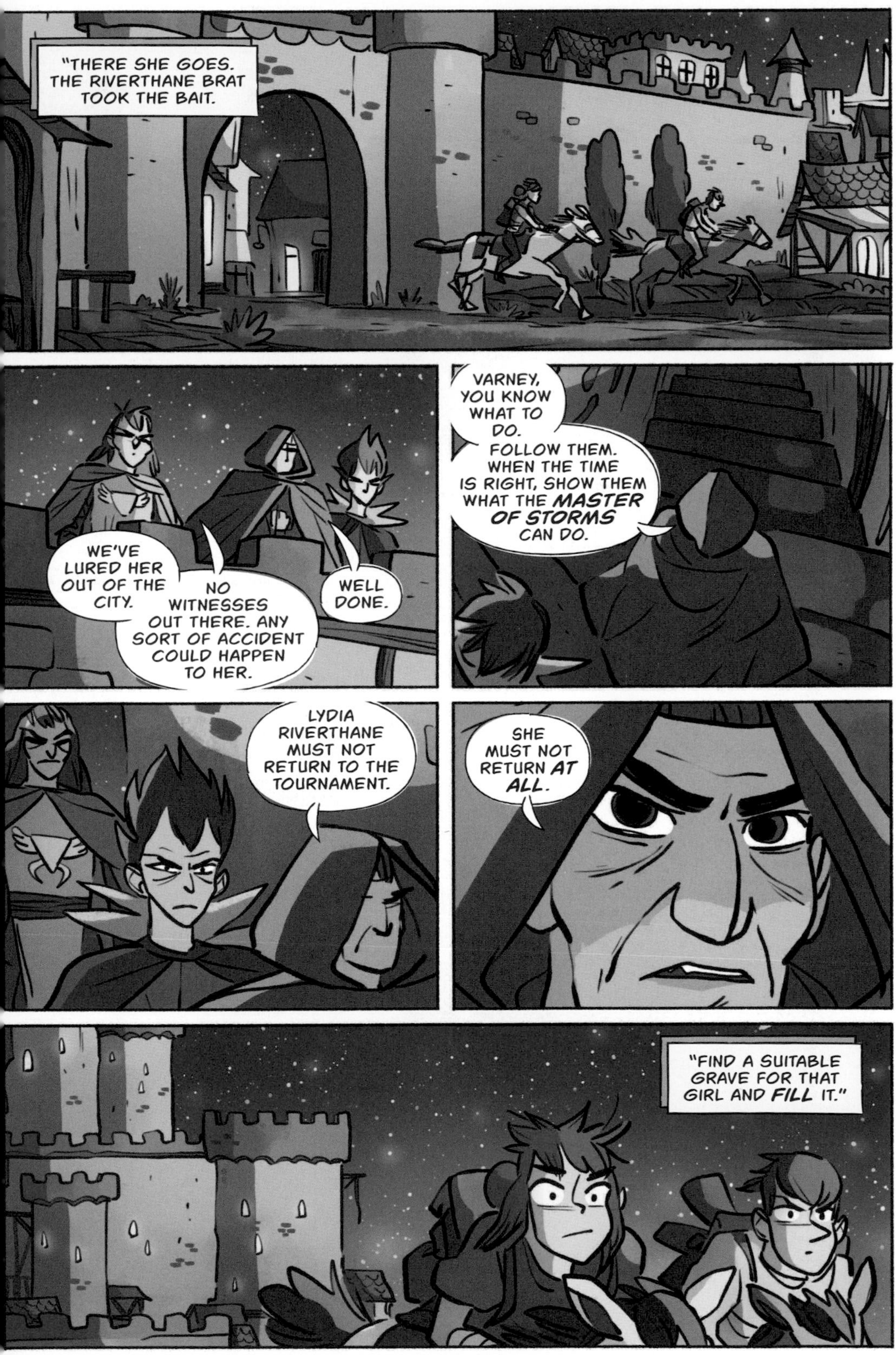
"THERE SHE GOES. THE RIVERTHANE BRAT TOOK THE BAIT.
WE'VE LURED HER OUT OF THE CITY.
NO WITNESSES OUT THERE. ANY SORT OF ACCIDENT COULD HAPPEN TO HER.
WELL DONE.
VARNEY, YOU KNOW WHAT TO DO.
FOLLOW THEM. WHEN THE TIME IS RIGHT, SHOW THEM WHAT THE MASTER OF STORMS CAN DO.
LYDIA RIVERTHANE MUST NOT RETURN TO THE TOURNAMENT.
SHE MUST NOT RETURN AT ALL.
"FIND A SUITABLE GRAVE FOR THAT GIRL AND FILL IT."

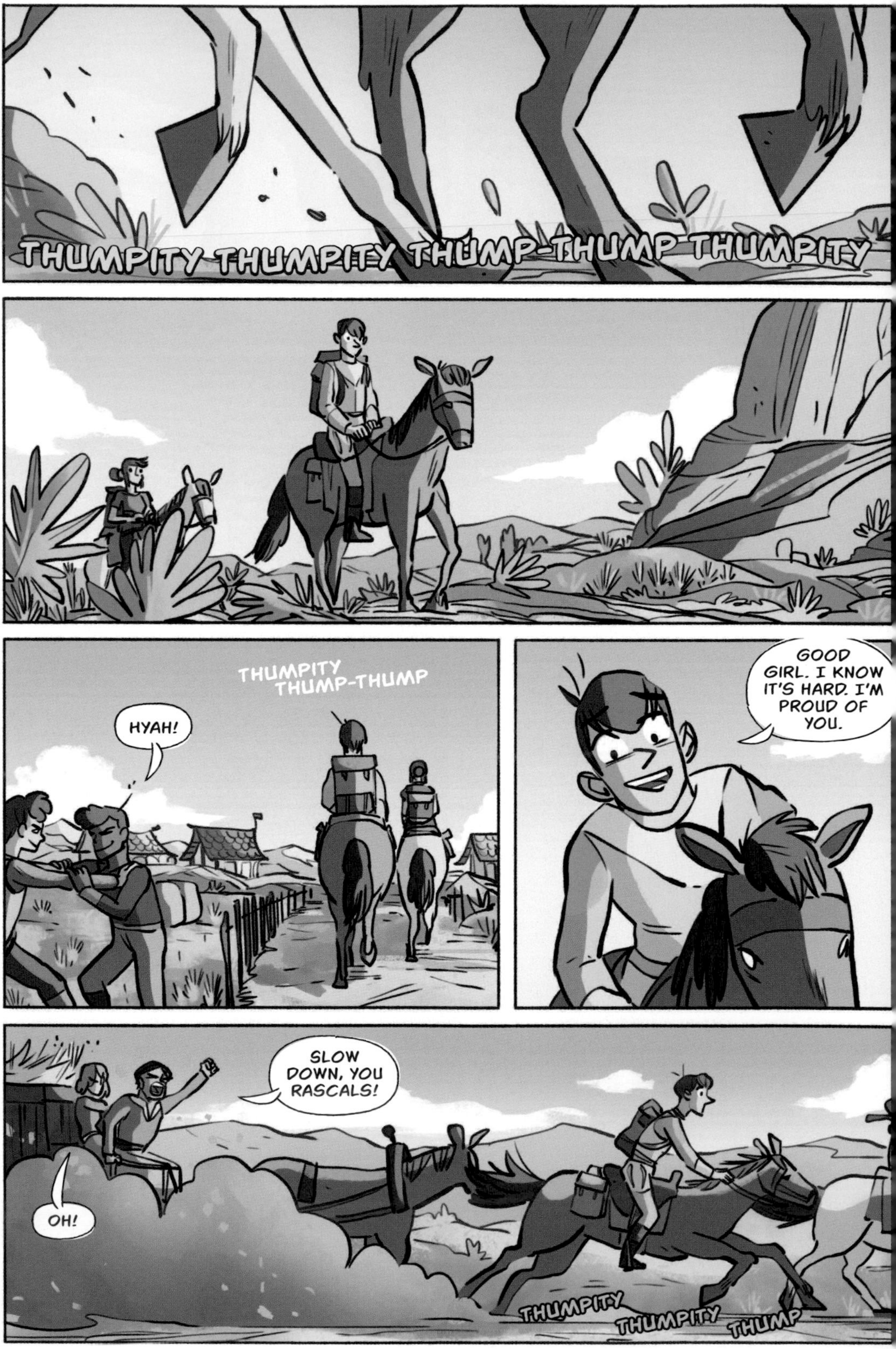
THUMPITY THUMPITY THUMP-THUMP THUMPITY
THUMPITY THUMP-THUMP
HYAH!
GOOD GIRL. I KNOW IT'S HARD. I'M PROUD OF YOU.
SLOW DOWN, YOU RASCALS!
OH!
THUMPITY THUMPITY THUMP

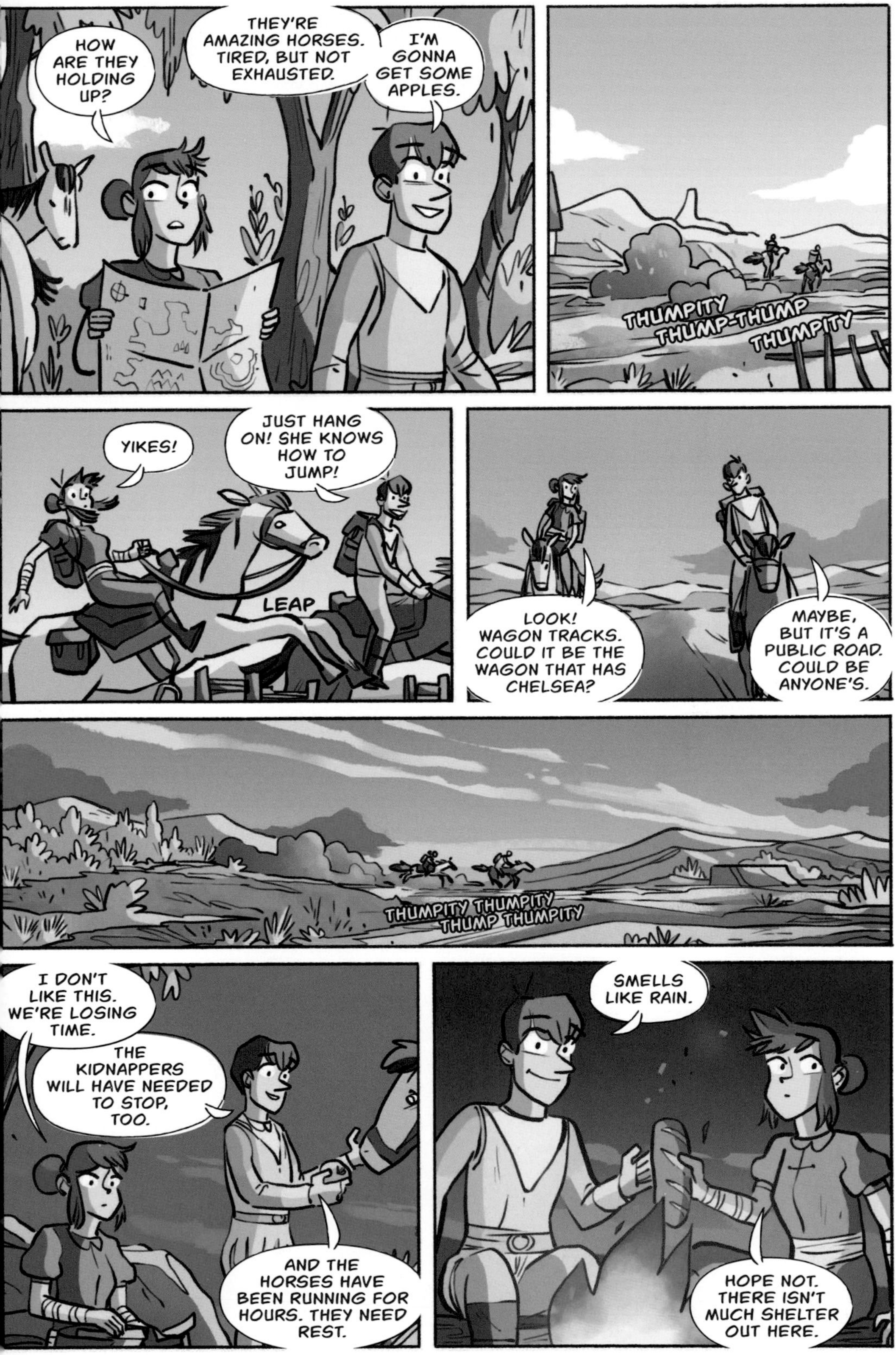
HOW ARE THEY HOLDING UP?
THEY'RE AMAZING HORSES. TIRED, BUT NOT EXHAUSTED.
I'M GONNA GET SOME APPLES.
THUMPITY THUMP-THUMP THUMPITY
YIKES!
JUST HANG ON! SHE KNOWS HOW TO JUMP!
LEAP
LOOK! WAGON TRACKS. COULD IT BE THE WAGON THAT HAS CHELSEA?
MAYBE, BUT IT'S A PUBLIC ROAD. COULD BE ANYONE'S.
THUMPITY THUMPITY THUMP THUMPITY
I DON'T LIKE THIS. WE'RE LOSING TIME.
THE KIDNAPPERS WILL HAVE NEEDED TO STOP, TOO.
AND THE HORSES HAVE BEEN RUNNING FOR HOURS. THEY NEED REST.
SMELLS LIKE RAIN.
HOPE NOT. THERE ISN'T MUCH SHELTER OUT HERE.

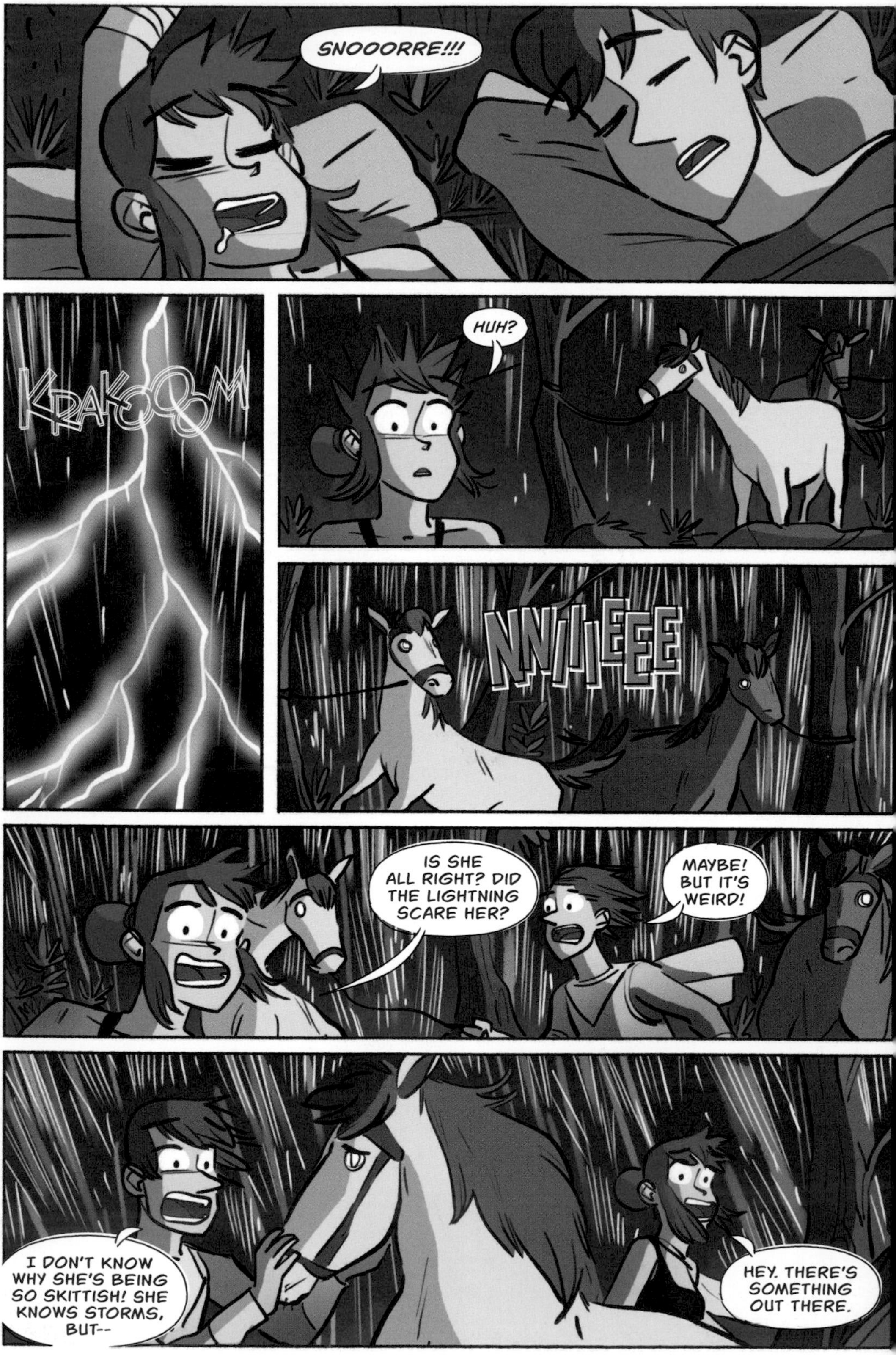
SNOOORRE!!!
KRAKOOOOM
HUH?
NNIIIIEEE
IS SHE ALL RIGHT? DID THE LIGHTNING SCARE HER?
MAYBE! BUT IT'S WEIRD!
I DON'T KNOW WHY SHE'S BEING SO SKITTISH! SHE KNOWS STORMS, BUT--
HEY. THERE'S SOMETHING OUT THERE.

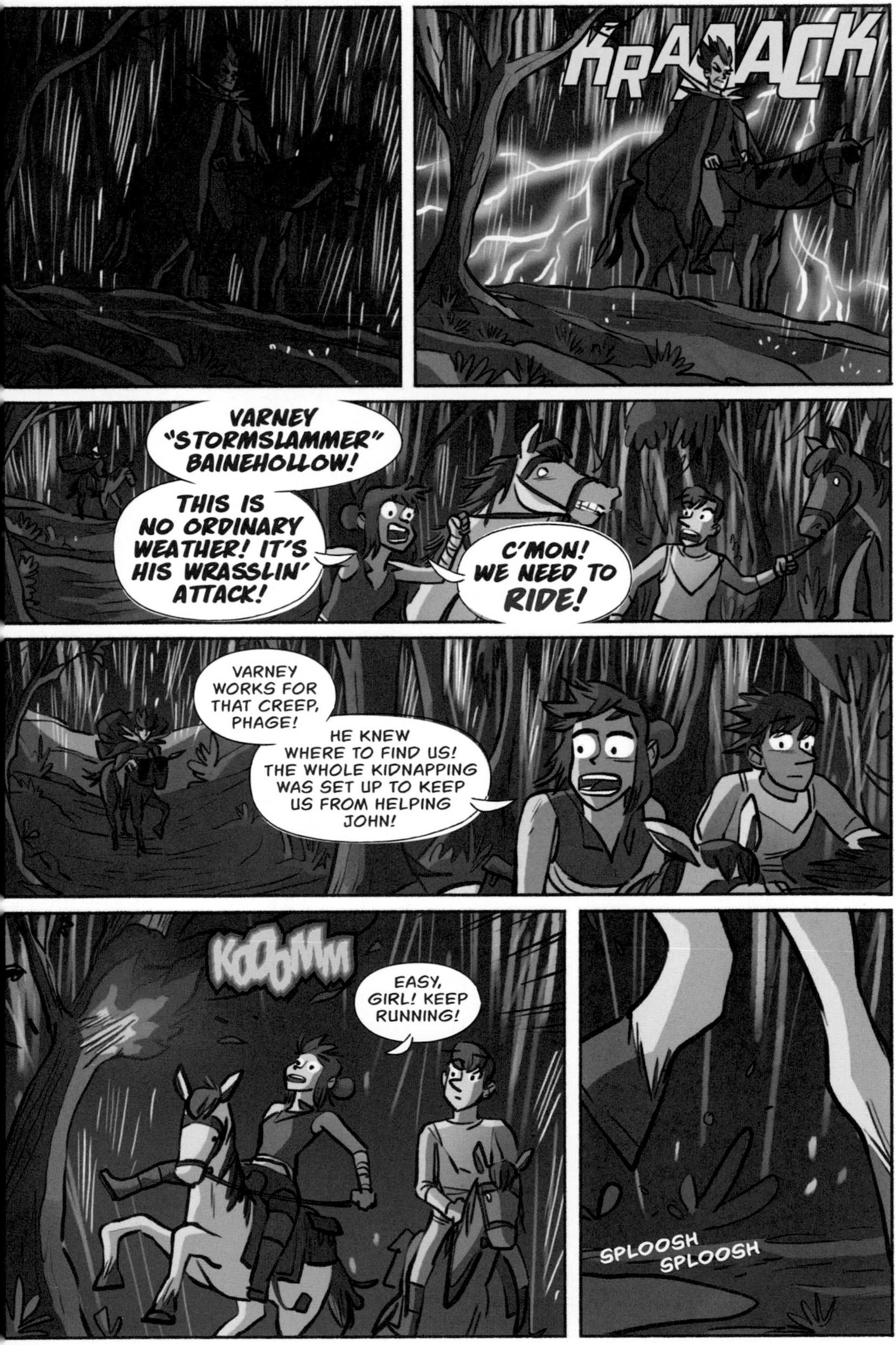
KRAAAACK
VARNEY "STORMSLAMMER" BAINEHOLLOW!
THIS IS NO ORDINARY WEATHER! IT'S HIS WRASSLIN' ATTACK!
C'MON! WE NEED TO RIDE!
VARNEY WORKS FOR THAT CREEP, PHAGE!
HE KNEW WHERE TO FIND US! THE WHOLE KIDNAPPING WAS SET UP TO KEEP US FROM HELPING JOHN!
KOOOMM
EASY, GIRL! KEEP RUNNING!
SPLOOSH SPLOOSH

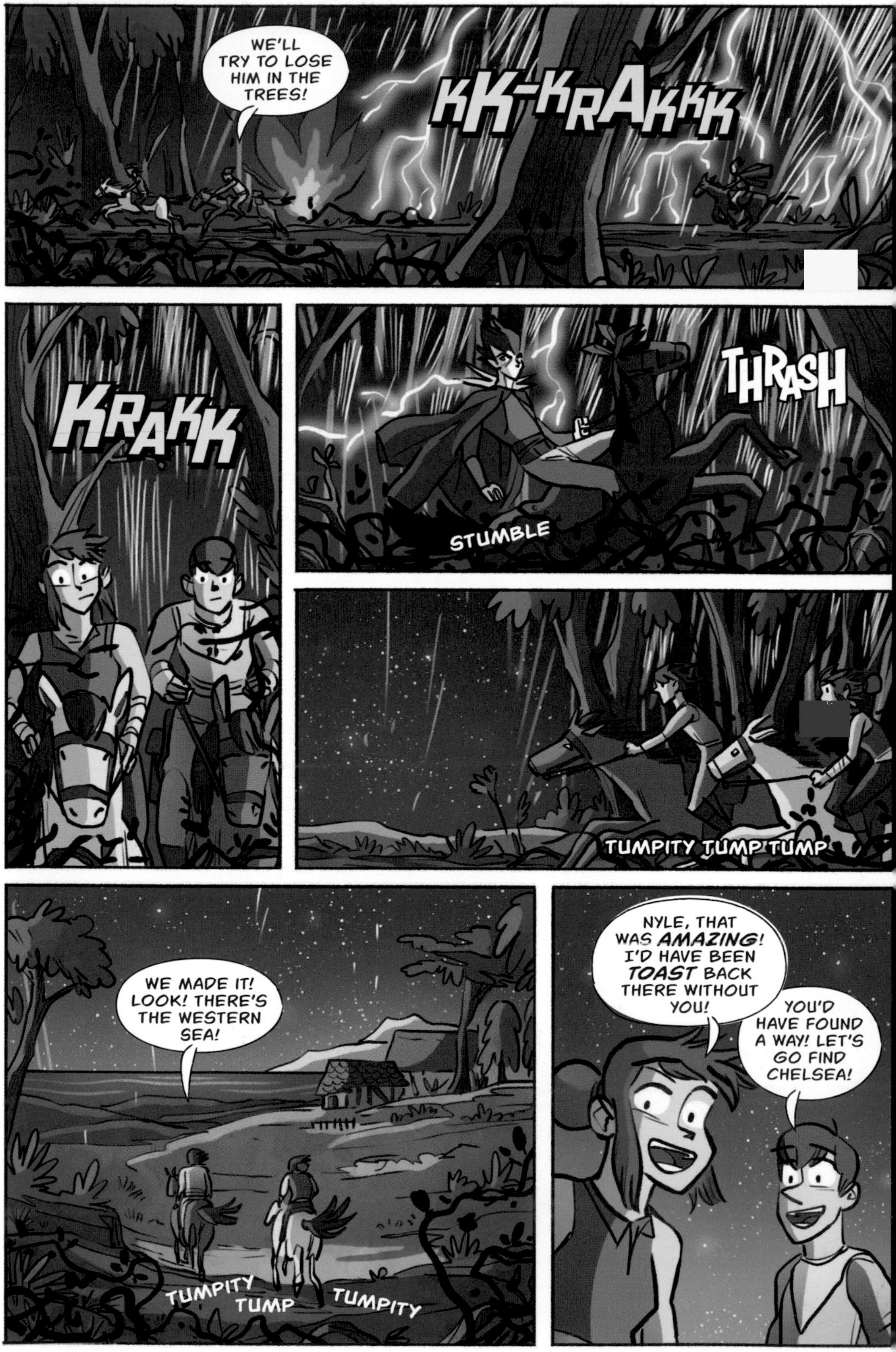
WE'LL TRY TO LOSE HIM IN THE TREES!
KK-KRAKKK
KRAKK
THRASH
STUMBLE
TUMPITY TUMP TUMP
WE MADE IT! LOOK! THERE'S THE WESTERN SEA!
TUMPITY
TUMP
TUMPITY
NYLE, THAT WAS AMAZING! I'D HAVE BEEN TOAST BACK THERE WITHOUT YOU!
YOU'D HAVE FOUND A WAY! LET'S GO FIND CHELSEA!

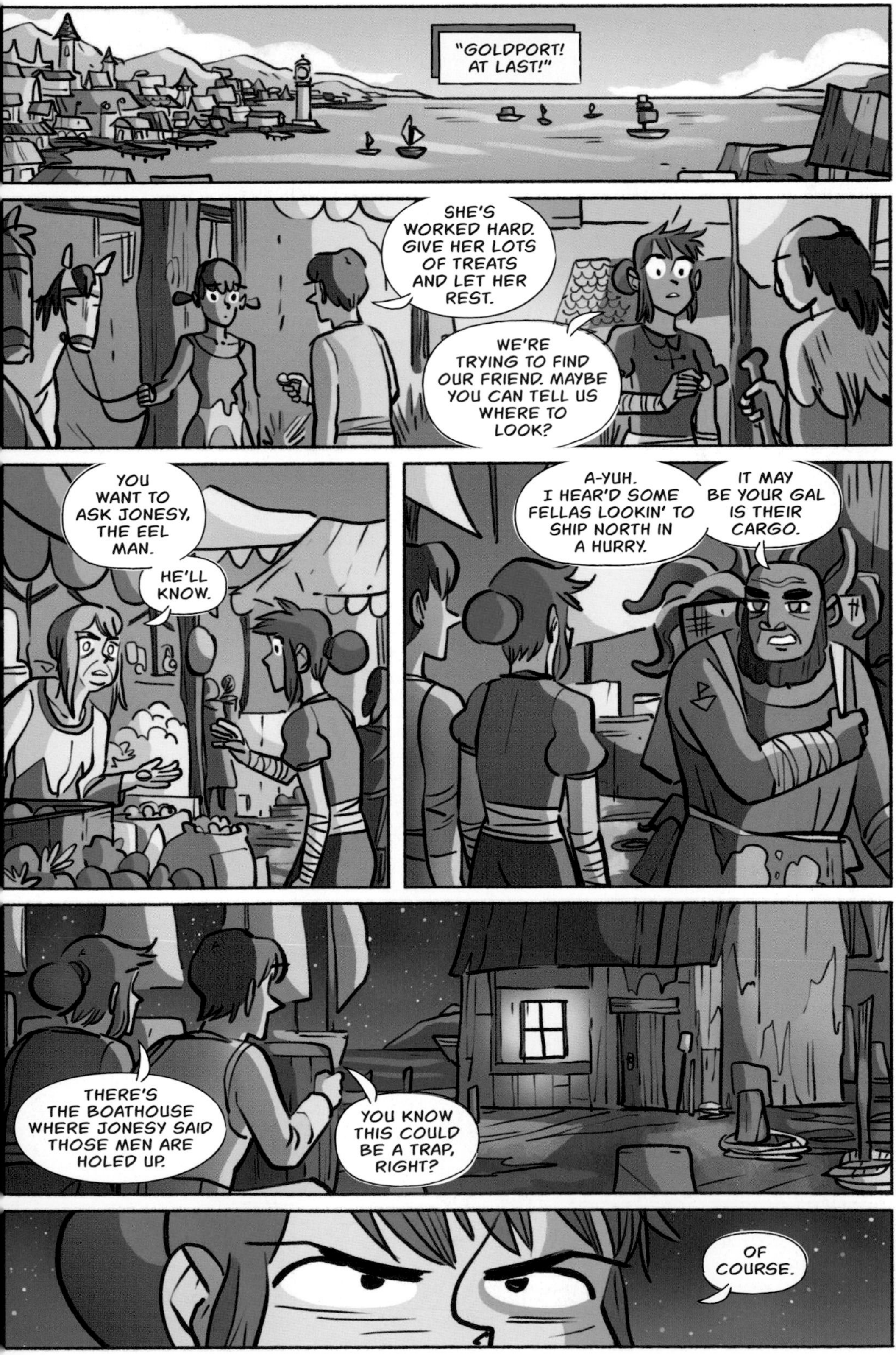
"GOLDPORT! AT LAST!"
SHE'S WORKED HARD. GIVE HER LOTS OF TREATS AND LET HER REST.
WE'RE TRYING TO FIND OUR FRIEND. MAYBE YOU CAN TELL US WHERE TO LOOK?
YOU WANT TO ASK JONESY, THE EEL MAN.
HE'LL KNOW.
A-YUH. I HEAR'D SOME FELLAS LOOKIN' TO SHIP NORTH IN A HURRY.
IT MAY BE YOUR GAL IS THEIR CARGO.
THERE'S THE BOATHOUSE WHERE JONESY SAID THOSE MEN ARE HOLED UP.
YOU KNOW THIS COULD BE A TRAP, RIGHT?
OF COURSE.

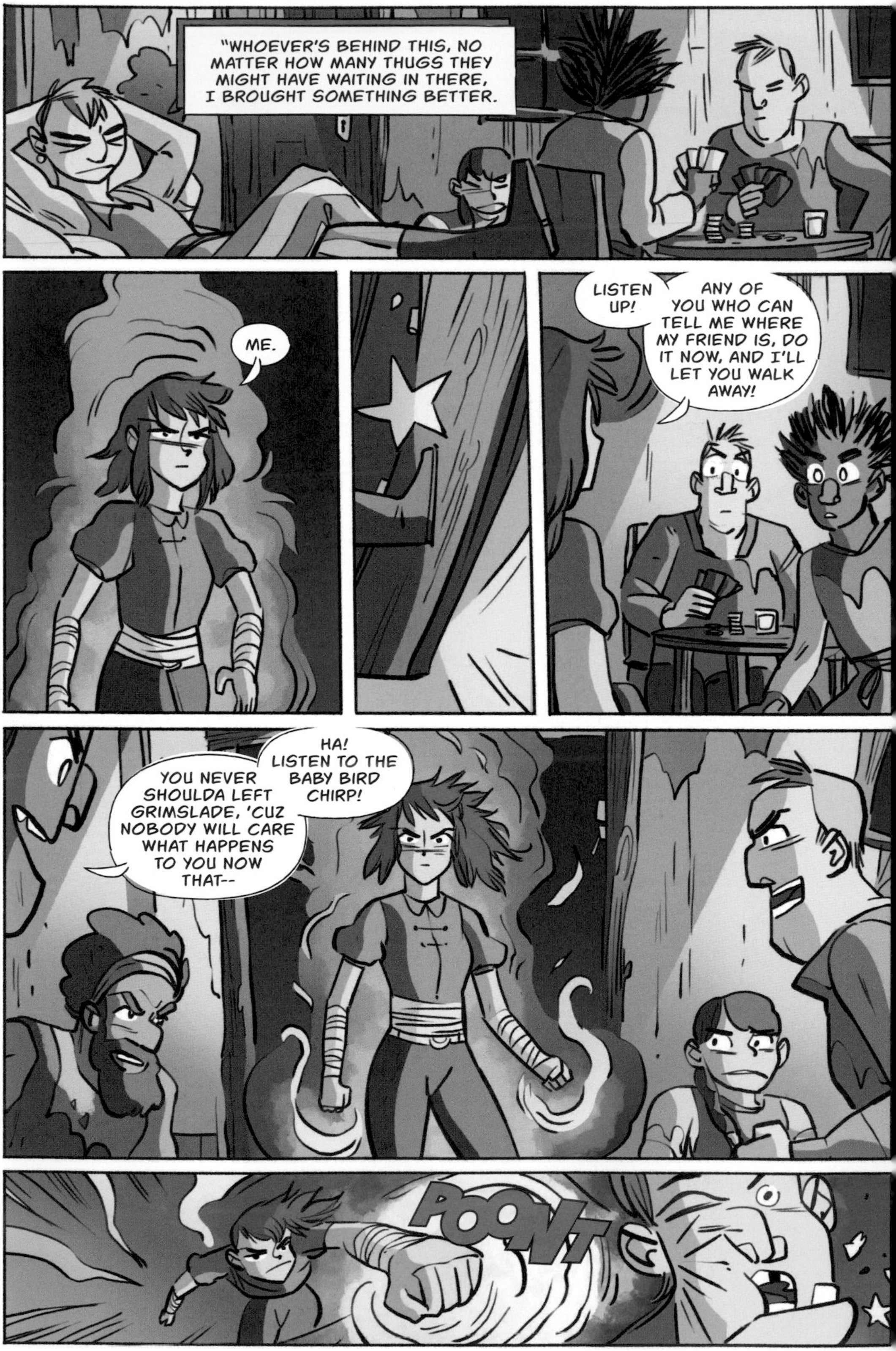
"WHOEVER'S BEHIND THIS, NO MATTER HOW MANY THUGS THEY MIGHT HAVE WAITING IN THERE, I BROUGHT SOMETHING BETTER.
ME.
LISTEN UP!
ANY OF YOU WHO CAN TELL ME WHERE MY FRIEND IS, DO IT NOW, AND I'LL LET YOU WALK AWAY!
HA! LISTEN TO THE BABY BIRD CHIRP!
YOU NEVER SHOULDA LEFT GRIMSLADE, 'CUZ NOBODY WILL CARE WHAT HAPPENS TO YOU NOW THAT--
POOMT

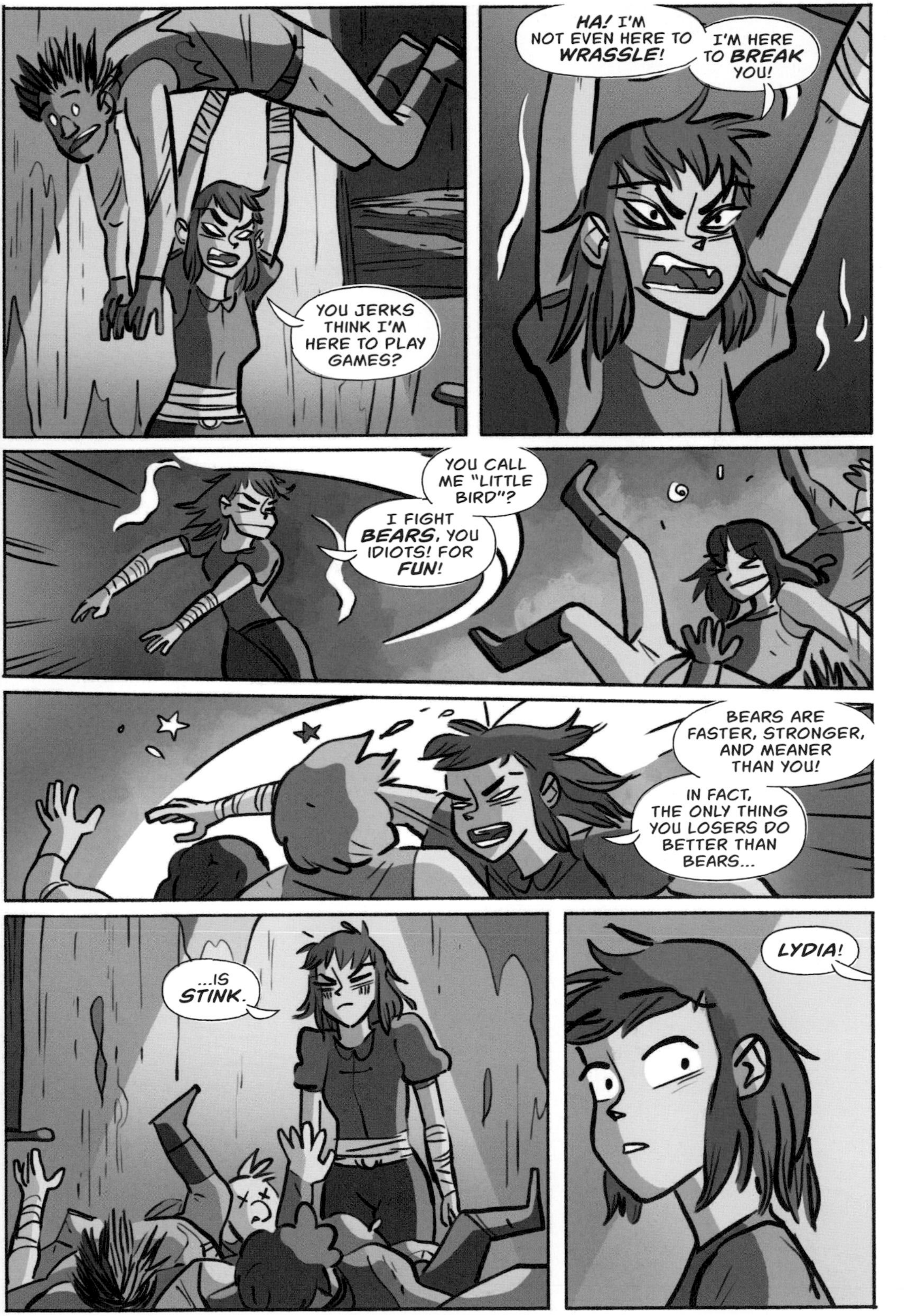
YOU JERKS THINK I'M HERE TO PLAY GAMES?
HA! I'M NOT EVEN HERE TO WRASSLE!
I'M HERE TO BREAK YOU!
YOU CALL ME "LITTLE BIRD"?
I FIGHT BEARS, YOU IDIOTS! FOR FUN!
BEARS ARE FASTER, STRONGER, AND MEANER THAN YOU!
IN FACT, THE ONLY THING YOU LOSERS DO BETTER THAN BEARS...
...IS STINK.
LYDIA!

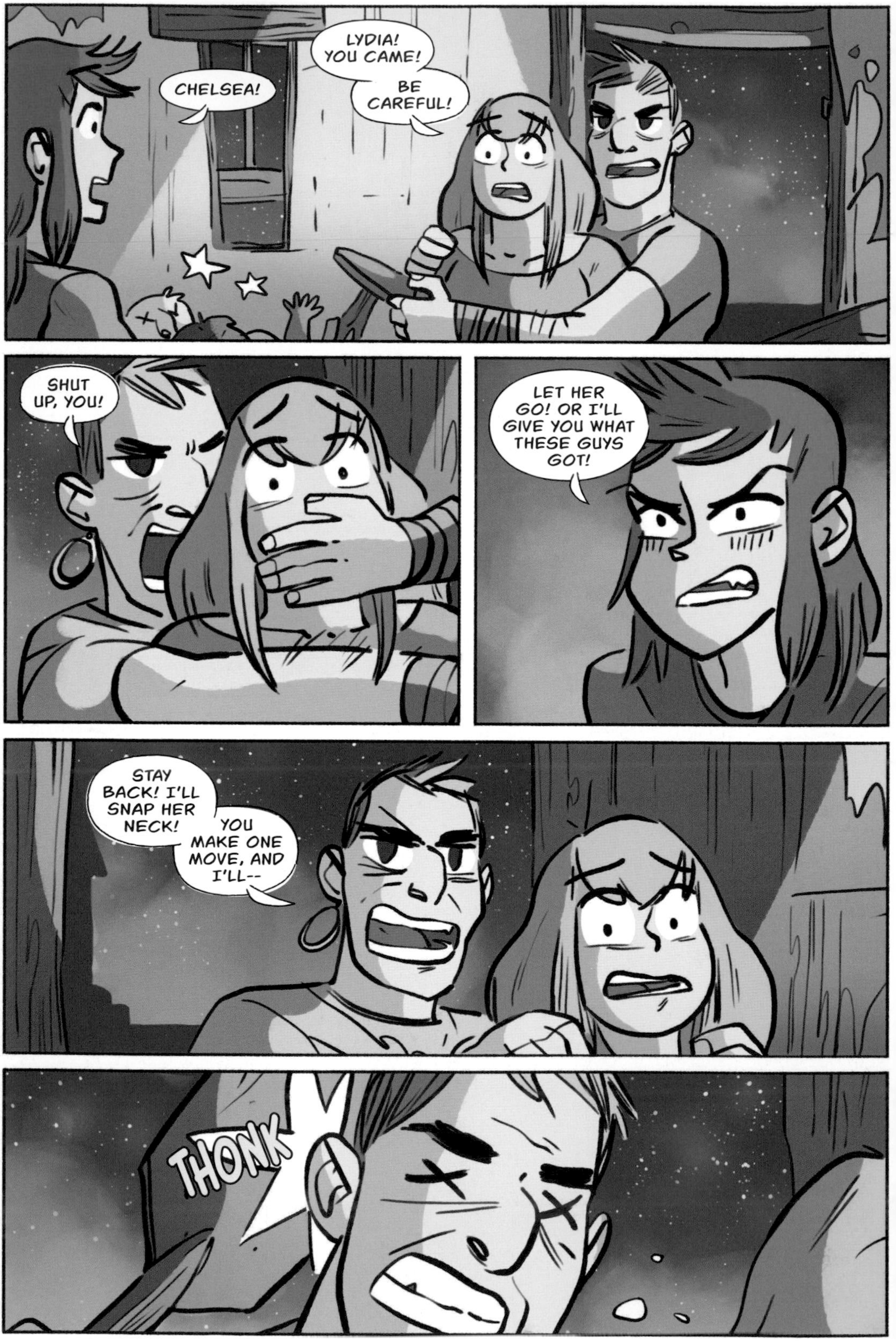
CHELSEA!
LYDIA! YOU CAME!
BE CAREFUL!
SHUT UP, YOU!
LET HER GO! OR I'LL GIVE YOU WHAT THESE GUYS GOT!
STAY BACK! I'LL SNAP HER NECK!
YOU MAKE ONE MOVE, AND I'LL--
THONK

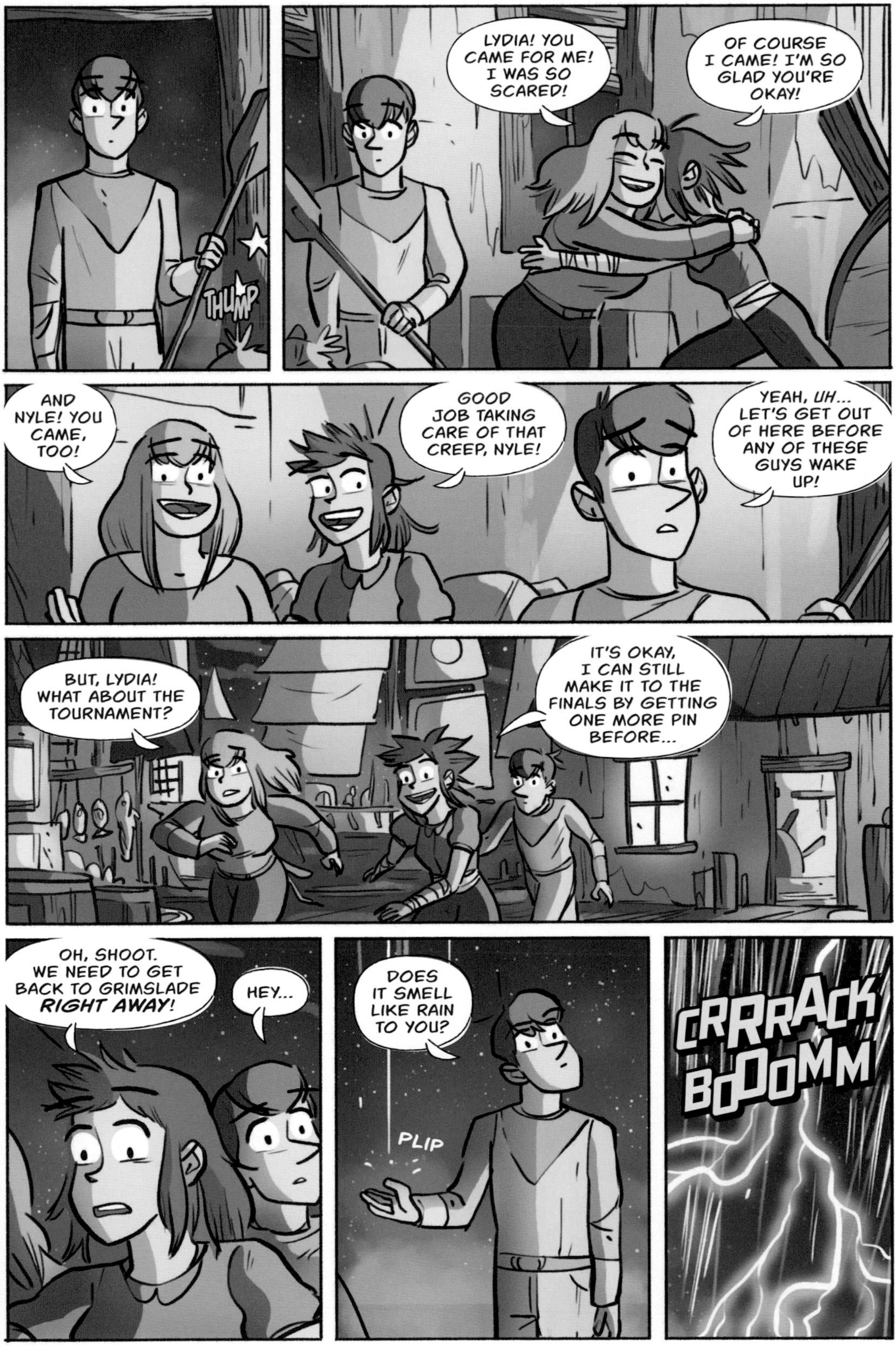
THUMP
LYDIA! YOU CAME FOR ME! I WAS SO SCARED!
OF COURSE I CAME! I'M SO GLAD YOU'RE OKAY!
AND NYLE! YOU CAME, TOO!
GOOD JOB TAKING CARE OF THAT CREEP, NYLE!
YEAH, *UH*... LET'S GET OUT OF HERE BEFORE ANY OF THESE GUYS WAKE UP!
BUT, LYDIA! WHAT ABOUT THE TOURNAMENT?
IT'S OKAY, I CAN STILL MAKE IT TO THE FINALS BY GETTING ONE MORE PIN BEFORE...
OH, SHOOT. WE NEED TO GET BACK TO GRIMSLADE ***RIGHT AWAY***!
HEY...
DOES IT SMELL LIKE RAIN TO YOU?
PLIP
CRRRACK BOOOMM

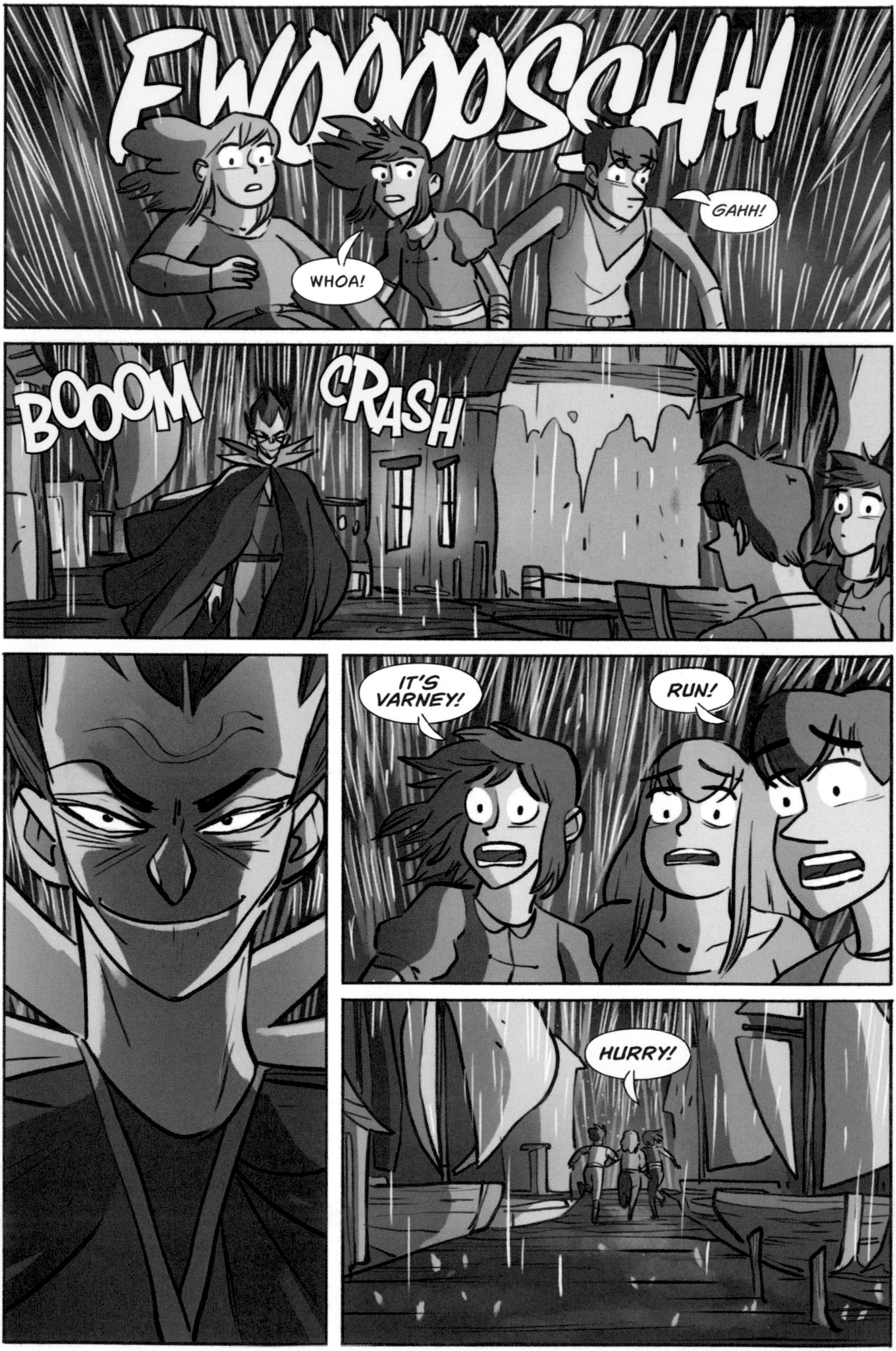
FWOOOOSCHH
WHOA!
GAHH!
BOOOM
CRASH
IT'S VARNEY!
RUN!
HURRY!

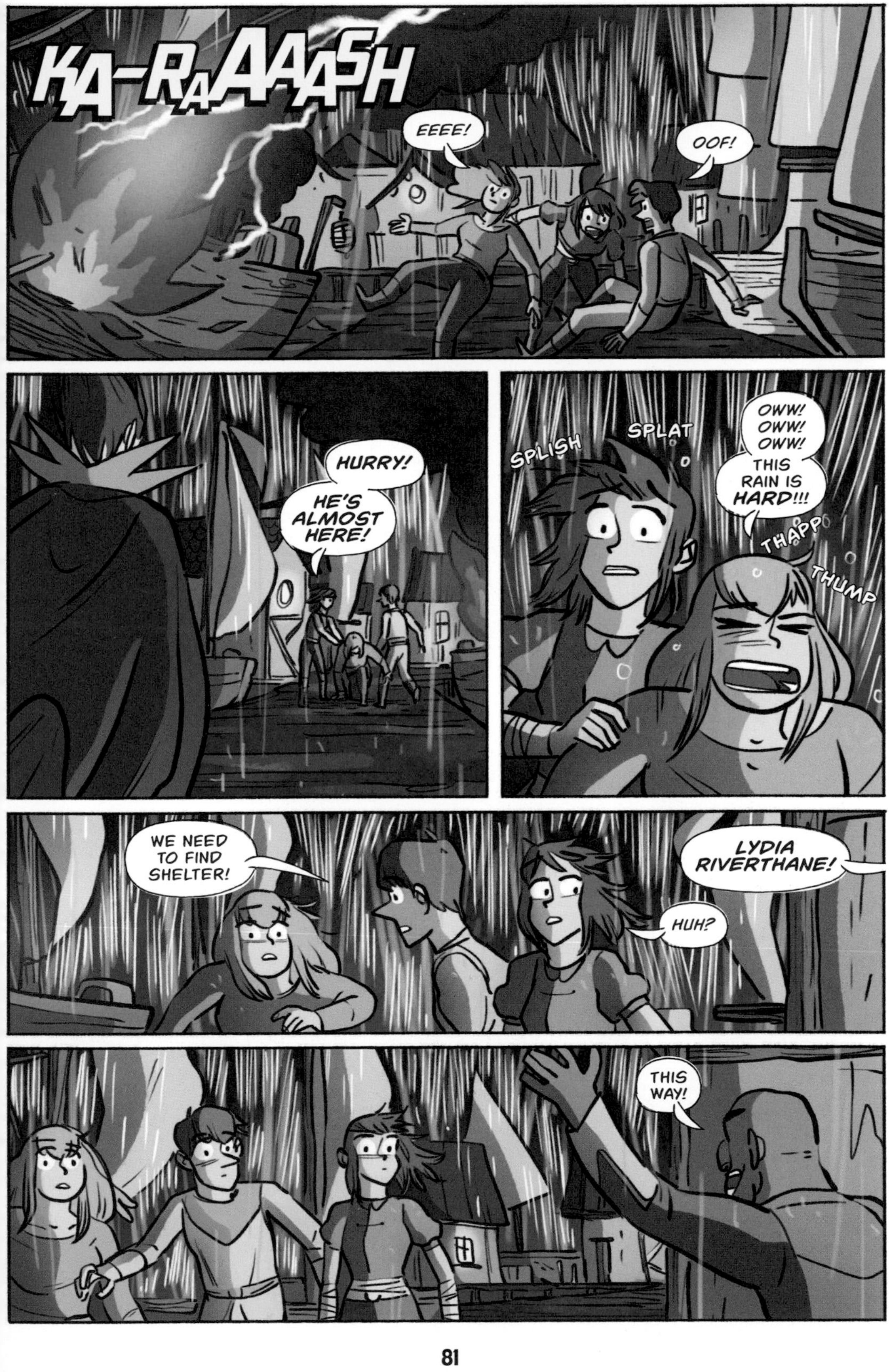
KA-RAAAASH
EEEE!
OOF!
HURRY!
HE'S ALMOST HERE!
SPLISH
SPLAT
OWW! OWW! OWW! THIS RAIN IS HARD!!!
THAPP
THUMP
WE NEED TO FIND SHELTER!
LYDIA RIVERTHANE!
HUH?
THIS WAY!

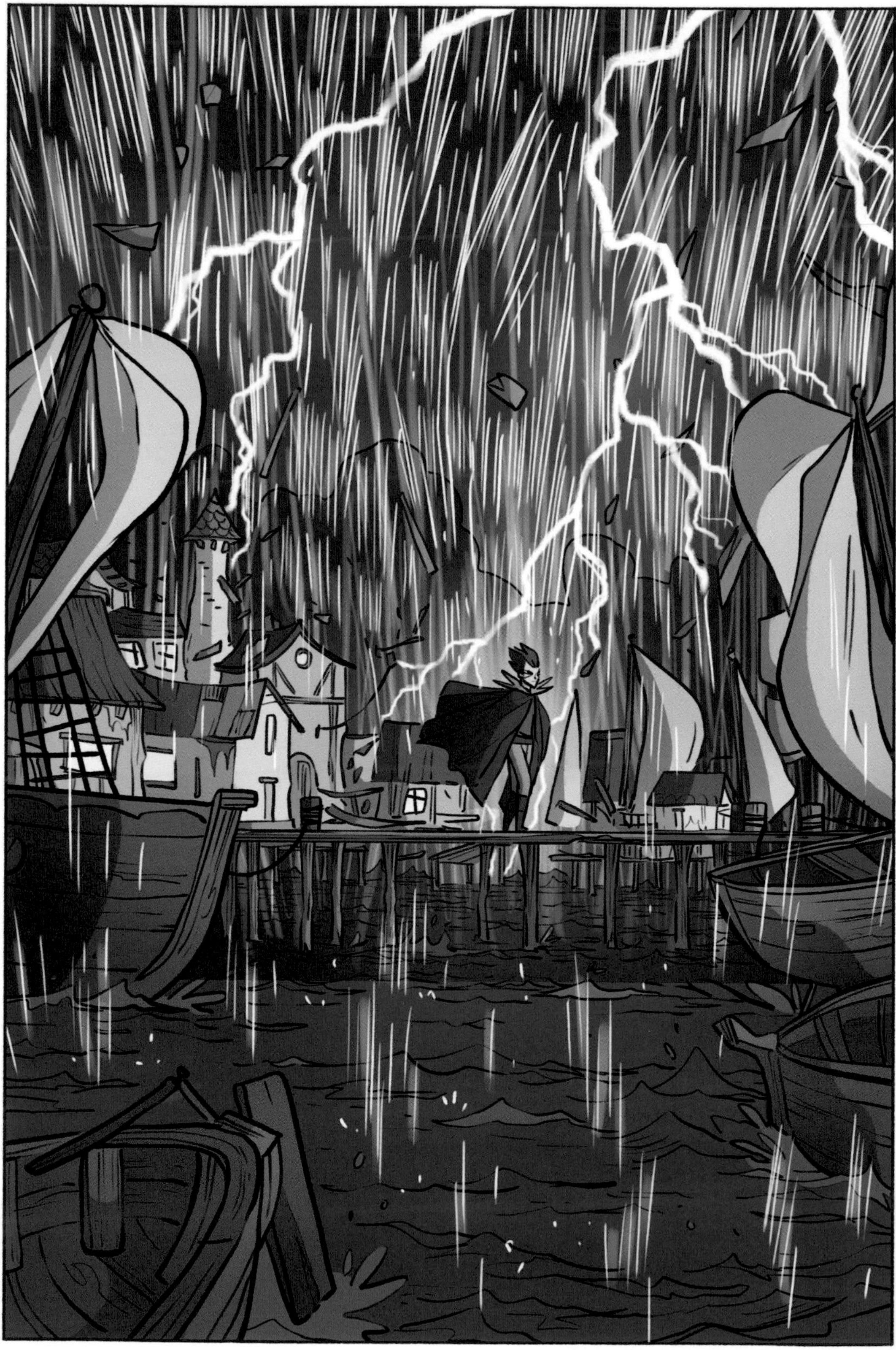

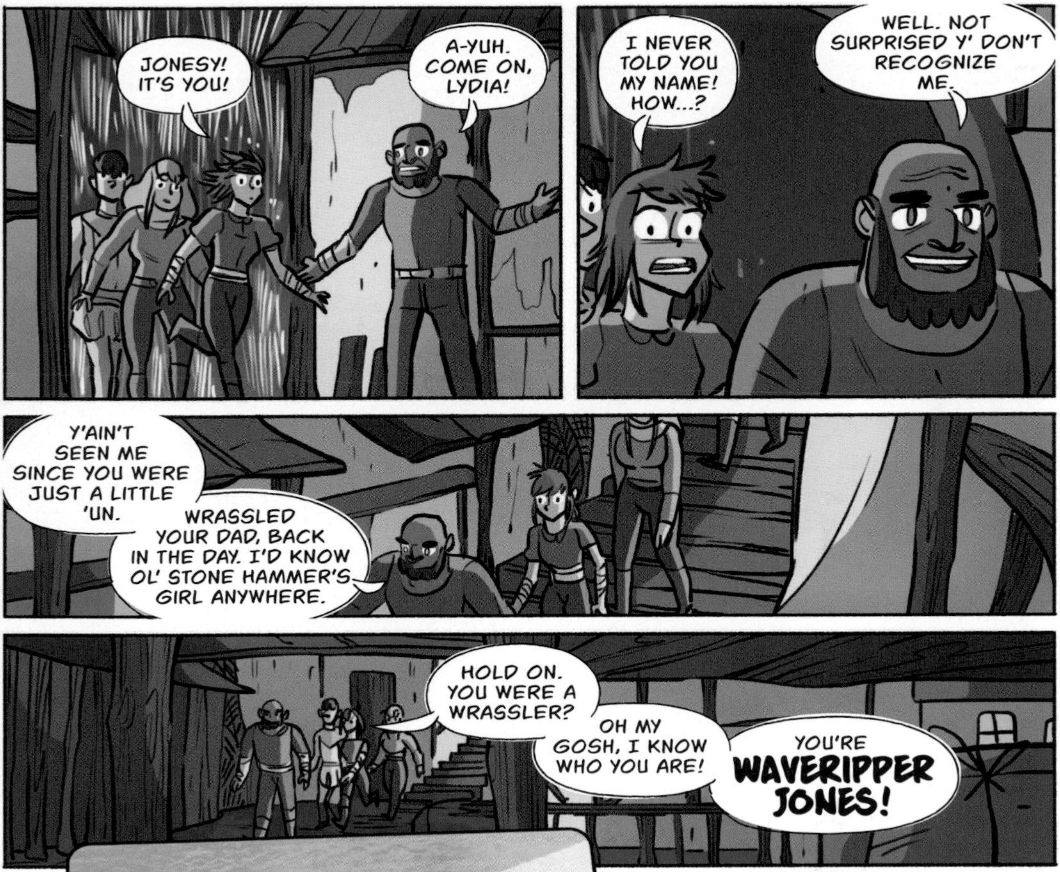
JONESY! IT'S YOU!
A-YUH. COME ON, LYDIA!
I NEVER TOLD YOU MY NAME! HOW...?
WELL. NOT SURPRISED Y' DON'T RECOGNIZE ME.
Y'AIN'T SEEN ME SINCE YOU WERE JUST A LITTLE 'UN.
WRASSLED YOUR DAD, BACK IN THE DAY. I'D KNOW OL' STONE HAMMER'S GIRL ANYWHERE.
HOLD ON. YOU WERE A WRASSLER?
OH MY GOSH, I KNOW WHO YOU ARE!
YOU'RE WAVERIPPER JONES!

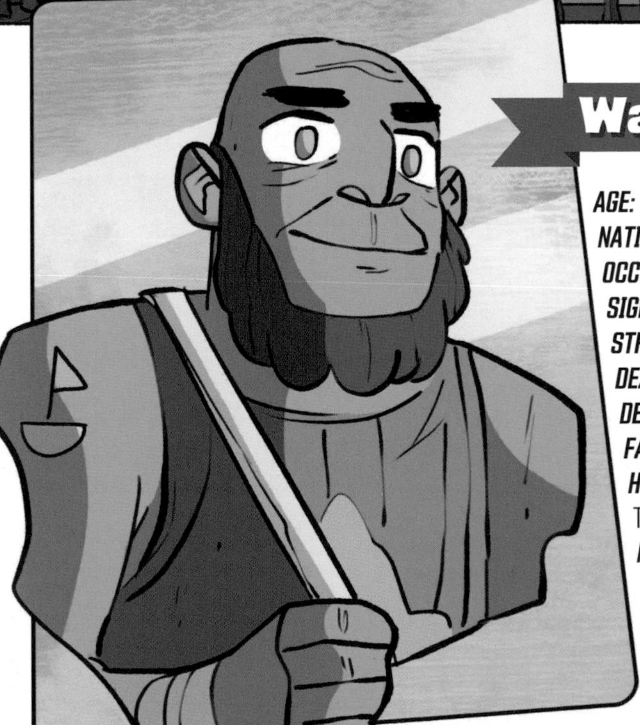

BONUS STAT CARD!

Waveripper Jones

AGE: 53 years old
NATIONAL RANKING: (retired)
OCCUPATION: Old Sea Salt
SIGNATURE MOVE: Waveripper
STRENGTH: 16
DEXTERITY: 12
DETERMINATION: 16
FAVORITE FOOD: Eel Spaghetti
HOBBIES: Fishing, Pipe Smoking, Telling Sea Stories
NOTES: Waveripper Jones, known as The King of the Canvasback River, is responsible for clearing out the Dread River Pirates of '78, helping free the waterways, and restoring trade to the city of Grimslade.

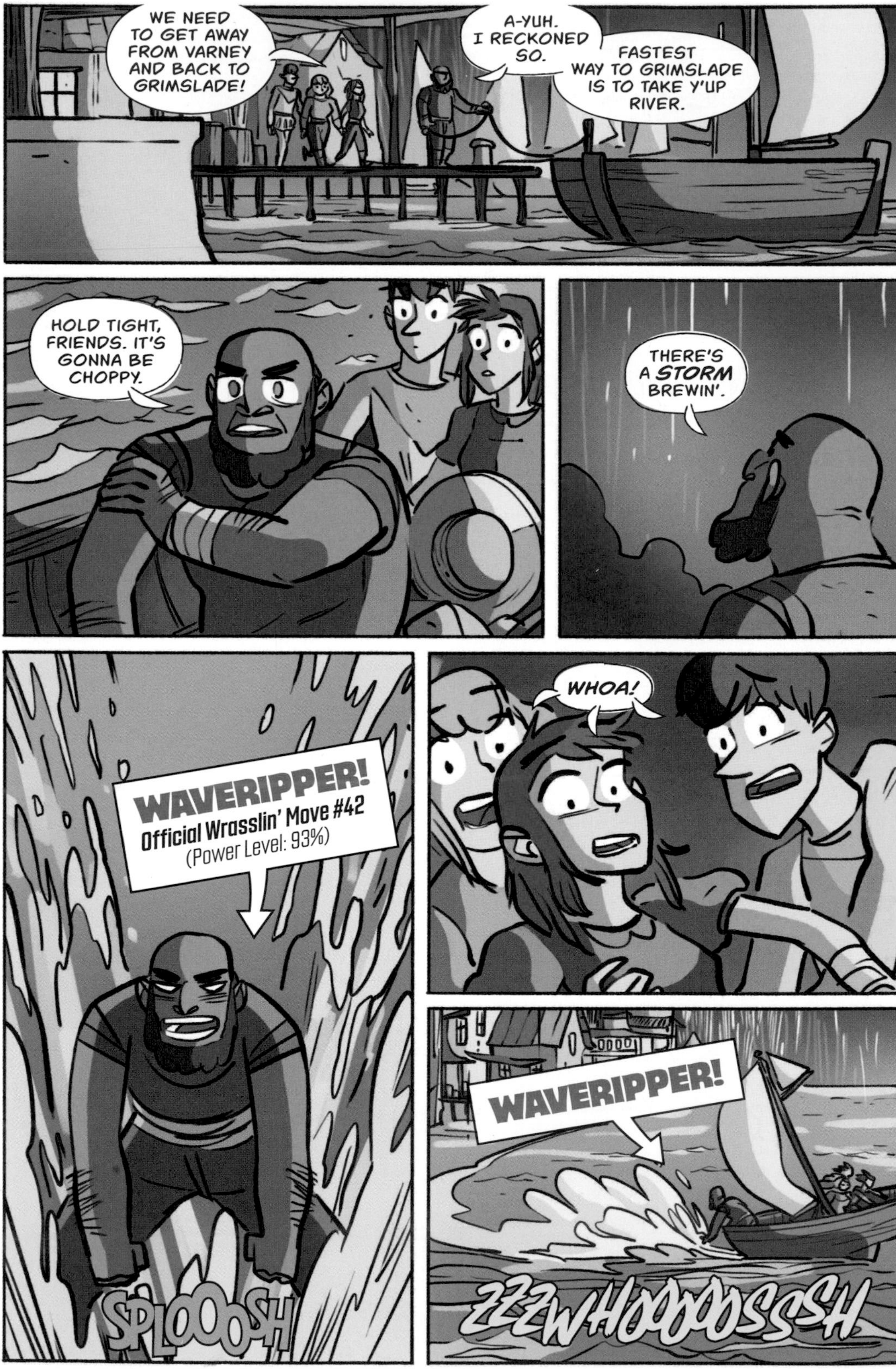
WE NEED TO GET AWAY FROM VARNEY AND BACK TO GRIMSLADE!
A-YUH. I RECKONED SO.
FASTEST WAY TO GRIMSLADE IS TO TAKE Y'UP RIVER.
HOLD TIGHT, FRIENDS. IT'S GONNA BE CHOPPY.
THERE'S A STORM BREWIN'.
WAVERIPPER!
Official Wrasslin' Move #42
(Power Level: 93%)
SPLOOOSH
WHOA!
WAVERIPPER!
ZZZWHOOOOOSSSH

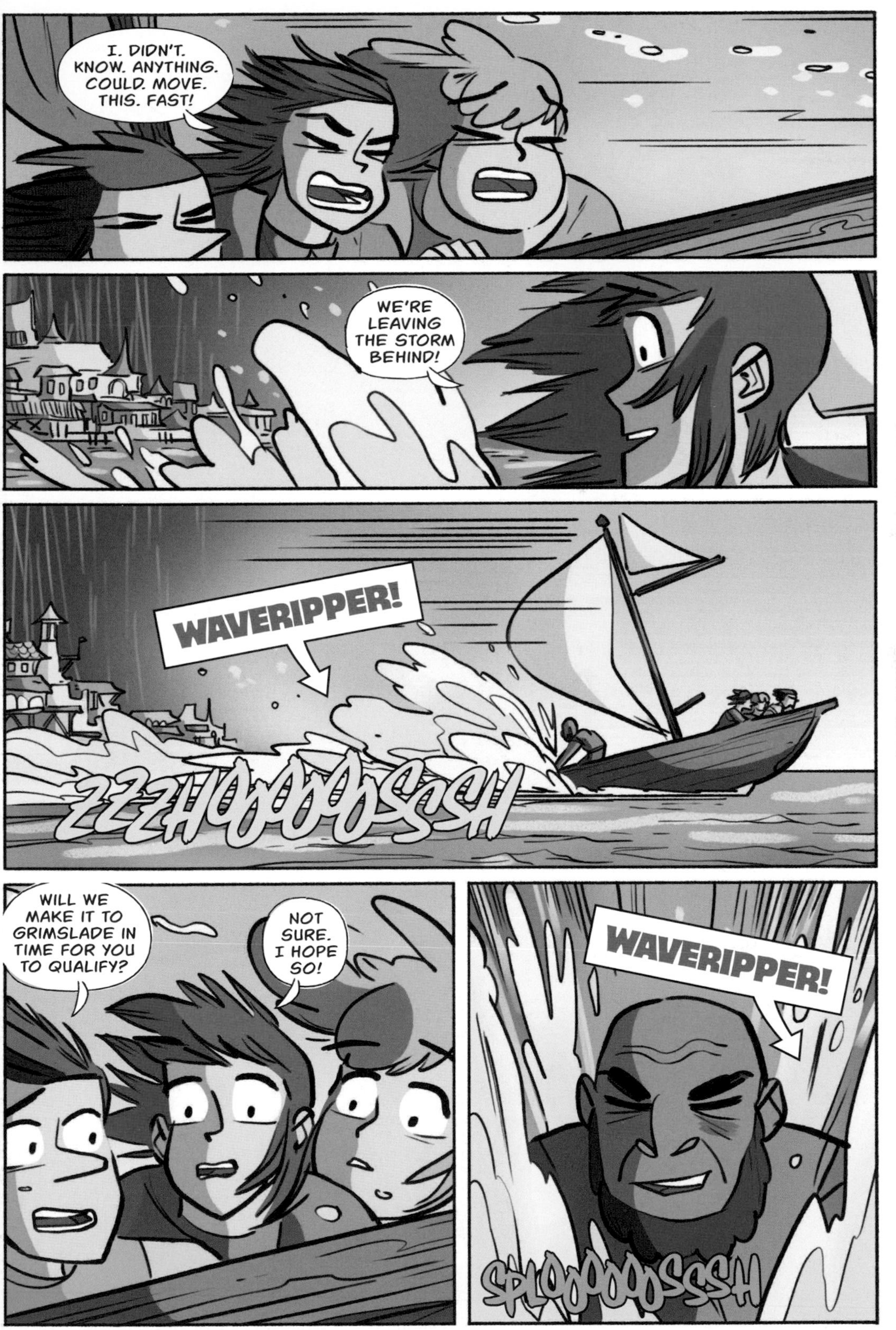
I. DIDN'T. KNOW. ANYTHING. COULD. MOVE. THIS. FAST!
WE'RE LEAVING THE STORM BEHIND!
WAVERIPPER!
ZZZHOOOOOSSSH
WILL WE MAKE IT TO GRIMSLADE IN TIME FOR YOU TO QUALIFY?
NOT SURE. I HOPE SO!
WAVERIPPER!
SPLOOOOOSSSH

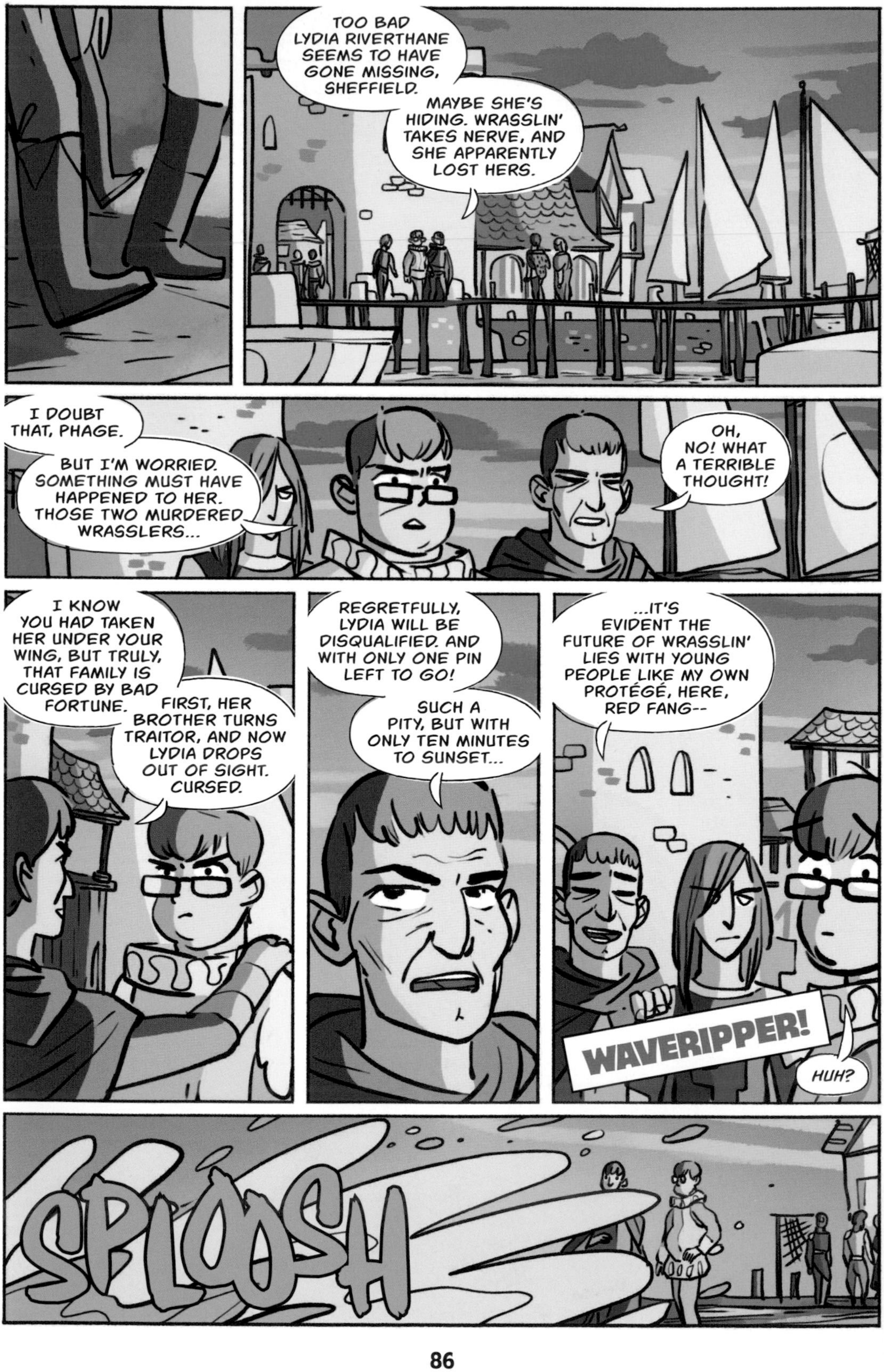

TOO BAD LYDIA RIVERTHANE SEEMS TO HAVE GONE MISSING, SHEFFIELD.
MAYBE SHE'S HIDING. WRASSLIN' TAKES NERVE, AND SHE APPARENTLY LOST HERS.
I DOUBT THAT, PHAGE.
BUT I'M WORRIED. SOMETHING MUST HAVE HAPPENED TO HER. THOSE TWO MURDERED WRASSLERS...
OH, NO! WHAT A TERRIBLE THOUGHT!
I KNOW YOU HAD TAKEN HER UNDER YOUR WING, BUT TRULY, THAT FAMILY IS CURSED BY BAD FORTUNE.
FIRST, HER BROTHER TURNS TRAITOR, AND NOW LYDIA DROPS OUT OF SIGHT. CURSED.
REGRETFULLY, LYDIA WILL BE DISQUALIFIED. AND WITH ONLY ONE PIN LEFT TO GO!
SUCH A PITY, BUT WITH ONLY TEN MINUTES TO SUNSET...
...IT'S EVIDENT THE FUTURE OF WRASSLIN' LIES WITH YOUNG PEOPLE LIKE MY OWN PROTÉGÉ, HERE, RED FANG--
WAVERIPPER!
HUH?
SPLOOSH

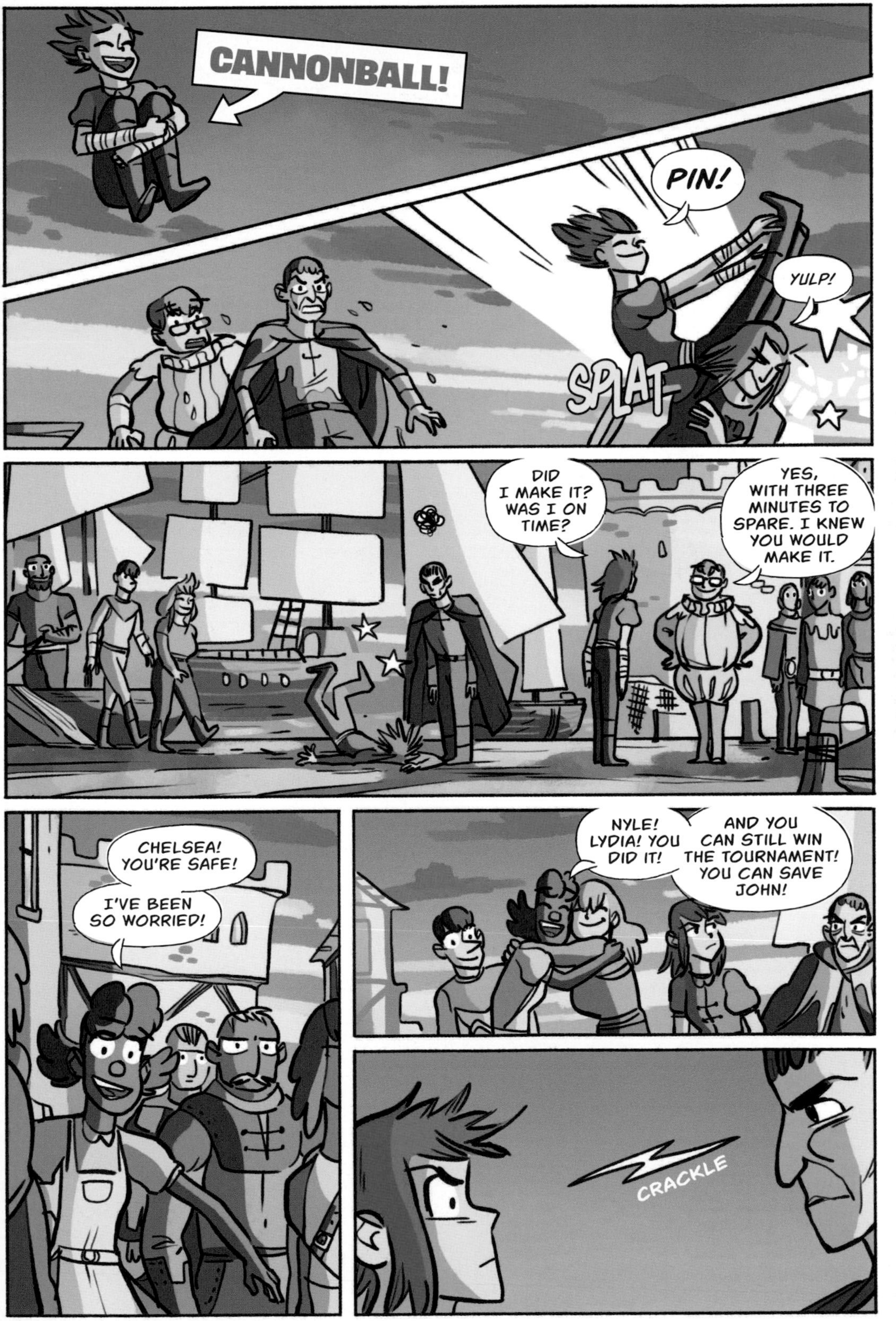
CANNONBALL!
PIN!
YULP!
SPLAT
DID I MAKE IT? WAS I ON TIME?
YES, WITH THREE MINUTES TO SPARE. I KNEW YOU WOULD MAKE IT.
CHELSEA! YOU'RE SAFE!
I'VE BEEN SO WORRIED!
NYLE! LYDIA! YOU DID IT!
AND YOU CAN STILL WIN THE TOURNAMENT! YOU CAN SAVE JOHN!
CRACKLE

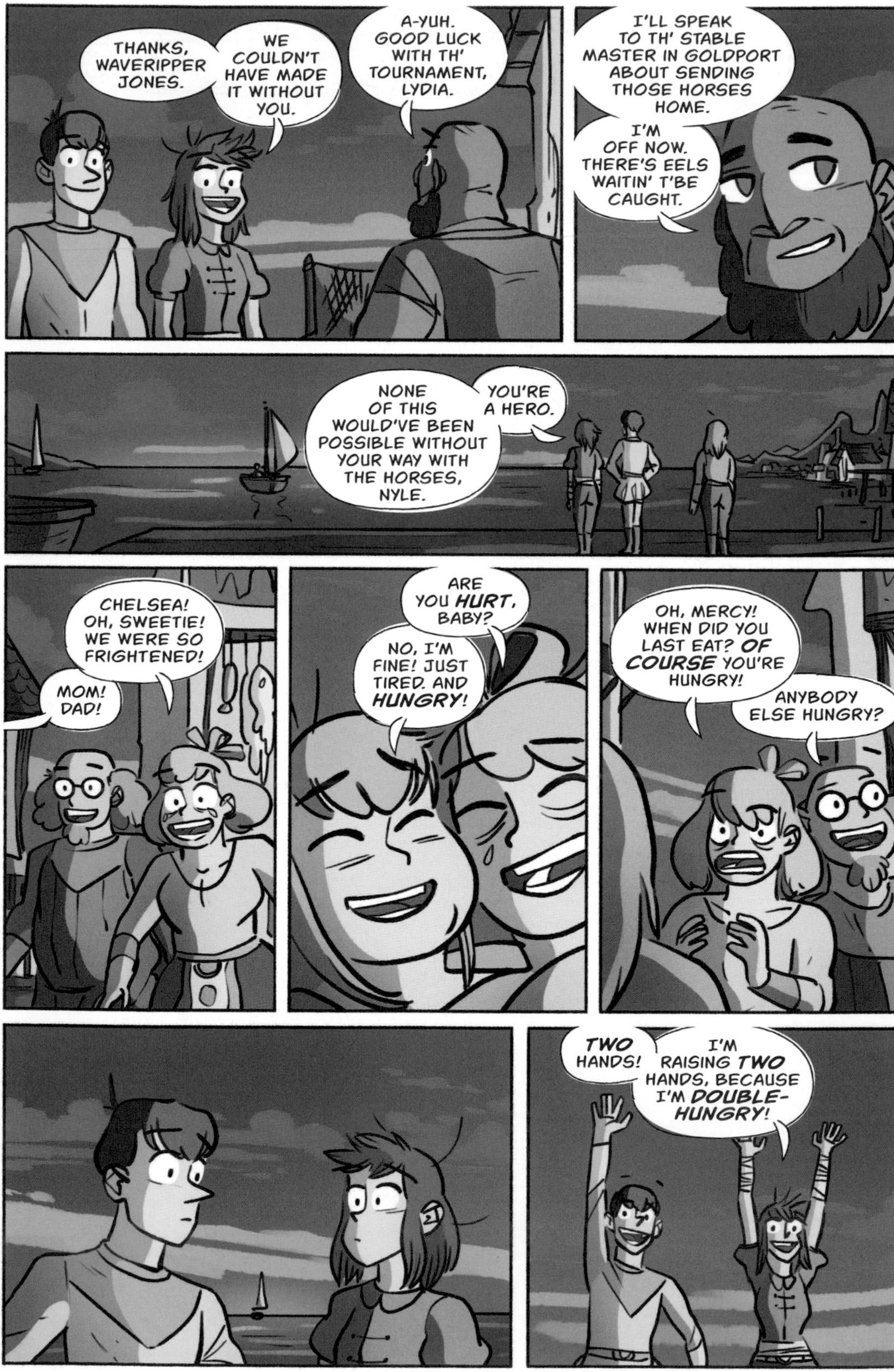
THANKS, WAVERIPPER JONES.
WE COULDN'T HAVE MADE IT WITHOUT YOU.
A-YUH. GOOD LUCK WITH TH' TOURNAMENT, LYDIA.
I'LL SPEAK TO TH' STABLE MASTER IN GOLDPORT ABOUT SENDING THOSE HORSES HOME.
I'M OFF NOW. THERE'S EELS WAITIN' T'BE CAUGHT.
NONE OF THIS WOULD'VE BEEN POSSIBLE WITHOUT YOUR WAY WITH THE HORSES, NYLE.
YOU'RE A HERO.
CHELSEA! OH, SWEETIE! WE WERE SO FRIGHTENED!
MOM! DAD!
ARE YOU HURT, BABY?
NO, I'M FINE! JUST TIRED. AND HUNGRY!
OH, MERCY! WHEN DID YOU LAST EAT? OF COURSE YOU'RE HUNGRY!
ANYBODY ELSE HUNGRY?
TWO HANDS!
I'M RAISING TWO HANDS, BECAUSE I'M DOUBLE-HUNGRY!

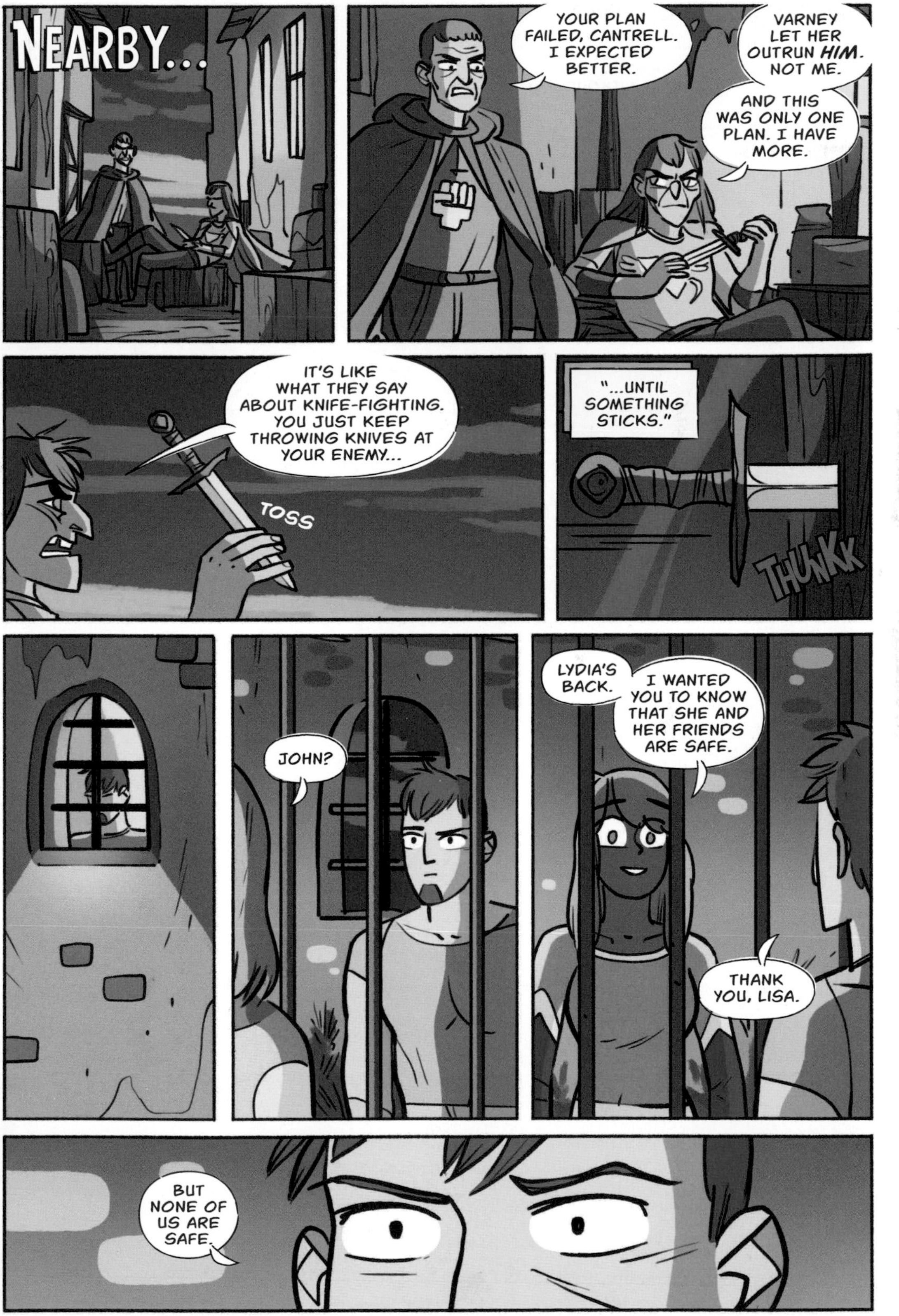
NEARBY...
YOUR PLAN FAILED, CANTRELL. I EXPECTED BETTER.
VARNEY LET HER OUTRUN *HIM*. NOT ME.
AND THIS WAS ONLY ONE PLAN. I HAVE MORE.
IT'S LIKE WHAT THEY SAY ABOUT KNIFE-FIGHTING. YOU JUST KEEP THROWING KNIVES AT YOUR ENEMY...
TOSS
"...UNTIL SOMETHING STICKS."
THUNKK
JOHN?
LYDIA'S BACK.
I WANTED YOU TO KNOW THAT SHE AND HER FRIENDS ARE SAFE.
THANK YOU, LISA.
BUT NONE OF US ARE SAFE.

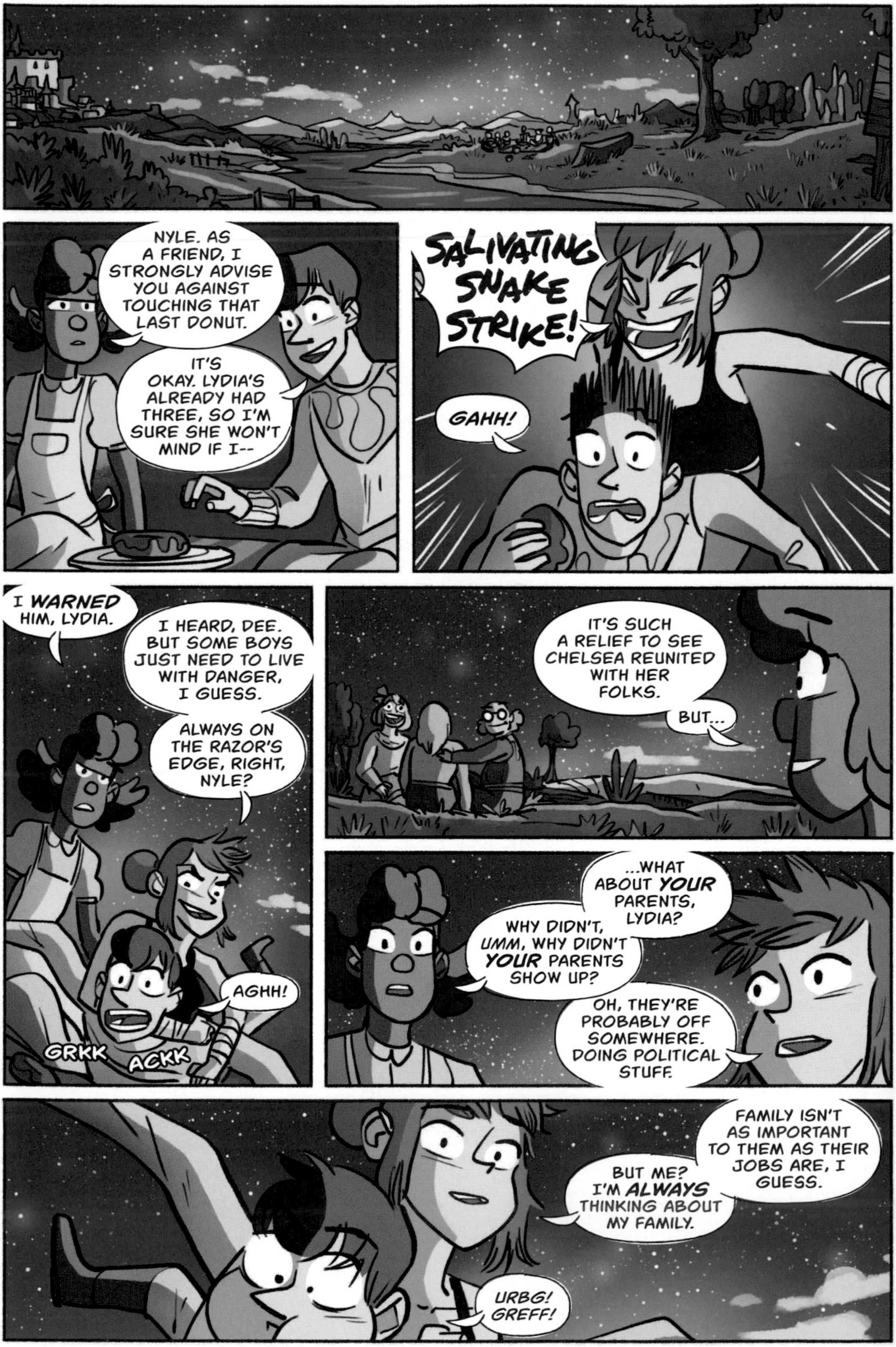
NYLE. AS A FRIEND, I STRONGLY ADVISE YOU AGAINST TOUCHING THAT LAST DONUT.
IT'S OKAY. LYDIA'S ALREADY HAD THREE, SO I'M SURE SHE WON'T MIND IF I--
SALIVATING SNAKE STRIKE!
GAHH!
I WARNED HIM, LYDIA.
I HEARD, DEE. BUT SOME BOYS JUST NEED TO LIVE WITH DANGER, I GUESS.
ALWAYS ON THE RAZOR'S EDGE, RIGHT, NYLE?
AGHH!
GRKK
ACKK
IT'S SUCH A RELIEF TO SEE CHELSEA REUNITED WITH HER FOLKS.
BUT...
WHY DIDN'T, UMM, WHY DIDN'T YOUR PARENTS SHOW UP?
...WHAT ABOUT YOUR PARENTS, LYDIA?
OH, THEY'RE PROBABLY OFF SOMEWHERE. DOING POLITICAL STUFF.
FAMILY ISN'T AS IMPORTANT TO THEM AS THEIR JOBS ARE, I GUESS.
BUT ME? I'M ALWAYS THINKING ABOUT MY FAMILY.
URBG! GREFF!

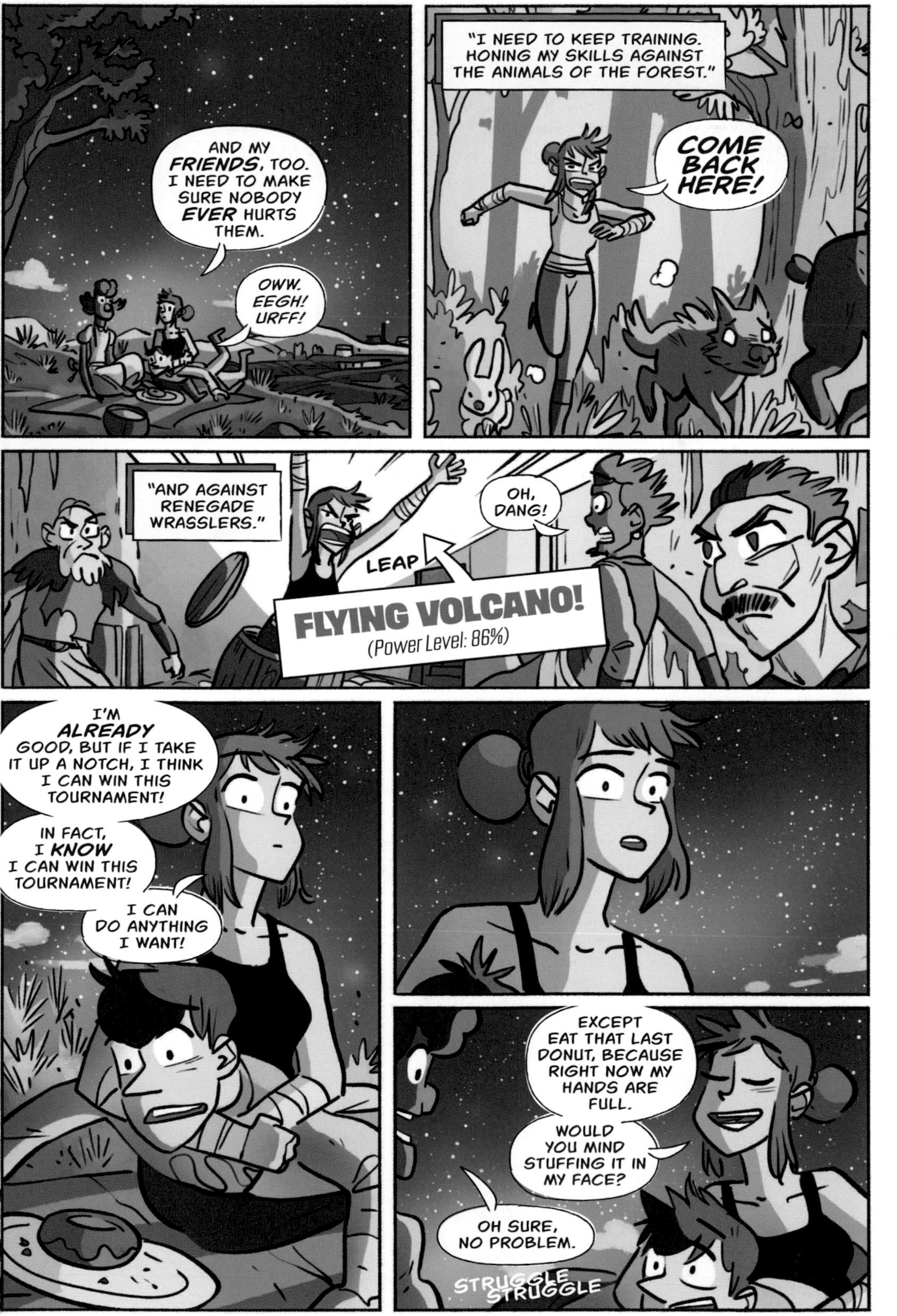
AND MY FRIENDS, TOO. I NEED TO MAKE SURE NOBODY EVER HURTS THEM.
OWW. EEGH! URFF!
"I NEED TO KEEP TRAINING. HONING MY SKILLS AGAINST THE ANIMALS OF THE FOREST."
COME BACK HERE!
"AND AGAINST RENEGADE WRASSLERS."
OH, DANG!
LEAP
FLYING VOLCANO!
(Power Level: 86%)
I'M ALREADY GOOD, BUT IF I TAKE IT UP A NOTCH, I THINK I CAN WIN THIS TOURNAMENT!
IN FACT, I KNOW I CAN WIN THIS TOURNAMENT!
I CAN DO ANYTHING I WANT!
EXCEPT EAT THAT LAST DONUT, BECAUSE RIGHT NOW MY HANDS ARE FULL.
WOULD YOU MIND STUFFING IT IN MY FACE?
OH SURE, NO PROBLEM.
STRUGGLE STRUGGLE

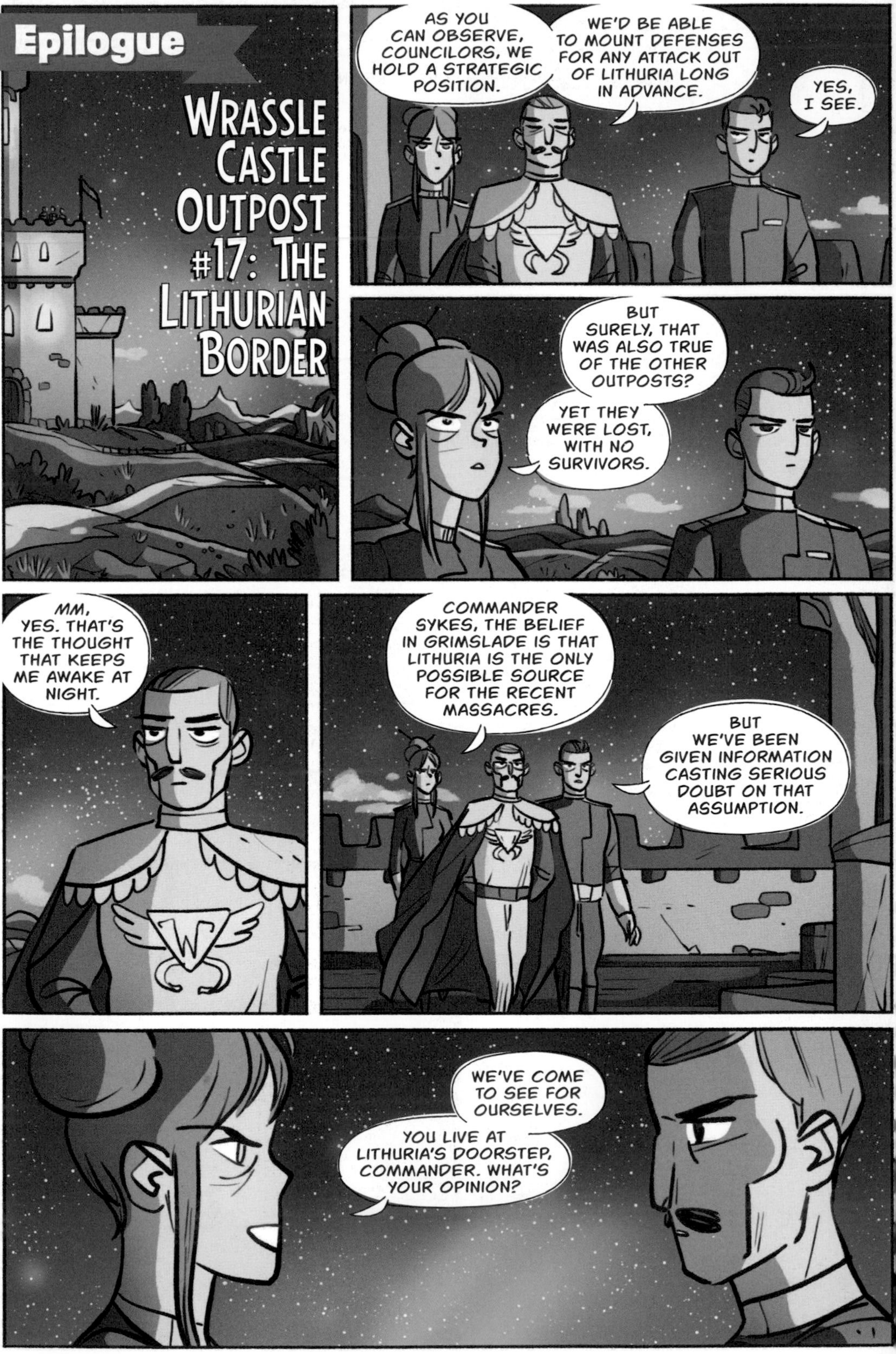
Epilogue
WRASSLE CASTLE OUTPOST #17: THE LITHURIAN BORDER
AS YOU CAN OBSERVE, COUNCILORS, WE HOLD A STRATEGIC POSITION.
WE'D BE ABLE TO MOUNT DEFENSES FOR ANY ATTACK OUT OF LITHURIA LONG IN ADVANCE.
YES, I SEE.
BUT SURELY, THAT WAS ALSO TRUE OF THE OTHER OUTPOSTS?
YET THEY WERE LOST, WITH NO SURVIVORS.
MM, YES. THAT'S THE THOUGHT THAT KEEPS ME AWAKE AT NIGHT.
COMMANDER SYKES, THE BELIEF IN GRIMSLADE IS THAT LITHURIA IS THE ONLY POSSIBLE SOURCE FOR THE RECENT MASSACRES.
BUT WE'VE BEEN GIVEN INFORMATION CASTING SERIOUS DOUBT ON THAT ASSUMPTION.
WE'VE COME TO SEE FOR OURSELVES.
YOU LIVE AT LITHURIA'S DOORSTEP, COMMANDER. WHAT'S YOUR OPINION?

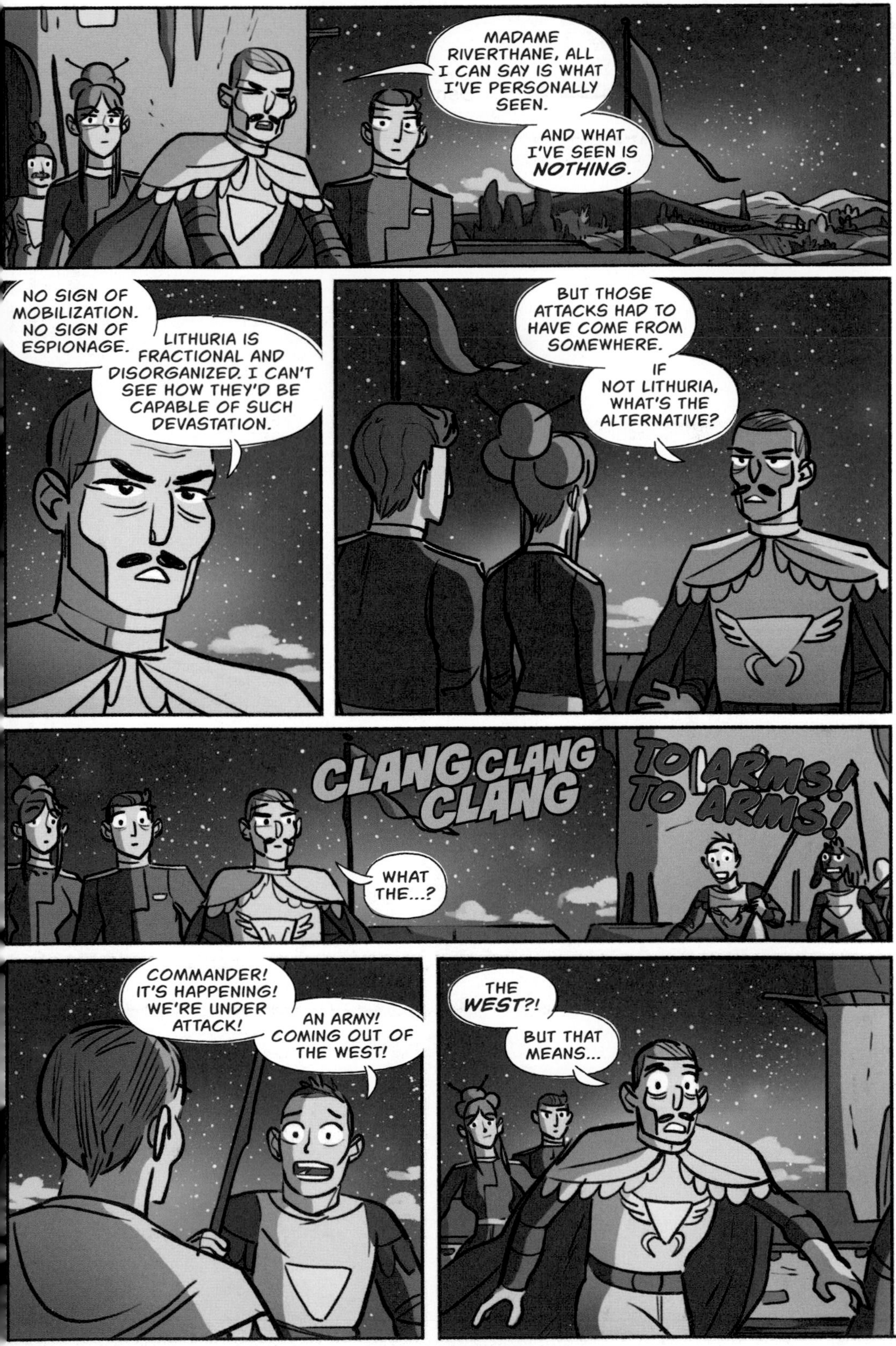
MADAME RIVERTHANE, ALL I CAN SAY IS WHAT I'VE PERSONALLY SEEN.
AND WHAT I'VE SEEN IS *NOTHING*.
NO SIGN OF MOBILIZATION. NO SIGN OF ESPIONAGE.
LITHURIA IS FRACTIONAL AND DISORGANIZED. I CAN'T SEE HOW THEY'D BE CAPABLE OF SUCH DEVASTATION.
BUT THOSE ATTACKS HAD TO HAVE COME FROM SOMEWHERE.
IF NOT LITHURIA, WHAT'S THE ALTERNATIVE?
CLANG CLANG CLANG
WHAT THE...?
TO ARMS! TO ARMS!
COMMANDER! IT'S HAPPENING! WE'RE UNDER ATTACK!
AN ARMY! COMING OUT OF THE WEST!
THE *WEST*?!
BUT THAT MEANS...

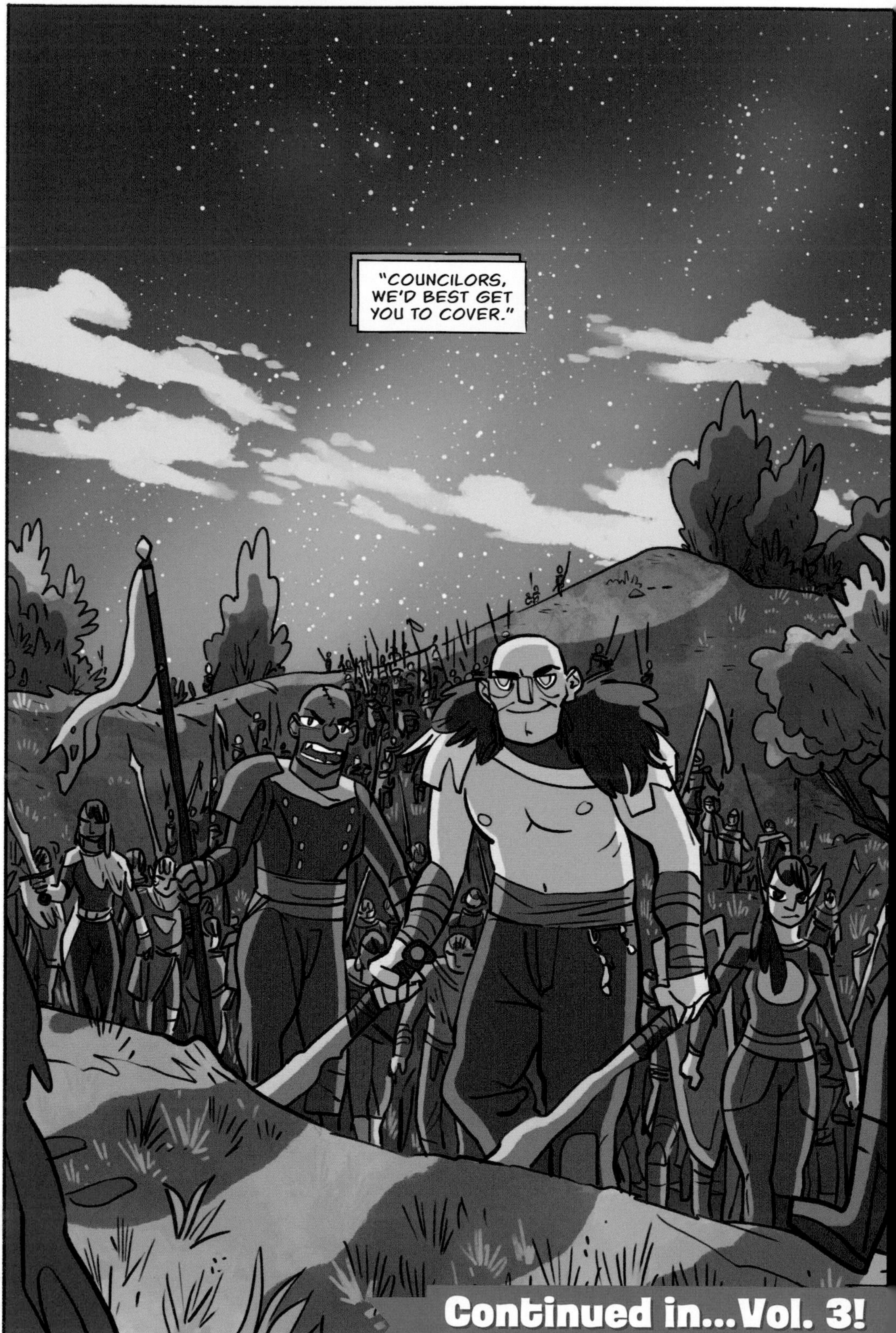
"COUNCILORS, WE'D BEST GET YOU TO COVER."
Continued in...Vol. 3!

NEXT TIME

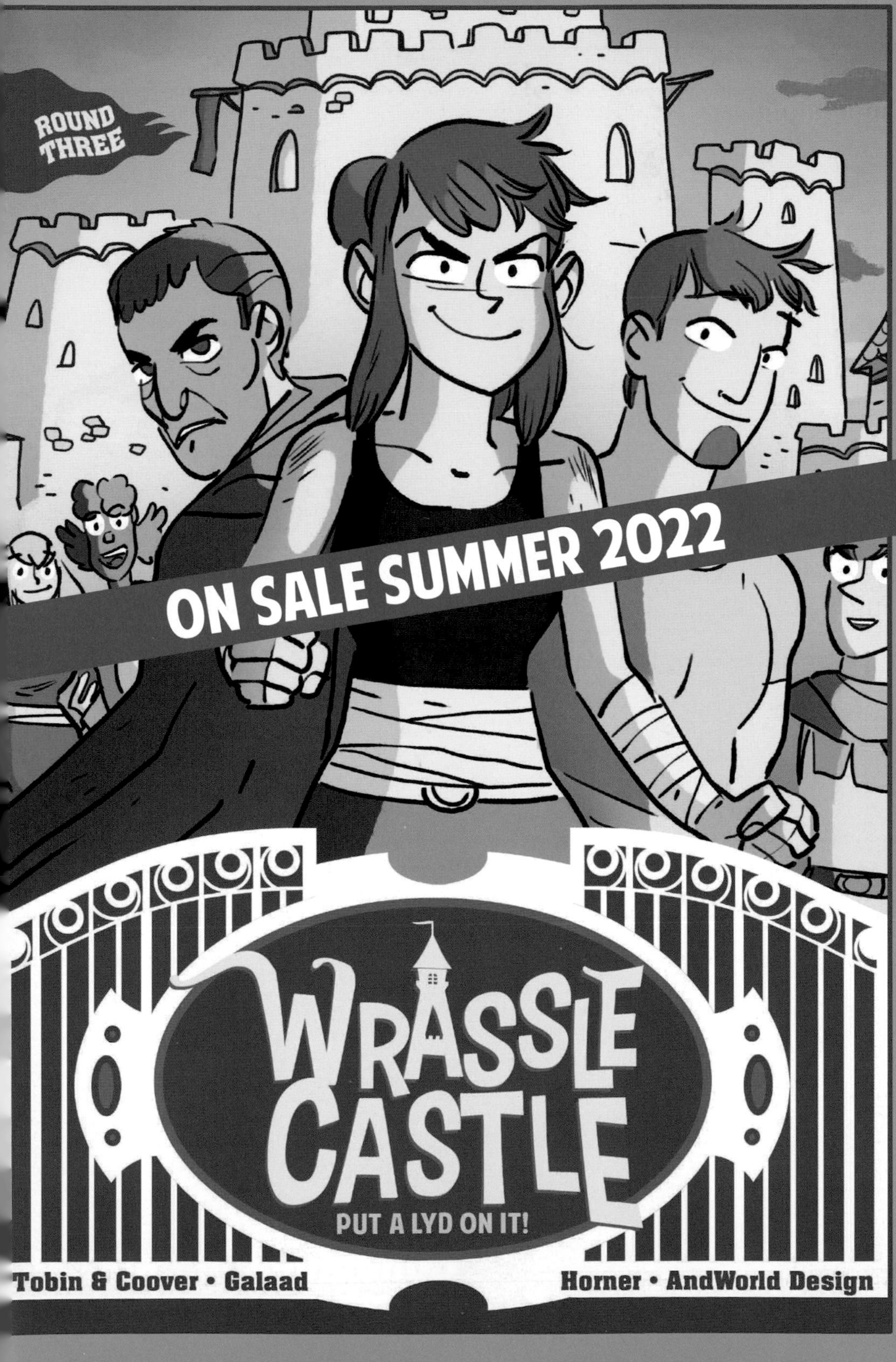

ROUND THREE
ON SALE SUMMER 2022
WRASSLE CASTLE
PUT A LYD ON IT!
Tobin & Coover • Galaad
Horner • AndWorld Design

"MEAN" COLLEEN

NATIONAL RANKING: STILL COUNTING.
SIGNATURE MOVE: TRUTH BOMB
(HIGHEST POWER LEVEL: NUCLEAR)

NOTES: COAXED FROM THE COMFORT OF HER
COMIC-DRAWING CAVE BY THE PROSPECT OF
CO-WRITING A FANTASY WRASSLIN' ADVENTURE,
COLLEEN HAS BEEN TRAINING HER AUTHORING
MUSCLES BY BENCH PRESSING COMPUTER
KEYBOARDS AND EATING RAW WORD DOCS
FOR BREAKFAST.

"TEN TOES" TOBIN

NATIONAL RANKING: 7,898,653 (ON A GOOD DAY)
SIGNATURE MOVE: NAPALANCHE
(HIGHEST POWER LEVEL: 98%)

NOTES: AS A FERAL CHILD IN THE IOWA WILDERNESS,
PAUL WAS RAISED BY A KINDLY PAIR OF PULP
MAGAZINES AND EVENTUALLY JOINED HUMAN SOCIETY
AFTER PASSING THE LEGALLY-REQUIRED POTTY
TRAINING TEST ON ONLY THE FOURTH TRY. HE ENJOYS
FRENZIED STORMS AND AN ASTONISHING RANGE OF
THINGS MOST PEOPLE CONSIDER STRANGE.

"ÚLTIMO DISEÑADOR
EXTRAORDINARIO"

NATIONAL RANKING: OFF THE CHART.
SIGNATURE MOVE: EXPLOSIVE PENCIL OF DEATH
(HIGHEST POWER LEVEL: DEADLY)

NOTES: ONCE DEFEATED VEGETA IN SINGLE COMBAT.
OR WAS IT IN HIS IMAGINATION?

"RABBLE ROUSIN" REBECCA

NATIONAL RANKING: LOW!
SIGNATURE MOVE: BEFUDDLE!
(HIGHEST POWER LEVEL: ?!?)

NOTES: CAN BENCH PRESS UP TO 2 CATS AT ANY
GIVEN TIME!